T0167108

SCALP

SCALP
AN INDIAN WESTERN

David C. Dillon

iUniverse LLC
Bloomington

SCALP

iUniverse books may be ordered through booksellers or by contacting:

iUniverse LLC
1663 Liberty Drive
Bloomington, IN 47403
www.iuniverse.com
1-800-Authors (1-800-288-4677)

ISBN: 978-1-4759-9796-5 (sc)
ISBN: 978-1-4759-9797-2 (ebk)

Printed in the United States of America

iUniverse rev. date: 07/18/2013

Contents

Preface

My father got me interested in reading westerns at an early age. It is one of the things we shared together. I will always remember talking with him about the Powder Valley westerns and the adventures of Pat, Sam, and Ezra.

The only way I would even try to write a western was if I could come up with a totally different idea. With this book I have.

David C. Dillon

Acknowledgments

A special thanks to Robin Wheeler Espejo, the model for the cover picture and Billie Kussman and her daughter for the use of the dress.

I am truly grateful for all who support me and especially my fans.

This book is dedicated to my mom, Joyce, my two daughters, Stacey and Kristie, and my two granddaughters, Ashley and Brooklyne.

A special thank you goes out to Grandma and Grandpa Brown who enjoyed or at least pretended to listen to my bear tales before I even went to school. They are the ones that called my stories bear tales because the stories always included a bear.

Chapter 1

GREASY GRASS RIVER

An arrow flew through the air from behind Gray Fox and stuck in the pine tree in front of him. Startled, he glanced over at the arrow and knew by its markings they had been spotted by Blackfoot scouts. He looked back and saw three scouts, rapidly closing in on him. They wouldn't miss with the next shot if he didn't do something immediately.

"Hurry, ride into the river and head north. I'll lead them away and find you later," Gray Fox shouted to his pregnant wife, Gentle Breeze.

He turned his pony south and kicked it in the flanks and held on as it leaped into a fast gallop. He headed into an open field to draw the Blackfoot scouts away from the river.

Looking back he saw two scouts following him and one heading toward his wife. Gray Fox raised his rifle and fired at the scouts. He watched as the one going north stopped and turned his horse around to follow after the other two scouts.

A couple shots were fired. One was close enough to hear the whiz of the bullet as it passed by his head. He lowered his head and tried to make his body as small as possible. He had to make it to the far end of this open meadow where he would have a better chance of surviving.

The forest was just ahead but the Blackfoot scouts were closing fast with their strong horses. He could hear the hooves of the other horses hitting the ground behind him.

He saw a steep ravine at the end of the field and rode his pony straight for it. As his pony headed down the side he jumped off and allowed his pony to go on ahead. He scrambled back to the top edge to try and get a shot off before the scouts got there. From the sounds of the hoof beats he knew the horse was extremely close to where he hid in the weeds.

He lay down on his back in the weeds with his rifle ready to fire as soon as the first Blackfoot rode over the steep hill. The first horse over the bank almost stepped on him. He raised his gun and fired. The rider threw both arms in the air and made a loud moan as he fell from his horse and hit the ground.

Gray Fox got ready to fire at the second rider but when that horse came over the edge of the bank it was right on top of him. The horse flinched and the rider flew off his stumbling mount and landed right on top of Gray Fox knocking his rifle on down the steep embankment.

Gray Fox drew his knife and jumped on top of the scout before the scout could get to his feet. They both tumbled down the sheer levee rolling over and over until they were at the bottom. Gray Fox slashed at the scout and cut him across the chest and upper arm.

The Blackfoot grabbed the hand holding the knife and bent Gray Fox over and to the ground. Gray Fox used his leg to sweep the legs out from under the scout making him fall backward to the ground. He slid his body in behind the Indian and wrapped his arm around the man's neck and applied a chokehold on the scout. He held on as the man squirmed, trying to get free.

The man clawed at Gray Fox's eyes but Gray Fox turned his head and held on choking the man with both arms. The man went limp and Gray Fox used his knife to stab his attacker in the chest.

He scurried to his feet and retrieved his rifle. He headed back up the slope to ambush the third rider. He hid down in the weeds and got ready.

He waited.

He listened but heard nothing. Gray Fox eased his way slowly to the top where he could look over the open grassland. Nothing was there. No Blackfoot scout. No horse. Just open field.

His heart raced. He had to find his pony and beat the scout back to the river. He cupped his hands together and blew into his thumbs making a flute sound. He flapped the fingers of the hand on top making the sound change back and forth. In a few minutes his pony came walking up beside him. He quickly mounted and headed back the way he had come, back toward the river.

He only rode a few minutes when he ventured upon something laying in the weeds that surprised him. He spotted a horse laying on its side with a man behind it pointing a gun at him. It was too late. He saw the flash from the barrel and felt his side burn like it was set on fire.

He fell from his horse. He lay still as his mind examined his body to tell him how bad he had been hurt. As best he could tell it was only a flesh wound. He thought. "Two can play this game."

He moved his hand down to his rifle and put his finger into the trigger guard then acted dead. He listened as the Blackfoot walked slowly over to him. He could tell exactly where the man stood. When the footsteps stopped Gray Fox opened his eyes, lifted his gun and fired catching the scout completely by surprise.

Gray Fox watched as the man's mouth dropped open and his eyes grew wide. The scout, wearing a blue Cavalry shirt with the number seven on the sleeve, staggered a few steps sideways, closed his eyes and collapsed backward to the ground.

The greatest battle in the history of the world, her world, was about to begin and she would be the only woman there. The world as she knew it was about to change. The world would be better than it had ever been in her entire life in just a day or so.

Every nation Gentle Breeze could think of had warriors here. This would be their last great stand. This would be the battle that stopped the annihilation of her people. The enemy had moved into the area and stole their land and killed the buffalo, stole their horses and slaughtered and massacred her people. The enemy would no longer be able to exterminate her relatives. Her people would be free once again.

Gentle Breeze and her husband, Gray Fox, sat on their ponies high on a ridge overlooking the Greasy Grass River as it was called by her people, the Lakota. It had been a most difficult journey. Gentle Breeze would be giving birth to her first child before the next full moon, the strawberry moon. They had left their village over two weeks ago but now they were here.

Gentle Breeze was a beautiful young woman with dark eyes and long dark hair that she parted in the middle and had it tied on both sides with leather straps made from deerskin. She wore red beads in her hair that her mother gave her when she was a little girl. The beads ran across the front of her hairline forming what looked like a hairband.

She had many suitors growing up but the man that caught her eye was a fast and strong warrior. He had muscles that made Gentle Breeze feel safe when she was with him. She loved the kindness he showed others but most of all she couldn't get enough of his smile. His smile was so powerful it not only lit up his face but also made her whole body tingle when she saw it.

She grew up with Gray Fox and they were joined together last fall during the moon of the colorful falling leaves. Gray Fox showed her attention in a way she liked and needed. He was interested in her as a person. He listened to her ideas and seemed to value her company. He made her laugh during times when life was more of a struggle than fun and when food was scarce and people were going hungry.

Gray Fox was the love of her life. He was in her heart forever. She was going to be with him always. This was the very reason she was with him now, here at the upcoming battle site. She could not bear to send him off to the fight without being there to help in any small way she could.

From the ridge they could see thousands of teepees below and Indians completely covered the basin where the Greasy Grass River ran into the Big Horn River. She had never in her life seen that many Indians in one place. It seemed that all the Indians from the four winds had come to take part in this battle that would put an end to all the Indian wars and suffering. It would stop the white man once and for all.

Her husband, Gray Fox, dismounted and walked the ponies along the top of the ridge over to where there was a thicket of trees and bushes. He helped Gentle Breeze to the ground and helped her find a place to sit near a path made by either deer or elk that led into the thicket.

Gray Fox walked away and when he returned he had an armload of grasses to make a comfortable place for Gentle Breeze to rest.

"This is a nice spot. You'll have to stay here until I can return. I'm leaving our food and water for you," Gray Fox said.

"I've made it this far and I want to go with you the rest of the way," Gentle Breeze answered.

"No, I won't have it. The only reason I allowed you to come this far was because I saw you following me the second day I left. Women aren't allowed to even be here. I love you and you have to keep our child safe. That's even more important than what I'm doing."

"You're right. If I have to ride down one more hill your son may arrive before we get to the camp."

"My son? Are you sure it's a boy?"

"Pretty sure."

"How do you know?"

"A mother can tell. Why, do you doubt me?"

"Never."

Gray Fox went over and put his hand on Gentle Breeze's swollen belly. The baby kicked and Gray Fox smiled and his face lit up with pride.

"Just think, after this battle, the white man will never hunt or try to kill our son," he said.

Gentle Breeze smiled. "Yes, after this is all over our son will be the one hunting them down. You mark my words."

"I believe you. How could it not be?" Gray Fox snickered.

Gentle Breeze got up and helped Gray Fox arrange her camp the way she wanted it. She had lived only sixteen summers but knew how she wanted things done. She had a strong will and got her way most of the time. Gray Fox, only being one summer older, gave in to avoid any conflict or disagreement that he knew he would lose anyway.

At midday, Gentle Breeze took the food pouch and got them both a piece of buffalo jerky and fry bread. She took out a cloth, opened it, and handed Gray Fox a few dried peach slices to eat. They sat in silence and ate. She did not want to think about him leaving soon but that was the only thing on her mind.

After the meal, Gray Fox stood and went to hug her good-bye. She pulled away. She looked down at the Indian camp below. She looked back at Gray Fox then down at the ground. He held her face then tried to give her a kiss but she turned her head.

Gray Fox held the lead strap of his pony and jumped up so his waist was over the back of her pony. He then held the pony's mane as he swung his leg over the back and sat. He handed down his blanket for Gentle Breeze to keep for him.

"Here, this'll keep you warm at night. Now, don't build a fire. I don't want the army to see the smoke and find you," he said.

Gentle Breeze reached over to take the lead strap of her pony. Gray Fox pulled it away and said, "I'm not leaving your pony."

"You're taking my pony too? But why? Are you afraid I will follow?"

"No, I don't want the pony to give away your location. I want you to be safe."

"But that's my pony. I want it here with me."

"I don't tell you no very often but this time I am. Besides, this way you will be part of the battle. I'll ride your pony and kill many of our enemy and someone will ride my pony and do the same." His head dropped just for a moment. He looked up and said, "It's time now for me to go."

Gentle Breeze picked up the water bag made from a big horn sheep's stomach and gave it to her husband. He shook his head no but she insisted. He took the bag and got a drink before handing it back to her.

Gentle Breeze laid the water bag down and ran back over to Gray Fox and pulled his arm down. As he leaned toward her she put both her arms around his neck and hugged him tighter than she had ever hugged him before. She was just going to hang on to him as long as she possibly could. As long as she was holding on he couldn't leave.

The trip and carrying the child had worn her strength down. She felt her grip loosen and soon her arms dropped from around his neck.

"I love you. Come back safe," she said as Gray Fox turned the ponies and headed down toward the Indian camp.

With tears forming in her eyes she watched him for as long as she could. She saw him ride into the camp where he was greeted and then surrounded by so many other Indians that it wasn't long before he blended in with the rest of the warriors and she couldn't tell which one was Gray Fox. Every once in a while she would get a glimpse of her pony and knew the rider was her husband.

From her camp on the ridge high above the Greasy Grass River, she could see the entire Indian camp. She could hear some of the hollering floating up to her from the excitement below. She thought she saw Chief Sitting Bull and wondered if she would be able to see Chief Crazy Horse with him. She looked to see if Gray Fox would ride with them or another group.

In the middle of the afternoon, Gentle Breeze spotted a large dust cloud to the south. Her heart jumped into her throat. She knew this dirt was being stirred up from horses arriving and was hoping it was another tribe coming in to join the warriors.

She heard a bugle sound and knew it was starting. She heard a great roar of cheering from the Indian camp as they scrambled to get on their horses and get ready for battle. All she could do to help was pray to the Great Spirit to keep them safe and let them be victorious. She also asked the Great Spirit to allow her, a woman, to help fight this battle in some small way that would make a large difference.

There was a double line of soldiers coming up the Big Horn River valley going north toward the Indian camp. She heard the first gunshot, which made her jump like she was just stung by a bumblebee. She could see smoke come from the guns and several seconds later the sound would reach her ears. She watched as the first Indian was shot and fell to the ground. "Please don't let that be Gray Fox," she said out loud.

It was hard for her to watch. Anger and fear rose up inside her like a small river during a hard rain. She had to look away for a moment. Her eyes followed the top of the ridge as she listened to the gunshots and yells from below. What was that she saw? Someone dressed in blue, a hundred yards away, was standing out on a ledge waving two white flags.

She noticed when this soldier moved the flags to the left the soldiers below moved to the left and the same thing happened when he moved the flags to the right, the soldiers moved to the right. When he held the flags straight up the soldiers in the middle moved forward. This man was signaling the army and moving the soldiers to where they could do the most damage.

Panic filled her heart. She ran to her blanket and unrolled it. She picked up the knife her father had made with an elk antler handle and a very long and sharp blade of steel. She headed toward the soldier with the two flags.

There was no trail to follow. She had to climb over rocks and through brush. At one spot she had to climb down a ravine and back up jagged rocks to the other side. She was slow getting there because of her condition but she wouldn't stop to rest. She couldn't stop to rest because lives were at stake, maybe Gray Fox's life.

She spotted a horse wearing an army saddle tied to a tree and knew the soldier would be just ahead. She moved as quietly as she could as she made her way toward the edge of the cliff. She spotted the soldier just ahead standing out on a ledge still waving the flags.

She got down and crawled. She moved like she had seen a mountain lion do once, very slow, and stopping after each movement of her arms or legs. She picked the places to put her hands down so no sticks or rocks would make a noise.

She crawled within ten feet of the man when she hit her shin on a jagged rock and that made her wince with pain. The soldier heard the noise and turned around. When he saw her he dropped his flags and pulled out his pistol. Gentle Breeze saw the surprised look on his face.

She said, "You would shoot a woman about to give birth to a child?" She sat back on her knees with the knife still in her hand.

The soldier froze for a moment and she could see the puzzled look in his eyes as he looked her over. He lowered his gun.

"Great Spirit, help me!" she yelled as she rose up and swung her arm back and threw the knife as hard as she could at the man.

He pointed his pistol at Gentle Breeze but it was too late. Her knife sunk deep into the man's chest. He dropped to his knees, pulled out the knife then fell forward to the ground lifeless.

Gentle Breeze took a few moments to rest and to catch her breath. Her heart was beating fast and it took time for her to settle down.

She had an idea. She walked over to the edge of the cliff and picked up the flags. She waved them in the direction the soldiers had entered the valley. She watched as some of the riders retreated. The army looked confused and she watched as Indians took advantage of the army's retreat and killed several of the soldiers while they were moving back.

She waved one flag to the left and one flag to the right and watched as the army parted allowing the Indians to move up the middle and do much damage to the troops.

She held the flags high in the air and crossed them. This made the soldiers stop where they were. She watched as Indians advanced and pushed the army back.

She waved the flags again for the army to retreat. A few soldiers moved back but this time a bugle sounded and the Cavalry move forward. Her trick was no longer working. She threw the flags down and stepped back from the edge.

She had done what she could to help fight the battle. She knew her people could use all the help they could get. Every soldier that died meant another Indian warrior would live. She wished there was more she could do.

When she was ready she retrieved her knife and picked up the pistol. She wanted to take the horse back with her but knew of no way to get the horse across the ravine she had climbed through. She knew Gray Fox was right when he had said her pony would give her away. That is exactly how she had found the man with the flags and now he was dead.

It took Gentle Breeze a long time to return to her camp. It was nearly dark when she got back. Her stomach growled from hunger and her muscles ached but something else was wrong. She doubled over from sharp pains down below where she carried the baby. The pain didn't last long but it came again and again and hurt more each time.

Chapter 2

The Battle Ends

Gentle Breeze was more frightened than she had ever been in her life. She wanted to hide because she couldn't very well go get any help. She hurried and moved all her bedding grass, food, and blankets down the animal path that went inside the thicket of bushes. Here she was out of sight and felt somewhat safer. She figured some deer had once stayed here to keep out of sight and be in the cool shade during the heat of the day. She found comfort in thinking that maybe they even had their off spring in here.

Gunfire could be heard even after dark had set in. Gentle Breeze wanted Gray Fox to return to her at nightfall, especially now. She knew this wouldn't happen with the battle still going strong. She could smell gun power once in a while and sometimes smoke from teepees burning. She had no way of knowing if the Indians were winning or being killed like so many other battles her people had fought.

She was worried about Gray Fox but that worry was interrupted. She had a pain below her stomach that wouldn't stop. She got a piece of buffalo jerky from the food pouch to bite down on so she wouldn't scream. She could feel the baby drop down and move to come out. She squatted down and pushed with her abdomen muscles.

She wanted to scream and had trouble breathing. She bit down hard on the jerky. She was straining with all her might. She was running out of strength. She had to stop and get her breath back. She was holding on to the branches of a bush just to keep her balance. The pain never stopped.

She could feel the baby slip out and drop to the ground. When the newborn landed on the ground it started to cry. Instincts took over for Gentle Breeze as she cut the cord and tied it and cleaned herself and her gift from the Great Spirit. She wrapped the baby using one corner of the blanket and let it nurse at one of her full breasts.

Gentle Breeze was so tired from the long, hard trip, killing the man with the flags, and now giving birth to this tiny new life that she was about to fall asleep, even with all the gunshots below. She was ready to pass out. She curled up in a ball under the blanket with her baby cuddled up to her stomach.

"Great Spirit, please protect me and my baby boy," she said just before her eyes closed.

The next morning, gunshots and yells woke Gentle Breeze. She checked the baby and he was sleeping. He was a beautiful baby boy. She hadn't been able to see him in the dark to see what he looked like. He was so precious and so beautiful. A life had been born to replace so many that were dying.

Gentle Breeze had to inspect every inch of her new little boy. She ran her finger across the back of his hands and opened up his fists and stroked every finger. She ran her hand across the top of his head and had to touch the little bit of soft, dark hair on the sides and back of his head.

She straightened out his little legs and rubbed his feet. She patted his belly. She took a finger and ran it across his lips. She had to touch his eyelids and she grinned as she touched his nose and saw his face wrinkle up. She kissed her infant with no name on the forehead.

One of the gunshots was very loud. It sounded like it was right outside her hiding place. She was startled and even the baby jumped and started to fuss. She moved the child to her breast and the tiny newborn quieted down as he sucked his breakfast.

Gentle Breeze felt something warm and furry with her foot. When she looked to see what it could possibly be she sat straight up and gasped. She froze with fear.

Sleeping at her feet were two dog-like animals. When she sat up both wolves looked at her and with their tails down they slowly moved back to the entrance of the path that led inside the thicket.

One of the wolves watched down the path leading out and the other sat and watched Gentle Breeze and her son. Strangely enough Gentle Breeze didn't feel any danger.

A stick broke and outside someone grunted. Both wolves turned to look. Gentle Breeze saw the hair stand up around the necks of the two animals. The wolf near the entrance made a low growling sound. The other wolf walked over and stood between Gentle Breeze and the opening. He looked at her and then at the baby.

Another very loud shot was fired just outside the thicket that made both wolves flinch. Someone moaned and Gentle Breeze saw the bushes moving along the path coming into the hidden birthing hideaway. Black boots and a pair of legs wearing blue army pants appeared and were scooting backward into her lair.

The man crawled back far enough to where he had more room and he sat up. The arrow sticking out of his thigh caused the man to moan from pain. The man looked around and met a pair of eyes, only inches from his face. Gentle Breeze watched as the sunburned face of the man turned pale, a ghostly white.

Before the man could raise his pistol the wolf beside him jumped at his throat. The other wolf gave out a mean and angry growl and attacked the man by biting the hand with the gun. The two wolves were snapping and growling and jumped on top of the man. The wolves sunk their teeth deep into the man's flesh and shook their heads causing him to yell.

Gentle Breeze heard fear in the screams of the soldier as the army man tried to fight the wolves off. He didn't fight very long before he went limp. The two wolves pulled at his arms and dragged him out of the thicket.

Gentle Breeze exhaled a grateful sigh of relief. The Great Spirit had sent her two of her ancestors in wolves' bodies to keep her safe. There was no other way to explain what had just happened.

Gentle Breeze made sure her son was all right and that he was covered. By the time she made it out of the thicket the wolves and man were gone. She saw no signs of the wolves or the dead man; only drag marks on the ground leading down the rocky and steep backside of the ridge.

She went over to see what the battle looked like. She sat beside a large rock where she could look out over the battle area without being seen. There were so many dead bodies all across the battlefield. She could see soldiers dressed in blue, Indians, horses and ponies lying scattered across the basin. Her heart filled with a deep sadness.

She strained to see her pony but it was nowhere to be found. Maybe that was a good sign. Gentle Breeze struggled to keep her spirits positive.

She watched as a small line of soldiers moved forward. She could see a larger group of soldiers off to the rear behind the Indians. She gritted her teeth and frowned. From her vantage point she could see that if the Indians attacked the smaller group the larger bunch of soldiers would then attack the Indians from behind.

She watched as Chief Sitting Bull and his men ran away from the small group of soldiers almost like they were afraid and by doing so had run right over the larger group before they were prepared. She watched as the Indians wiped out this entire group of white dogs.

Gentle Breeze could tell the main battle was almost over. There were fewer and fewer soldiers. She watched as some of the white men took cover in rocks near some cliffs. She saw a group of warriors attack them and fight until all the white men were dead.

Another group of whites were held up in a canyon. She watched as Indian warriors climbed the walls of the canyon and surrounded the men and trapped them inside. It was just a matter of time before those men would cross over the bridge to the other side to be with their ancestors.

Her heart skipped several beats. She saw her pony. Her pony had a rider and when the pony turned around she could make out the rider was Gray Fox. He threw a spear and hit a man in blue standing with a rifle in front of his horse. The man in blue dropped his gun and fell to the ground. Gray Fox had killed the soldier.

She hurried back into the thicket and grabbed the baby. Her emotions were running wild. With tears in her eyes she said a prayer, "Great Spirit, please let Gray Fox see his son."

She ran to a clear spot and held the baby high. She saw her pony turn and ride away from all the others. She watched and held her baby up and when she did her pony reared up on its hind legs. She could see Gray Fox wave with his rifle. At that moment she held her breath as tears burst forth and ran down her cheeks in an unending stream, blurring her vision. She wished she could see his face. With her heart beating hard and fast she took in a deep breath.

"I was right. It's a boy. I've named him Two Wolves," she screamed as loud as she could scream. She heard the words 'Two Wolves' echo off the canyon walls twice. She felt sure Gray Fox had heard her.

At the sound of a bugle coming from the far side of the battlefield she watched as a group of soldiers gathered together on top of a small knoll. She saw a man waving a sword and the last of the men were standing with him as they all loaded their guns and got ready for the next Indian attack.

The man waving the sword had an arrow sticking in his leg and was bleeding from a hole in his side. He looked like he was giving orders to the others. He motioned with his sword in such a flurry that his hat fell from his head. Gentle Breeze noticed something different about this man. She had never seen a man with long yellow hair before.

She watched her pony for as long as she could keep track of it. She lost sight of her pony as it ran with many other ponies and horses into the dust and smoke of battle. At least Gray Fox was alive and he had seen his baby boy.

Less and less gunshots were being fired as the day wore on. Late in the evening of that second day the battle was over. There were no more white soldiers left standing. There were many Indians riding around helping those Indian warriors that had survived but were wounded. Some Indians walked across the battlefield and would fire a shot into any white man still moving or breathing.

Several of the tribes were gathering together and heading off in different directions. They didn't bother with the teepees; all of those were torn down or burned. Chief Sitting Bull and his men rode off towards the north.

Soon Gray Fox would be coming back. She felt joy in her heart. Her people had won. Things would be different from now on.

She waited.

She was still waiting the next morning because Gray Fox hadn't returned. The smoke of battle had cleared. She searched the battlefield with her eyes from where she stood above the valley but the only ones left were the ones on the ground. All the tribes had moved on.

There was no sound of any kind. No sound from galloping horse hooves. No more gunfire or battle cries could be heard. No birds sang. No crickets chirped. No leaves rattling in the wind. Smoke from some smoldering teepees rising straight up into the air was the only movement below.

Then her worst fear rose up and grabbed her and shook her. She saw her pony standing alone with no rider. She knew. She dropped to her knees with her baby in her arms and wailed a death chant as loud as she could. It didn't matter now how loud she could chant because there was no one left to hear her.

Gentle Breeze and Two Wolves cried.

Chapter 3

THE SWEAT LODGE

Two Wolves woke early. Today was the day he had been looking forward to for sixteen summers. He was going to go with the warriors and a few others his age to purify his body and spirit. He had heard his uncle say the chief would be there and that made this special. The chief didn't always go to every sweat lodge ceremony.

Gentle Breeze's brother stuck his head in the flap of the teepee. "Two Wolves, I need you to go with me today. I have to ride over to the Pine Ridge Agency to take care of some business. We'll be gone most of the day."

"You know what today is and we aren't going to the agency. Stop trying to fool me. What time am I supposed to be at the lodge?" Two Wolves asked.

"At midday. I'm going over now to help build the lodge and gather the rocks and wood for the fire," Brave Hawk, his uncle said.

"I'm ready now so I'll go with you and help."

"What about something to eat before you run off? You know after the ceremony you'll be gone a few days so you best eat something before you go," Gentle Breeze said.

Two Wolves hugged his mom and said, "I love you, Mother, but I can't eat. Besides, I'm supposed to fast today. Uncle Brave Hawk, I'm ready."

He left with his uncle. As they were riding over to where the sweat lodge would be built Two Wolves asked, "Do I become a warrior today?"

"You were born a warrior. Never forget that."

"I know, but according to our way of life and what our people believe, after today am I accepted as an adult warrior?"

"This is the first step. You go into the sweat lodge and sweat away the impurities of your body. You will pray and clean your spirit. The chief will talk with all the young men and give them wisdom. The second step is your vision quest. There, you will see what the Great Spirit wants you to know. The last step is the great hunt. When you kill your first large animal and give the meat to our people then you are a man, a warrior."

"Uncle Brave Hawk, tell me the story again of how you and my father got your names," Two Wolves said.

"Before either of us was born, our mother saw a hawk and a gray fox in a field. She watched as they fought with each other. The hawk would swoop down to grab at the fox but the fox was too crafty and always got away from the hawk. When the fox tried to get the hawk, the hawk would fly and circle back around to get the fox. Neither one of the two could get the best of the other one. This went on for some time as our mother watched.

"A nearby eagle saw what was going on and moved in to get the fox. The hawk would have no part of it and chased the eagle away. Also, another fox, a red fox, came to join the hunt but the little gray fox ran it off. It was as if the gray fox and the brave hawk protected each other from outside forces. But neither of the two could outsmart the other. They were equal in their hunting skills.

"Mother wanted to always remember this scenario. When it was time to have her baby she was surprised to have two boys, your father and me. She named us Brave

Hawk and Gray Fox so we would always be equal and watch out for each other.

"I'm sorry I couldn't do that at Greasy Grass. Your father saw you just before he was shot in battle. He pointed for me to look and I saw you too. I watch over him now by looking after you and Gentle Breeze the best I can."

"I know, and you've done a great job. Mother thinks so too. We couldn't have made it without you. Was Gray Fox great in battle?"

"Yes, he really was. He killed more soldiers than I could keep count of. Yellow Hair had a couple of arrows in him but the shot from Gray Fox's rifle brought Yellow Hair to his knees. Then another shot finished Yellow Hair off. Gray Fox was a great warrior. Gentle Breeze is a great warrior too. I'm sure you'll follow in their footsteps."

They stopped and tied their horses to a small bush at the edge of a large field where several men were working. The men had the frame of the lodge standing up and were covering it with buffalo hides. The holy man was there wearing his headdress of deer antlers. He pointed showing some men where the door going into the lodge had to be. The door had to face east.

"What's our job?" Two Wolves asked.

"I'm the fire overseer. You can help me make the fire pits. We need to make a large one outside and a smaller one inside. The one outside is for the fire to heat the rocks and the one inside won't have a fire. It'll be to hold the hot rocks as water is poured over them to make steam used to make everyone sweat."

They went to work. Before long they had both pits dug and a large amount of fire wood beside the outside pit. "We're ready to collect the rocks. Follow me down the hill to the creek bed and we'll start carrying them up here."

Once at the creek Two Wolves watched to see what size rocks his uncle was gathering. He then started picking up every rock he could find that was about the same size. He held all he could carry on one trip and started back up the hill.

"Hold on there," his uncle said. "Most of your rocks are the wrong kind."

"Wrong kind? They're all rocks aren't they?"

His uncle grinned. "Yes, but most of the rocks you gathered will crack or break apart with the heat of the fire."

"What's the difference?"

"Set your load down. Now look at this one," the uncle said pointing to one of the larger rocks. "It has lines running down the sides. That means it was made in layers. It could even explode when heated. We need the ones that are solid and strong. We want only rocks like that to send us their energy if we're to be solid and strong warriors. We don't want energy that will make us explode or crack apart."

They lined the edge of the pit with many rocks just the right size to be carried or rolled inside without being dropped.

"How will you get the hot rocks into the lodge?" Two Wolves asked.

"The Great Spirit has made each of us with a gift."

"And you have the gift of carrying hot rocks?"

The uncle laughed. "Yes, I'm a fire starter. I'll show you that in a few minutes. To carry hot rocks I have to use this limb with a fork. I scoop up the rock from underneath and the rock sits in the Y of the fork. That allows me to carry it inside to the other smaller fire pit."

"Fire starter, huh. Do you use magic?"

"Almost. Now take my tomahawk and chop some of these longer limbs into pieces that will be easier to burn. It won't be long now." The uncle then took a bucket down to the stream and got water to be used inside the lodge.

At midday the chief arrived. He wore a long sleeve shirt and buckskin pants. He had two braids, one down each side of his head. He was wearing a headband made from dyed porcupine quills. Two Wolves was disappointed that the chief wasn't in his full Indian ensemble with his headdress full of eagle feathers. After all, this was a big event for Two Wolves.

The chief greeted each of the men by grabbing their forearms and looking each of them in the eyes. "Light the fire, and observe our fire starter. Then I want the men going into the sweat lodge to come over here with me."

The uncle put some dried grasses at the bottom of the fire pit. He then added a handful of small dried sticks. He took out a pouch and sprinkled some black dust over the fire pit. He stood back and pulled out a rock of flint. Next he hit the flint using the back edge of his hunting knife. When one of the sparks landed in the fire pit there was a loud whoosh sound and all the wood burst into flames at the same time.

Two Wolves jumped back and noticed everyone else do the same. Some of the young men's eyes grew very wide and their jaw dropped down.

"That is magic," Two Wolves said.

His uncle moved his mouth over to Two Wolves' ear and whispered, "Gun powder. Now shhhhh."

Two Wolves' uncle put some smaller pieces of wood into the pit. As the flame grew more wood was added so the flames would heat the rocks along the sides.

The young men gathered around the chief. "I've seen each of you grow from a baby into a man. I am proud of all the young men from our tribe. Starting today you are no longer boys. From now on you must not think of your needs but of the needs of our people. Times are very hard. Our people have suffered much. We have many that aren't as strong as they once were. They need your help if we're to survive as a people. It's now your job to provide and protect the ones that can no longer do this for themselves. We owe them much. They are the ones that saved us and fought for us when you were too small to feed your own bellies. Take off your shirts and pants and follow me inside the sweat lodge where each of you will get a chance to tell me what's in your heart."

The chief held the lodge door flap open and motioned for the young men to enter. He handed each young adult a piece of cloth to sit on. He waited for the medicine man to go in then he went in and found a seat on the ground.

Two Wolves watched in anticipation as the medicine man held up a bundle of sage and set fire to it. He blew out the flames and allowed it to smolder. He said a prayer to the Great Spirit. The powerful way he talked to the Great Spirit made Two Wolves feel that the Great Spirit was in the lodge with him. After the prayer the holy man walked by each young man waving the smoke over their body and through their hair.

The elders rolled the hot rocks into the lodge and into the shallow fire pit. Next Two Wolves' uncle carried in the bucket of water and set it beside the rocks and left, closing the lodge flap. The chief picked the bucket up and poured some of the water over the rocks. The water crackled and hissed as the water turned into steam that filled the sweat lodge.

It didn't take Two Wolves very long to figure out why they took off their shirt and pants. The lodge heated up in a hurry from the steam and he was sweating as if he had run all the way there on the hottest day of the year. It was getting hard for him to catch his breath.

One of the boys couldn't stop giggling. The chief grabbed the boy's arm and pulled him up.

The chief then spoke to the others. "There's nothing wrong with being a boy. We all grow at different speeds. All the wild flowers don't bloom on the same day. Do all the leaves fall from the trees on the same day when the winter winds come? We have to accept people that are not in the same place as ourselves. That does not mean they are wrong. It only means we're in different places and that is okay. It's good to be who we are. As we cross a stream, no two people can stand on the same rock at the same time without one of them falling. Today we are crossing a great stream. Make sure you get your balance first then you can help another."

The chief looked at the boy whose arm he was holding. "You must leave. I invite you to join me at the next sweat lodge ceremony." The boy dropped his head and moved the lodge door flap and went outside.

Two Wolves welcomed a breath of fresh air as the door opened. That didn't last very long though as a couple of elders rolled in some more very hot rocks and more water was poured over them.

The holy man waved the smoldering bundle of sage and looked up. He was softly saying a prayer and motioned for all to do the same. Two Wolves didn't know what to pray so he asked the Great Spirit to protect his mother and to protect him.

The chief held up a peace pipe filled with rabbit tobacco and lit the pipe. He took a puff then said, "We will pass this pipe along. While you hold the pipe you will only speak truth. When it's your turn, take a puff then speak from your heart. Since I have the pipe and took a puff I'll go first.

"The great war is over. The white man took our land. We did not lose. We survived. Now we are fighting another battle. We are fighting for our place in this new time. In my heart I know there will be great warriors from our people. I know that some of us will be great leaders and great teachers and great healers. We are in the process of changing our way of life. We don't have to give up our beliefs; we just need to find ways in this new time to make them work without all the violence."

The chief passed the peace pipe over to the young man sitting next to Two Wolves. The young man took the pipe and held it over his head then took a puff.

He said, "I want our people to find happiness. I want my family to have enough food so they won't go hungry. I don't know how to make this happen but I'll look for the answers as I follow my path."

He passed the pipe over to Two Wolves. Two Wolves took the pipe and held it above his head then lowered it and took a puff. The smoke went into his lungs and he had to cough.

Two Wolves said, "I want our people to be free in this new time. I want justice and for our people and for them to be equal. I feel in my heart that this is possible. We're fighting a new kind of battle. In this new battle we need to learn the white man's ways and use what is helpful. We can throw the rest away. Only then can we find our place among the whites in this new era. There are too many whites to take our land back but we still have our respect and our way of life even if we have to change some in order for us to survive. If we make the same mistakes we have always made then we will remain in the condition we're in now. We must learn to make better choices."

He passed the pipe on to the next person. This man was older and had been to many sweats before. He raised the pipe and then took a puff. He said, "The white man kills the buffalo just because he can. The meat lays on the ground and rots. It poisons Mother Earth. The whites will not learn before they poison the water and the air also. We don't have to be like them. Always respect Mother Earth and you will have respect for yourself."

The pipe was passed around until every young man had a turn, then it was returned to the chief.

The chief stood and said, "I am proud of what I've heard here today. You all are indeed men. Now our holy man will give you instructions about your vision quest." The chief opened the door flap and went outside leaving the door open.

The holy man stood and said, "This is an exciting time in your lives. Your lives will only go faster from now on. To enjoy it and make the most out of it you must be ready. Starting now you'll become men. You only have one more major step to accomplish. So, are you ready to die?"

Chapter 4

THE VISION QUEST

All the young men stood and were looking back and forth at each other. Two Wolves' eyes became big as he looked around startled. He wasn't ready to die. He wiped the sweat from his forehead. Looking around at the others he saw each of them had a serious, almost fearful look on their faces. He swallowed hard.

The holy man started laughing. "I don't mean you will leave your body and cross over today. But you will leave your childhood life and enter into manhood. You'll all be given a canteen of water to take with you on your vision quest. You are not to eat any food while you're gone. Each of you will ride to a high peak or mountaintop and find a peaceful place to stay for a few days. Don't leave this spot. You are to pray until you receive instructions from the Great Spirit. You will know when that happens. After you receive your vision return here to me and I will help you understand the vision. Go now and be safe."

Two Wolves walked out of the lodge, he wiped the sweat from his face and shoulders with the cloth he had been sitting on. He quickly ran over and got dressed. His uncle came over and gave him a slap on the back and greeted him with a smile of pride.

"Where will you go for your quest?" his uncle asked.

"I have two places in mind but I'm not sure which one is the better place. Where did you go?"

"My first quest was up on Porcupine Ridge. It wasn't such a good place because it was near here, and there were too many others using it for their quest."

"That was my first pick. I'm also wondering about Eagle Cliff."

"We think a lot alike. Eagle Cliff is where I go now whenever I go on another vision quest. It's a half-day's ride. It's higher and more peaceful. Remember that spot near the top we went to once?"

"Where there's a hole in the rock making the rock look like a giant ring?"

"That's the place. I sat under the natural bridge. It gave me shade during the day and the cliff walls protected me from the wind at night."

"Okay, thanks Uncle Brave Hawk, I guess I need to get going. Watch out for Mother while I'm gone."

Two Wolves walked down and untied his horse and swung his legs over the horse's bare back and turned the horse southeast toward Eagle Cliff. He waved and rode away.

He had only been there once with his uncle but he remembered the way. He arrived a few hours before dark. He dismounted and took the bridle off his horse and used the leather straps to tie the horse's front legs together with enough strap for the horse to walk around. He knew if he tied the horse to a bush using the bridle the horse could starve. By tying the horse's legs together the horse could walk around and find food without going too far.

It took Two Wolves a couple of hours to make his way to the top and find the natural bridge. He made a place to sit down and relax under the giant ring. His stomach churned and made a growling sound. He rubbed his stomach then he went over and sat down to catch his breath.

He studied the natural bridge overhead. The bridge being all one solid rock with a giant hole running through it was beautiful. The rock had a yellowish orange color and seemed to glow from a distance when the sun struck it just right. Under this ring Two Wolves sat in the soft, reddish sand. This would make for a comfortable place to stay for the duration of his quest.

Two Wolves stood under the natural bridge and could see down both sides of the mountain. The side he'd climbed up was rocky while the other side wasn't as steep and had many pine trees growing creating a forest with lots of birds flying from tree to tree. He listened to the birds calling to each other and he knew he wasn't alone. He enjoyed hearing the birds as they sang out to each other. He relaxed as they welcomed him to the area.

It was quickly becoming dark. He knew he was going to stay up all night and pray. He looked forward to the challenge. If he fell asleep he could miss his vision.

He opened his hands toward the heavens and started praying. At first he just wanted his family to be safe and happy. He gave thanks for the many experiences that had made him a man. He continued praying about everything he could think of. He started getting sleepy so he chanted the songs his mother had taught him. He sang the songs he had learned at the gatherings in the springtime when tribes came together to dance, enjoy food, and celebrate.

His head grew heavy and his eyes started closing. He thought it would be a good idea to just listen to the sounds of the night. He heard wind moving leaves. He heard a coyote howling over on the next ridge. He heard an owl hoot not far from where he was sitting. There was a sound of some tiny creature scurrying through the pine needles on the ground near him. He nodded his head down and tried to locate the little mouse or whatever the animal was.

The next morning the sun woke him as it appeared shining through the giant ring and right into his eyes. He jumped up. He frowned when he realized he had fallen asleep. The sun had been shining for a while, but he did feel rested so maybe he could concentrate better today. He stood and stretched then sat down to pray.

As the day went on he ran out of things to say to the Great Spirit and he found it harder to pray. He had prayed about everything and everyone he could think of. His belly growled louder and whenever he took a drink it gurgled. He yawned then took a deep breath and let out a sigh. He stood and walked around in a circle to keep his legs from cramping from all the sitting.

By the end of the day Two Wolves found it easier to sit still. He thought about his mother and his friends but for that moment he had no worries. He adored the view from high up on Eagle Cliff and the air smelled sweet and fresh with the scent of pine. He enjoyed the refreshing stillness and he liked being there without any occurrences going on around him except for a few clouds floating by and changing shapes.

He sensed something strange happening. Two Wolves wondered if this was the start of his vision. He noticed that as he sat there concentrating on the fluffy clouds that he could burn a hole right though a cloud just by staring at it and thinking of nothing else. Maybe this wasn't him doing it and something that happened naturally as he watched the clouds.

He had to try this again to see if it was his thoughts or just nature. He concentrated his thoughts again as he stared at the cloud. And again a hole slowly opened as the cloud dissolved but only at the spot he stared at.

This amazed Two Wolves. He tried it again and again. Each time the cloud opened up at the spot he stared at. He was doing it. He found this exciting and wondered if anyone could do it or if he was special.

He saw a cloud that looked like a fish. He remembered the time he thought about becoming a fisherman. After thinking about it awhile he said to someone that he wanted to learn how to fish. Once he said it then he tried it. It wasn't long before someone gave him advice on how to catch fish and showed him what worked for them. And with the help of the Great Spirit providing the tools and experience needed in the form of other people that helped he became a rather good fisherman over time.

He realized that if he thought about something long enough he usually talked about it and what he talked about, in time, he usually ended up doing. And then what he did, if he did it enough, he would become. It all started with that first thought.

He wondered if this insight could be his vision. It was so simple but something he had to give deep thought to in order to see it. A thought became words. Words became action and that action became a way of life.

Two Wolves had his vision. But he didn't want to return home yet. He wanted to stay another day. Going back this soon would make him look bad. A vision quest wasn't supposed to be this easy.

That evening some storm clouds moved in. Two Wolves moved under an overhang and prepared for the rain. When the rain came he was in a dry place though he did get some mist of rain when the wind would blow.

It continued raining all night but he didn't mind. The storm turned into a soft light rain. The chill that came with it kept him awake. He enjoyed listening to the water hitting the rocks and trees.

He welcomed the morning sun. Two Wolves smiled at himself for not being tired or sleepy. Actually he felt pretty good and didn't feel hungry like he had the day before.

He sat and prayed but it didn't take long before he was all prayed out so he just sat to listen for a change.

Two Wolves stood and stretched and let out a groaning sound as he tried to reach the clouds with his hands. He heard another sound. It was a snort. He thought for a moment but the snort hadn't come from him.

He looked around to see what could have made the snorting sound. Standing about a stone's throw away he saw a sacred white buffalo. A sacred white buffalo hadn't been seen in this area since before the Great Sioux Wars started a long time ago. "How did you get up here?" Two Wolves asked not expecting an answer. He wanted to go over and touch it to see if it was real but he remembered he wasn't allowed to leave his spot for any reason.

The huge animal snorted again then put his head down to the ground to find some grass to eat.

"All whites aren't evil," a voice said. The voice seemed to be coming from the buffalo but Two Wolves couldn't tell with its head down to the ground and its mouth hidden in the grass.

"What does that mean?" Two Wolves asked again not expecting an answer.

The white buffalo looked Two Wolves right in the eye while chewing its grass. It lowered its head and took a step closer and started chomping on more grass.

"I'm white so some whites are good," the voice said.

"None I know of except for you," Two Wolves said.

"Are white cranes evil? Are mountain goats evil? Are white horses all bad?" the voice asked. The buffalo raised its head and looked at Two Wolves again as it walked several steps closer.

"No, but they aren't white men."

The white buffalo used its nose to rub its hind leg and lowered its head down to eat more grass. "All white men aren't evil."

This time Two Wolves didn't reply. He frowned and his eyebrows furrowed down closer to his eyes where he could see them. This was his vision quest? A white buffalo telling him there were some good white men? How could that even be true? How was it possible for him to carry on a conversation with a white buffalo? This was crazy.

He saw a thorn bush so he went over and grabbed a stem from the bush. He jerked his hand away as some thorns went into the palm of his hand. He looked at the couple spots of blood the thorns left. "Now if these punctures are here tomorrow then I'll know that this wasn't just some silly dream," Two Wolves said.

The white buffalo walked toward Two Wolves until it was almost within reach. It lowered its head into some tall weeds to find more food. "Sometimes one must become the enemy to survive."

Two Wolves was becoming more puzzled. "What does that mean? How can that even happen?" he asked.

The mighty buffalo raised its head. This time it started clawing the ground with its front hooves and snorted loudly. It charged right at Two Wolves.

This took Two Wolves by surprise and he jumped back. There was no place for him to go to get out of the charging buffalo's way. He was so shocked at seeing the buffalo coming at him that he raised his hands in the air and made a loud roar like a bear to scare the buffalo away. In doing this he slipped on a stone and lost his footing. He fell backward to the ground.

Two Wolves scurried to his feet only to find the buffalo was gone.

With his heart racing Two Wolves knew this was his vision. He didn't understand why he got a vision that couldn't possibly be true. He stayed another two days sitting under the natural bridge partly hoping for more but mostly because he didn't want to tell the holy man about his vision. Just to be sure that was the vision, he checked the palm of his hand and it was sore from the thorns.

He was getting weak from not eating so he made his way back down and looked for his horse. When he found his horse he leaned down to undo the leather straps around its legs and that is when he saw the hoof prints of a buffalo all over the ground next to the horse.

On the ride home, the sky had a few of those large fluffy clouds floating from west to east. Two Wolves did see one white cloud that resembled a buffalo and that cloud was going in a different direction than all the other clouds.

Two Wolves rode straight to the medicine man and found him sitting by a campfire in front of his teepee near the river that ran out of the Badlands. The medicine man was chipping some flint rock to form arrowheads. Two Wolves told him of the vision. "What does my vision mean?" he asked.

"Have you met every white man?" the holy man asked. "If not, then it's possible that you will find one that's good. A long time ago, in the land of the Shawnee, I have heard stories of a white man who was a chief named Chief Blue Jacket. I have met a few white men that I trusted and even liked as a man. As for becoming the enemy, I believe that to mean you must always be friends with yourself. Do not become your own worst enemy."

Two Wolves nodded. The explanation left him almost as confused as the vision. He thanked the medicine man and walked over and got his horse and headed home. He had been cheated. He had hoped his vision would have a life-changing event attached to it and the vision would help him make his world a better place. He wanted his vision to be something exciting. He didn't understand how the meaning of his vision could accomplish this. "Good white men, buffalo chips!" he yelled.

Chapter 5

THE HUNTING PARTY

Two Wolves had watched the hunting party leave and return for sixteen summers. He had always stayed at camp to protect the women and children. That is what the chief had told him he needed to do.

Earlier this spring Two Wolves had gone on a vision quest to complete the ritual of becoming a warrior. The Great Spirit had shown him a vision that he did not understand. In his vision, he became the enemy and saw that not all white men were bad. He felt the wisdom was false so he had put it in the back of his mind.

Since he did complete the vision quest, this summer he would ride with the hunting party to help find food for his people. He was finally becoming a warrior.

His people had been forced to move onto the Pine Ridge Reservation during his sixth winter. His people tried to remain free for as long as they could. The people were starving and many were sick so eventually they were captured and moved to the reservation.

Two Wolves had only heard stories of how large his tribe once was. He grew up hearing about how brave his father fought in the battle of Greasy Grass River that the white man calls the Little Big Horn. He had heard the stories of how he and his mother had killed the soldier with the flags but he doesn't remember any of the battle. He loved hearing about the time when they were powerful and free. Now there were but a handful of warriors left in his family clan.

Two Wolves knew how beautiful the land on the reservation looked. The land had a few mountain ridges and many rolling hills and lots of grasslands. Two Wolves had spent his youth riding and exploring the creeks and cliffs. The main problem with being on the reservation was that there was very little food and the Indians were not allowed to leave to find more.

Every year, though, the hunting party would sneak away and go into the mountains to hunt for food. Some years they would bring back a buffalo, which would feed them well for many months. The last few years had been sparse as far as finding meat.

More and more white towns were being built and whites were moving in at a faster rate to find gold in the Black Hills. The large Iron Horse brought in settlers and white hunters and they had killed most of the buffalo and only used the skins. They let the meat lay on the ground and rot.

"Two Wolves, are you ready to ride?" Brave Hawk, his uncle, asked.

"More than ready. We have our teepee strapped to our donkey and just waiting for you," he replied.

"Good. You will follow behind me. We'll make it to the edge of the reservation by nightfall and then travel by night to avoid being seen. We'll head north from there. Okay, mount up. We have a hard journey ahead of us."

Two Wolves excitedly ran over and picked his mother up and swung her around. "We are finally going."

"Yes, but don't act as though you ate loco weed for your last meal," Gentle Breeze answered.

"I couldn't be happier if I had eaten loco weed," Two Wolves said.

Two Wolves' cousin, Dawn, ran over and gave him a hug. "Be safe and bring me back a buffalo robe."

"Don't you worry about that. I will bring back a whole herd. This winter we will all get fat from all the meat I'll bring back home."

"Just don't tangle with any of those mean ole porcupines." Dawn started giggling.

Two Wolves gave a playful frown then ran and jumped up on the back of his horse. He remembered what Dawn referred to. A few years back they had been playing near a creek when Two Wolves heard a noise behind him. He was startled and slipped and fell. He ended up sitting on top of a porcupine. It took the rest of the day to get all the quills out of his hindquarters and he was still trying to live that down. For many moons after that he was known as Quill Butt.

By the time this hunting trip would be over, the last thing anyone would remember would be his encounter with that porcupine.

The horses started moving. Two Wolves and Gentle Breeze rode behind Brave Hawk with their donkey between the two of them.

During the second night of riding, Brave Hawk led the hunting party into a dead end canyon. "This is where we'll camp. I've camped here before and it's safe here. Set up the teepees tonight and get what rest you can. At daybreak the hunters will join me to start the hunt," Brave Hawk said.

Two Wolves helped his mom set up their teepee. As they were working he asked, "Mother, why don't they let you go on the actual hunt? You're a warrior. You fought in the battle with my father."

"Okay, I'll go and you can stay here and get ready to prepare the meat when I bring it back," she teased.

"No, thanks. This is my year to ride on the hunt. I was just wondering how you got to go into battle and don't get to go on the hunt."

"I wasn't supposed to be at the battle. I followed your father anyway. You were born during the battle that took his life so you were born a warrior. Since you will become a man with your first kill tomorrow I'll stay here and get ready to butcher all the meat you bring back. I have hunted before on my own when you were small. I had to feed you. Now you'll feed me and I'll prepare and dry the meat. That's my job now. You had better get some rest."

Two Wolves went inside to lie down. The harder he tried to go to sleep the more he tossed and turned. He was still awake when the sun rose the next morning.

As soon as he heard another person walking around he jumped up and said, "Mother, we're leaving. I have to go."

He ran out of the teepee to find Brave Hawk walking some horses down to a nearby creek for a drink. He saw a few others sitting outside and eating some fry bread for breakfast. It looked like any other day back on the reservation. He felt disappointed and confused as to why they were not mounting up.

He went over and grabbed the lead straps of his horse, his mother's horse, and the donkey and headed for the creek. When he caught up with Brave Hawk he asked, "We are going today, right?"

"Good morning. How did you sleep?" Two Wolves noticed a big grin run across the face of his uncle after he spoke.

"Good morning. I didn't sleep, not at all. But we are going here soon, yes?"

"Well, without any sleep maybe we should stay at camp today and wait for the buffalo to come to us. It'll be easier that way."

"Oh stop it. When are we going to leave?"

"Soon. Let the horses drink and go and wash your face. Then get you a bite to eat. After that we'll say a prayer and start the hunt."

When Two Wolves got back to his teepee, Gentle Breeze was up and fixing some food for him to take with him. "Good morning," she said. "Are you back so soon?"

"Why is everyone teasing me? I'm the only one ready to ride."

"If you are so ready then I guess you have eaten and fed the horses. Where's the food you are taking with you?"

Then it hit Two Wolves that there were chores to do and preparations to make before he could just ride off and find the buffalo. If he didn't hurry he would be the last man ready to go. He took the horses and donkey over to a grassy area and let them eat. When he returned Gentle Breeze had breakfast ready and a pouch of water and some food for him to take with him on the ride.

Before he finished Brave Hawk motioned for everyone to gather around. Two Wolves crammed the last few bites into his mouth and ran over to where the others were. They had to stand in a circle as Brave Hawk prayed to the Great Spirit for protection and guidance. "Great Spirit, we give thanks to the animals that you have chosen for us to take for food. They give their life so we may live. Let them know that we don't kill for the sake of killing and that we will use all they provide to do only good. Watch over us and be with us today."

The women burned sage and walked around fanning the smoke on all the warriors.

"Let the hunt begin," Brave Hawk announced.

Two Wolves started to run back to get his horse but his mom had the horse right behind him. He mounted and she handed him the food and water. From where he sat on his horse he could see the top of his mother's head. She always wore her hair with tiny red beads that formed small rows across the front. He leaned down and gave her a kiss on her forehead and turned his horse to join the others.

"Wait. Haven't you forgotten something?" she asked.

"Yes, sorry. I love you."

"Yes, that, but don't you need your rifle? Or are you going to sit on them to take them down?" Gentle Breeze handed him the gun.

"Mother, geeze. Enjoy teasing me for the last time. Today I will bring home more than porcupine quills." He rode off with the others and turned to wave and smile at his mother.

There were only seven warriors going. The women and a few of the older men stayed at camp to prepare for their return. He was proud to ride with such great warriors. Many of the men had fought with Chief Sitting Bull in the battle that took his father from him. Others had fought in many battles alongside Chief Crazy Horse and Chief Red Cloud.

They rode until they came to the end of the forest. Here the tree line opened up into a large grassy field. Two Wolves noticed that the men were walking the horses as they looked down at the ground.

Brave Hawk, pointing at three of the men, said, "You three go east and the rest of you come with me. We will meet back here after we find our kills."

The four remaining hunters walked the horses along the tree line heading west. Two Wolves kept an eye out for some large animal standing off in the distance that he could ride up and shoot. This walking was going too slow for Two Wolves.

"Wouldn't it be better if we rode fast and found some deer or antelope?" he asked.

"And just where would we ride to? Animals don't just stand there waiting for us to come along to kill them, you know. If we did what you said then they would see us coming and be gone when we got there. All we would find is tracks and droppings."

"Then how do we find anything?"

"See the pine tree here that has a dished out place on one side of its trunk? That's a tree a buffalo uses to scratch its back. They use the same tree and eventually the tree bark wears thin. This is a fresh marking made not too long ago. You can tell by the tree sap forming little beads inside the indentation. We also look for hoof prints. Those big prints over there are headed the other way so the three that went east may have a better chance catching up with them. See that smaller hoof print to your right? Now that one is an elk and it looks like he is headed for higher ground. Once we get nearer the top of this slope I'll send you around to the other side of this mountain. From there you'll be able to track him and get close enough to take a shot."

"Why do I have to go to the other side to get him? Isn't that a long way around?"

"Yes, but if we just keep following his trail he will just keep staying out of range in front of us. We'll end up growing old following him. The wind is to our back so he is watching and can smell us coming. When you go around you will be down wind and he won't know you are there. Dismount once over there and walk back toward us. Maybe you will see him and can sneak up and take a shot."

"What if I don't see him or if I miss?"

"Then he'll hear you and come back this way. We will stay here and spread out and wait. If you have to shoot from a far distance the bullet will drop and you will shoot under him. So, if he is far off when you shoot aim about a foot above his head."

"Do you want me to go around this ridge now?"

"Yes, but remember, once on the other side, tie your horse and walk. Elk, as most wild animals, look for movement more than anything else. Move slow and stay hid. Have your rifle cocked and ready so he won't hear the sound of the metal shell casing going into the chamber."

"This is a lot different than rabbit hunting, isn't it? With a rabbit I could just whistle and it would stop and look."

"Yes, this is different. A rabbit stops to see what the whistle is. For an elk, don't whistle because he will know what the whistle is and be gone."

It took Two Wolves a little while to ride to the backside of the ridge. He rode half way up then dismounted and tied his horse to a sapling. He cocked his rifle and slowly walked up the hill staying in the tree line and staying out of open sight.

Two Wolves was almost at the top. He stopped to search for an elk grazing. Then he spotted something moving. It was just like what his uncle had said. He saw the movement before he could make out the elk. The elk blended in with his surroundings and was hard to see except for the huge antlers that would tilt from side to side with the movement of his head and even those looked like tree branches.

The elk would walk a few steps then stop and look behind him. The elk acted as though he knew someone was back there. The elk stayed behind trees and there was no good shot to take. Two Wolves watched as the elk stretched out one of his front legs and used its nose to rub its lower leg. It walked between trees but always seemed to be behind a tree when it stopped.

Two Wolves saw an opening it had to move through to continue up the hill. This would be the only chance he would have at shooting the animal without him having to go back down and around to the next ridge. He got ready and waited.

The elk walked up to the clearing but stopped just before going into the open. It stood there so long that Two Wolves didn't think it would move on and wasn't sure if he would get a shot. The elk was making sure it was safe. The elk started moving forward again.

Two Wolves took aim. The elk walked into the open space. Two Wolves had his finger on the trigger and was starting to squeeze it. The elk suddenly jumped over a fallen tree and was now trotting to the other side to find the tree line.

If Two Wolves would have fired he would have missed but now he had to fire or his chance would be gone. He aimed his gun slightly in front of and just a little bit above the elk. The elk was only a few steps from the trees. Two Wolves pulled the trigger.

Blam!

The elk jumped toward the trees and was out of sight. Two Wolves looked up in surprise. He was sure he got it. He ran to the open section between the trees. He saw blood on the ground where the elk once stood.

Two Wolves walked a couple of steps ahead and there in the bushes was the elk lying on its side not moving. He did get it. He looked around to see who might have seen his feat but no one had caught up with him yet. He took a giant breath and waited for the others. He didn't even want to start dressing it out until someone was there to see his kill. He paced back and forth with pride while he waited for the others to arrive.

After a couple of days the hunting party was returning to camp. The hunt had been successful and they had all the meat their horses could carry. The three warriors that went off to the east together had brought back a medium sized buffalo. Two Wolves had downed an elk and was feeling very good about his hunting skills. He had learned a lot from his uncle and would always remember this hunt.

When they arrived at the mouth of the canyon where they had set up camp, Brave Hawk stopped them. Two Wolves saw a worried look on his face.

"Listen," Brave Hawk said. "Something's wrong."

The older warrior who was to guard the trail into the canyon was gone. Brave Hawk pointed to horse tracks going into and out of the canyon.

Brave Hawk dropped the meat from his horse. The others did the same. Brave Hawk took off riding as fast as he could with the others following. Brave Hawk stopped them again half way down the trail. Two Wolves pointed to the sky above where the camp was. The sky was filled with dark smoke. His heart was beating fast and he could feel it in his throat.

Chapter 6

THE BURIAL

Two Wolves saw Brave Hawk dismount. He and the others got off their horses. He started walking. With his gun in hand, he went toward the camp. It was eerie that no sound could be heard. He didn't know what to expect. He started running.

Two Wolves was the first one back to camp. The teepees were all lying on the ground and some were burning. All the horses were gone. He saw bodies lying in different directions where his people ran for their lives. He searched for Gentle Breeze but couldn't find her. Maybe she had made it our alive.

He ran over to his teepee that had been pulled over. He saw legs partly showing from under one side of the buffalo hide they used to cover the temporary home. He ran to her and pulled her free. It was Gentle Breeze. She had been killed; shot many times.

Two Wolves looked in horror. He didn't understand what he saw. The top part of Gentle Breeze's head was blood soaked. Someone had used a knife and cut the top part of her hair and scalp off. All that was left was blood where her long, beautiful, dark hair once was.

Two Wolves was numb. He wanted to feel sadness but he couldn't feel anything. He stared in disbelief. He stood and looked around. The six other warriors were in the same condition. They were walking around checking the bodies for life but found no one alive.

He heard Brave Hawk scream. Then one by one he heard the others finding their loved ones and screaming also. He could hear the others crying out and yelling.

Two Wolves's knees buckled and he had to sit down. He rolled Gentle Breeze over into his arms and held her. He sat there rocking back and forth holding her tight.

All the men were standing listening to Brave Hawk. After a few minutes Brave Hawk came over to Two Wolves and said, "We're going to track the devil men down that did this evil thing to our families. We must find and kill them because of what they did to our people. Are you coming with us?"

Two Wolves couldn't answer. He couldn't even speak. He shrugged his shoulders not knowing what to say or do. He felt very strange, very empty. He had always relied on his mother to make decisions like this. If he stayed he would be alone. He had never been alone. If he went he would still feel alone without Gentle Breeze to come back to.

What did he want to do? He wanted the white men to pay for this but he couldn't leave his mother just lying there on the ground. He blinked his eyes several times trying to see through the tears now filling his eyes and running down his cheeks.

Brave Hawk looked at the young man and answered for him, "You stay and bury our people. Take what meat you can take back to our village and then you can come and join if you are able."

Two Wolves nodded. "Won't you all be killed doing this?"

"Our families are gone. We'll get these white dogs even if it means we die also. We are warriors with nothing else to live for." Brave Hawk turned toward the others and said, "Let's get those white killers."

The six men ran back for their horses and Two Wolves could hear them ride off. He had to sit for a long spell before he could stand again. He walked back to his horse and walked it back to camp. When he returned he heard the donkey bray ahead of him at the far end of the canyon. It was the only thing left alive.

Two Wolves went over and led the donkey back to camp. He looked around to see if there was anything at all he could do before he started burying his people. The camp was in such disarray. He thought of the meat so he took the donkey back to where the men had dropped the meat and he loaded it onto the donkey. Seeing the meat reminded him how proud and happy he was just moments before but that didn't matter now.

Two Wolves made a stretcher much like the one that dragged the teepee to this canyon only this time instead of a teepee he loaded all the meat on several buffalo hides. He was going to save what he could. Saving the meat meant saving his people from hunger. He led the donkey back to where the camp used to be.

He picked up his momma and took her over to the grassy spot and laid her down. He wrapped her with a buffalo skin from the teepee. He went and found some sage and burned it over her body while he asked the Great Spirit to watch over her spirit.

Next he went to the creek and started gathering large rocks to cover her with. It was hard work and it took a long time. When her grave was done he turned around and sat on it.

A white man on horseback came toward him. He rode right up to Two Wolves pointing his rifle at him. Two Wolves wished the white man to be dead but he was too tired and sad to do anything about it. At that moment he didn't care if the man was going to kill him.

"Did you kill my people?" Two Wolves asked.

"Nope," the man said.

"Are you going to kill me?"

"Nope."

"Then I won't kill you either," Two Wolves said.

The man put his gun away and got off his horse. "Do you want me to help?"

"Nay."

"Looks like you could use it so I'll help you get more rocks. This is too big a job for one person." He then walked over and picked up one of the bodies and brought it back and laid it down beside the fresh grave. He then walked to the creek and started gathering large rocks to cover the body.

The white man was a thin man just a little taller than Two Wolves. He had seen about thirty summers. He was tan from being outside so much. He had a compassionate composer yet something about him said you didn't want to get this man riled up.

The two of them worked side by side for a long time before anyone spoke. Finally Two Wolves asked, "Are you a soldier?"

"Nope."

"Are you a rancher?"

"Nope."

"Maybe you come to find the yellow soft rocks?"

"Gold? Nope, I'm not a miner either."

Two Wolves had only met soldiers and a few ranchers in his life and had only heard about miners so he didn't know what else to ask.

Two Wolves watched the white man's mouth as they talked. He wanted to see this man's split tongue he had heard about from the elders of his tribe that all white men had. Talking didn't give much of a view so Two Wolves asked, "Can you do this?"

The white man looked over and Two Wolves stuck his tongue out as far as he could.

"You mean like this?" The white man stuck his tongue out then put his thumbs in his ears and waved his fingers.

Two Wolves didn't see any split in the man's tongue but the man looked real silly making that face. Two Wolves didn't want to laugh but the harder he tried not to laugh the more tickled he got until he broke out giggling.

They worked side by side for many hours. At the end of the day they had the last grave finished. Two Wolves, talking to himself, asked, "Why did the men that did this have to take the top part of my people's hair?"

"They took those scalps to turn in for money," the man said.

"I've never seen anything like this before."

"It's called collecting a bounty. Your war party was off the reservation so those men will get money for turning in the scalps of the ones they killed."

"A war party? We were a hunting party, not a war party."

"It doesn't matter. They will say you were a war party so they can make the money. What are you going to do now?" the man asked.

"I'll take the meat we killed back to my tribe."

"Isn't the meat spoiled by now?"

"No, I rubbed it in salt. It will last like that until I can get it back home."

Two Wolves went over and got his food pouch and offered some buffalo jerky to the man that helped. They sat and ate together. When they were done Two Wolves got on his horse and said, "I need to get started. If I ride all night then I can be back home by the end of the next day, or maybe early morning depending on how fast the donkey will go. I'll be able to ride faster since there are no teepees and no other people to travel with."

"I'll go with you to make sure you don't run into any more trouble."

"You're not afraid?"

"Nope. What's your name?" the man asked.

"Two Wolves. What do they call you?"

"Dayton Colt."

"I've heard of Colt before, the gun, Colt. You know of those?"

"Yep, my family makes them back east."

The two rode off going south. They rode for many hours into the night. Two Wolves had tears in his eyes most of the way. They stopped at a stream to let the horses drink. Two Wolves got off his horse and walked down to the stream. He splashed some cold water on his face. Two Wolves asked, "How much is a scalp worth? I want to know how many frog skins my mother was killed for."

"I really don't know. I collect a different kind of bounty."

"Then you do kill people for frog skins, umm, money."

"Sometimes I do. But I only kill the bad ones that have a reward on their head, like bank robbers, cattle thieves, or murderers. I have never killed an Indian nor do I want to."

"Killing bad white men isn't against the law?"

"It isn't as simple as that. The real bad ones have a poster or drawing of them with some facts like maybe where a scar is or how old they are or the type of hat they wear. It will also have how much reward they are worth. Some are wanted dead or alive and the ones wanted alive you have to take to jail. You have to prove you killed the right man on the poster to get the reward money."

"I don't want the money. I just want to kill the bad white men. I don't like white men too much." Two Wolves looked at Dayton Colt to see what he would say.

"That's okay, son. At times I don't like them much myself."

It was midday and Two Wolves was thinking about his vision quest. Maybe there were some good white people. Well, maybe one. He still didn't like the idea of turning into the enemy, but if it meant he could get revenge for his mother's death it would be worth a try.

"That's what I am going to do," Two Wolves said out of the blue.

"What's that?"

"I'm going to kill the bad white people, like you do. It's too late for my mother but I can save others by killing the bad people that hunt for scalps. Maybe I can even find the men that killed my people."

"True but you have a lot to learn before you just ride off and shoot people."

"Like what?" Two Wolves asked.

"Like how to use a hand gun among other things."

"Could you teach me?"

"It's a shame you're not white. It would be easier to stay alive. You may not want to hear this but you're Indian. You would lose your scalp too if you rode around like you are now. You would have to cut all your hair off to keep from being scalped. You would have to dress differently. Basically, you would have to act and look white or else you would be killed. I could teach you and get you started but are you willing to do all that?"

Two Wolves didn't answer. He was confused and didn't know what to do. He so much needed his mother's wisdom and advice right now. He felt lost without her. Being an adult warrior wasn't supposed to be this hard. He didn't know if he was ready to become the enemy.

Chapter 7

THE BOUNTY HUNTER

They rode all night and most of the second day and reached the tribe in the late afternoon. Two Wolves left the meat from the hunt with his Cousin Dawn's family. Everyone was cautious about Dayton Colt being with Two Wolves. Once Two Wolves told what had happened and how Dayton Colt helped him they accepted him being there.

As Two Wolves walked around where he lived he realized how empty it now was without his mother. He had friends and a few relatives but it wasn't the same. He had no reason to stay. He thought about joining up with the six warriors but inside he didn't think doing that would be best thing to do.

"What's your life like?" he asked Dayton as they sat together in front of the now empty teepee that used to be his and his mother's home.

"What do you mean?" Dayton asked.

"Do you have a home? Do you have friends?"

"I left my home back east, several years ago, to come out west. I wanted adventure. I found my adventure in hunting outlaws and bringing them in. As far as friends go, I have several. I have made friends wherever I go, in different towns and settlements or ranchers I have met on my journey, and now you."

Two Wolves didn't know what to make of being friends with a white man. The words made him cringe. He didn't think of Dayton as being his friend. This white man did help bury his people and he did ride back home with him. So maybe he was kind of a friend.

"You said you could teach me how to hunt bad white people. Were you serious?"

"Sure, I can get you started if that's what you want. I have an extra handgun I'll give you and take you along to find the next outlaw I'm after but I get to keep your share of the reward as payment for teaching you."

"That sounds fair enough." Two Wolves walked into the teepee. When he returned he had cut off all his hair as close to his scalp as he could cut it.

"No one will ever take my scalp for money," he said. "Let's get started."

"We'll need a few things. Grab your horse and donkey and we'll ride to the Pine Ridge Agency and get some supplies."

Two Wolves was quiet on the ride to the town on the reservation. His head got hot from the heat of the sun beating down on him. He wasn't used to that feeling. His long hair had kept the sun from burning the top of his head and it caused his neck to sweat, which cooled him off. Without his hair his whole body felt the full impact of the heat.

In town, they stopped at the general store. Dayton went inside while Two Wolves waited with the horses. Two Wolves didn't know what they needed nor did he have any frog skins or money to buy anything anyway.

Dayton brought out several bundles and handed them to Two Wolves. "Here, load these on the donkey. I'll be right back."

Dayton came to the door of the store and tossed out a Stetson cowboy hat. Two Wolves caught it and just held it in his hands looking at it. If he put this on his head then he had indeed become the enemy.

Dayton walked out carrying a saddle in his arms. "Put the dang hat on your head so I can show you how to put this saddle on your horse," he said. "The saddle isn't new but it's in good shape. There are only a few worn spots in the leather. This is better than a new saddle anyway. This one has been broke in already and will be more comfortable for you to use."

Two Wolves took a deep breath and put the hat on his head. His vision quest had now become true. He watched as Dayton showed him how to throw the saddle over the horse's back and how to strap it on. The horse fidgeted and snorted. It had never had something like this on its back before and showed its dislike.

"What now? We go after the bad guys?" Two Wolves asked.

Dayton laughed. "I don't think we're ready for that yet. Let's ride up into the Black Hills and camp a few days. There are a few things I still want to show you before we head south to catch the guy I'm after."

They mounted up and headed northwest toward the Black Hills. Two Wolves squirmed using the uncomfortable saddle. When riding bareback he felt like he was part of the horse. He was freer and had more control of what he wanted the horse to do. This saddle seemed to slow the horse down and gave the horse more control over the rider than the other way around. The only good thing Two Wolves liked about the saddle was he could use the stirrups to stand and stretch his legs once in a while when riding.

That night they stopped to let the horses rest and eat. They got some jerky and stretched out to relax. Two Wolves tried to stay awake. He jumped at any sound. The next sounds he heard were birds chirping as the sun rose.

They rode on until late that afternoon and they made camp on top of a foothill covered with trees. They could see down both sides of the hill and know when anyone came their way. The trees hid them and provided shade.

Dayton took one of the bundles off the donkey and opened it. He handed Two Wolves a shirt and a pair of Levi jeans to put on. Two Wolves found the jeans to be stiff and not soft at all compared to the buckskin pants made from deerskin he was wearing. He spent a few minutes pulling his left knee then his right knee up to his chest to get the jeans to at least fold in the right places so he could move and bend his legs when he walked.

The jeans were too long and the end of the legs covered his toes. Dayton showed him how to fold them over and roll them up at the bottom edge and into a cuff that fit his legs better.

The cowboy boots were the hardest to get on and use. They weren't fancy, just plain black leather with high tops. Two Wolves found the boots were very uncomfortable and hurt his feet when he walked. Two Wolves was stumbling around trying to get used to how much the boots hurt his feet. His ankle gave way and he fell to the ground.

Dayton looked at him and said, "You have the boots on the wrong feet."

Two Wolves felt embarrassed and silly so he said, "But these are the only feet I have." Two Wolves smiled.

Dayton chuckled then said, "Funny." But then he broke out laughing at Two Wolves's remark.

Two Wolves sat back down and removed the boots and put them back on the right way. He could walk much better but they still weren't as comfortable as his moccasins.

Dayton threw him a tiny gun that he called a Colt .41 Caliber Derringer Circa. "You should always have a back-up gun. Keep this one in your boot. It'll only give you one shot but this little gun's one shot will take down a charging bull."

Two Wolves thought the gun was a good idea. He didn't like walking in his boots but now he had to walk in them and have a gun in one of them.

"I'm getting hungry. Do you want me to go and hunt down some meat for supper?" Two Wolves asked.

"No need." Dayton went over and pulled out a tin can and threw it to Two Wolves. "We can eat this tonight and maybe find something fresh for tomorrow."

Two Wolves held the can and asked, "What's this?"

"Beans."

Two Wolves tapped on the can with his knuckles. "Won't we have to cook this an awfully long time to get it tender enough to eat?"

"No, they're ready to eat now."

"Sorry, I've never seen beans like this before. I've seen dried beans that came in sacks." Two Wolves lowered his mouth to the can and tried to nibble off the top edge.

"Wait. Let me show you. I thought you knew how to open the can. Here, use your knife like this and cut out the top of the tin." Dayton put his knifepoint on the top and gave the handle a tap until the blade went into the can. He cut in a circle around the top moving the knife blade back and forth until the top could be folded back thus opening the can and exposing the beans inside.

"Thanks," Two Wolves said. He didn't say another word about the can. He had never seen a tin can before and didn't want Dayton to think he was trying to eat the can. He would rather let Dayton think he was just trying to open it.

After they ate, Dayton said, "We need to go get some water for the horses. We'll leave them here hidden in the trees so they won't be spotted."

Both men walked down the hill to a stream. Two Wolves got a drink but had no idea how to get the water back to the horses since neither of them had a pail or water pouch to carry the water in.

He watched as Dayton took off his hat and dipped it into the creek and pulled it out full of water. He was amazed that the water didn't run out. Two Wolves grinned at the thought of wearing a water pouch on your head that protected your head from the hot sun and had a brim that provided shade. For the first time he liked the hat because it now had a purpose other than just hiding the fact he had cut off all his hair.

Two Wolves was beginning to realize there was more to becoming a white man than he first thought. The white man's ways were very strange and different than the way he had been raised. The white man's clothes felt binding and the way they rode their horses with saddles just didn't feel right. And he wasn't sure he could ever run again, at least while wearing those stiff boots.

Two Wolves did like the cowboy hat and how whites could carry food in small tins; that was handy.

Being with Dayton wasn't as bad as he thought it would be. Dayton was kind enough and didn't seem to want anything back from Two Wolves. He was certainly interested in helping for some strange reason.

That evening, Dayton handed Two Wolves a holster and helped him put it on and adjust it to fit. He then handed Two Wolves a six shot Colt .38 and a box of shells.

"This is one of my spare guns and you can have it. Don't load it yet. We need to work on your draw first. To be a good shot and be fast on the draw will take weeks of practice. Watch and do what I do." Dayton drew his gun very slowly and showed the proper way to draw.

Two Wolves learned fast. It was embarrassing to learn how to shoot from a white man but he was willing to do it. He had handled handguns before but never owned one until now. Two Wolves worked hard trying to get faster and faster with his draw.

"You're doing one thing wrong," Dayton said as he watched.

"I'm getting faster. What am I doing so wrong?"

"You're just drawing to be fast. Pretend every time you draw it's for real and your life depends on it. How you practice is how you'll do in real life. If you just draw to be fast, you'll be fast but if you draw to kill then you'll be less likely to get shot. Go against me and you'll see what I mean."

Two Wolves faced Dayton with his gun in his holster, ready. He slapped his hand down to the handle of his Colt. He saw Dayton going for his gun and Dayton's gun was coming out ahead of his. Dayton's gun was very smooth moving out of the holster.

Two Wolves got very excited and nervous. He tried to beat Dayton so he went as fast as he could. He got his gun out first but then the barrel got caught on the leather edge of the holster and came out of his hand and dropped to the ground.

"Bang," Dayton said. "You were faster. You had me but you only worked to be faster not to kill me. Now you can see the difference."

"Okay, I see what you mean. We leave in the morning to go after the bad guys?"

Dayton laughed. "I think we'll do best to stay here a few more days. Maybe tomorrow we can put bullets in your gun and see if you can hit anything before riding off and catching an outlaw."

Chapter 8

THE CATTLE DRIVE

Two Wolves gained confidence as he learned about some of the white men's ways. There were many new things he had not known. He was skilled at tracking and knew they were on their way to find the bad guys so with this part of the training he would do much better. But before he could show off his tracking skills he had to master the handgun.

"Today, let's ride on up into the mountains to shoot. That way it'll be harder to tell where our shots are coming from because the sound bounces off the mountain ranges and cliffs," Dayton said. He poured some coffee into one of the tin cans and offered Two Wolves a cup.

Two Wolves took the cup and took a sip of the coffee. He made a sour face and spit it out. "How do you drink that stuff?"

"You don't like my coffee?"

"Hell no. It tastes and looks like bitter roots or mud. I was thinking it might taste like soup. I watched as you took some of the beans and crushed them into powder to make this nasty drink. I don't even think bugs will drink this stuff."

"You may be right. It takes an acquired taste I guess. You'll learn to like it." Dayton finished his cup and then he took several deep breaths of the fresh morning air.

They got on their horses and rode toward the mountains. When they got to a concave overhang they stopped and got off and tied the horses to some bushes.

Dayton opened his saddlebag and pulled out a box of shells and handed them to Two Wolves.

"Load up and let's see how you do," Dayton said. Dayton showed Two Wolves how to put the bullets into the gun. He also showed him where to put the extra bullets in the tiny leather loops that ran around the entire gun belt.

Two Wolves played with the gun. He tossed it from hand to hand. He twirled it around and spun it with one finger in the trigger guard. He had to get a feel for the balance of the firearm. He knew from throwing spears that balance was an important key to mastering this revolver.

Two Wolves knew how to handle the six-shooter. He had no problem standing and shooting and could hit the target from a good ways off. When it came to drawing and shooting he wasn't nearly as good. He had trouble drawing fast enough and hitting the mark at the same time. He would need to get in more practice before he was in an actual standup gunfight.

Dayton set up the two tin cans on a rock about twenty yards away. Two Wolves shot at the tin cans until he could hit them most of the time. Next Two Wolves put his gun in his holster then drew his gun and shot at the tin cans. At first he couldn't come close to hitting them but with practice he could either hit the cans or hit right beside them.

"You're picking up this shooting thing pretty fast. For what little practice you have had you are getting better with each shot. We'll head out tomorrow and ride south," Dayton said.

"Where're we heading to?"

"We'll go down into Nebraska and join up with a cattle drive heading to a market town in Kansas. I've heard that a couple of the Wild Bunch gang is going to rustle the herd."

"So, we're only after some ole cow thieves?"

"Doesn't sound too exciting, huh? These guys are mean. They ride with the Wild Bunch Gang and rob trains and banks and kill whoever gets in their way. Now, is it more to your liking?"

"Yep, are we going to take out the whole gang? How many are in this gang?" Two Wolves asked.

"No, at least I hope the whole gang isn't in on this."

"Why? Don't think we can take them?"

"It would take an army to take out the whole gang. They're the meanest bunch of outlaws around. They have thirty or forty guys sometimes. I doubt they'll use more than just a couple to take over the cattle drive."

"How'll we know which are the bad guys and which are the cowboys?" Two Wolves asked.

Dayton smiled then said, "The ones stealing the cattle are the outlaws. That'll be the ones we want."

Two days later they ran across the tracks created by the cattle drive. They followed the trail another day before they saw the dust stirred up by the slow moving herd heading east. Two Wolves and Dayton rode out of sight and off to the side just observing what was going on.

"Watch and learn what the cowboys are doing so when you ride in you can join the cattle drive. I'll flank the herd and stay out of sight until we figure out when the rustlers are going to make their move," Dayton said.

"How'd you find out that this cattle drive was going to be hit?"

"I overheard a man with only one ear talking in a saloon last week. I guess he had a few too many and was bragging to his friends about it."

"Wouldn't it be better if I were to stay out here and follow the herd? I'm good at tracking."

"You're right about that but I want to see if you can pass off as a cowboy. You need to get your feet wet. Besides, I'll know better than you when to make our move if and when the outlaws show up. After you ride in, find out what you can but don't let anyone know what we're up to. Can you handle that?"

"What do I tell them about why I'm there?" Two Wolves asked.

"Just say you are looking for work. Take the donkey with you and you can tie him to the chuck wagon. I'll ride in later or catch you off alone and then we can trade any information we've learned."

"See that?" Two Wolves said as he pointed to a lone set of horse tracks coming out from the cattle herd. "I saw a set of tracks going in just a mile or so earlier."

"Good eye. That could be a sign that something is going to happen soon. Keep your wits about you down there," Dayton said.

Two Wolves rode down to where the cattle were walking. He passed a cowboy and waved. "Who do I see about helping you all?"

"The trail boss is over there. He's the one on that dapple-gray horse. His name's Bart," was the reply.

Two Wolves rode over to the dapple-gray horse and rode alongside the man. He was very nervous but asked, "Are you Bart? I'm looking for work."

"Yep, kid, have you ever been on a cattle drive before?"

"No, but I'm willing to learn. I'll work hard if you give me a chance."

"Can you use that gun you're wearing or is it just a show piece?"

"I can."

"I pay a dollar a day but since you're new to this type work I'll give you half that. Still want to work?"

"Sure, I have to start somewhere," Two Wolves said.

"Okay, what's your name kid?"

Two Wolves had not thought about a different name other than his Indian name. He started to say Two Wolves at first then wasn't sure what to say. He didn't want to sound Indian as that would give him away. "I'm a . . . a . . ."

"Kid?"

He was even more nervous. "No . . . ah . . ." He had no idea what to say. His mind raced but he just couldn't think fast. He had to think of a name or say something.

"Well, Noah, go on over to the chuck wagon and let Chad know you're on the payroll. After that go to the back of the herd and help keep those steers moving forward."

He rode over to the chuck wagon and asked, "I work here now. Are you Chad?"

"Yessir," was the reply.

"Can I leave my donkey tied on the back of your wagon?"

"Yessir, just tie him next to the two milk cows. He'll be fine. Whenever you hear my dinner triangle ring that means the food is ready to eat"

"Okay, thanks."

At the back of the herd he found one other cowboy. Two Wolves, now called Noah, watched and did what the other cowboy did. Mostly they had to ride up behind any steer that had stopped and nudge it into moving ahead. If any of the cattle went off to the side of the herd they had to ride over and head it back in the right direction.

The other cowboy at the rear of the herd was just a boy. The boy's horse was brown with a black mane and tail. The boy was a tall, young, skinny kid and Noah thought he was barely in his teens. He wore a long sleeved shirt and a cowboy hat that sometimes slipped down over his eyes as he rode. He had a red bandana tied around his neck. This boy had uncommonly blues eyes that Noah had to stare at them a few minutes.

Noah could tell he was being watched and from afar; the feeling that someone was looking at him. He could tell where Dayton was at any given moment because of the birds rising from the trees up on the ridge over to the side of the herd. He hoped that no one else noticed. He would have to give Dayton some tips on how to prevent scaring all the birds later when they met up.

The herd wasn't very large, only sixty to seventy, maybe eighty steers at the most. It was hard to tell exactly. The cattle were strung out over one or two hundred yards while they stopped to graze. When the herd was moving they were strung out over a quarter mile.

Riding behind the herd made Noah's throat dry from all the dust. Noah was glad when the herd slowed to a stop at the end of the day. He heard the black wrought iron triangle and saw everyone heading for the chuck wagon. Noah joined them for supper. Noah took his tin plate that Chad handed him and walked over to a spot and sat down to eat.

It would be easy to make off with this amount of cattle with very little help. Noah counted only a dozen or so cowboys, Bart the trail boss, and the cook that drove the chuck wagon. This wasn't very many men to protect the cattle if they were going to be stolen by rustlers.

The young boy came over to sit with Noah. "Hi, I'm Clayton, Clayton Murphy. You're new here."

"Yep, I just started today. Name is T . . . ah, Noah. How far are we going with these cows?" Noah asked.

"We have about two more weeks until we get to Fort Wallace. That's where we're headed. I'm to meet my dad there and head back home with him," Clayton said.

"Where's home?"

"Wyoming. How about you?"

"Don't have a home right now. Used to live north of here."

"Where ya headed?" Clayton asked.

"Not sure right now. Just drifting and looking for work," Noah replied. He then sat his plate down and let out a big burp.

Clayton giggled.

Noah looked over at him and said, "Excuse me that was a big bear burp."

Clayton laughed, strained just a little, and then farted.

Noah put his fingers up and pinched his nose shut and waved the air with his other hand.

Clayton said, "Excuse me that was a big bear fart."

Noah laughed. He liked Clayton because he thought fast on his feet. He knew right away he and Clayton would get along.

Bart, the trail boss, walked up and said, "Clayton, you take the first watch then around two in the morning come and get Noah here and break him in; show him what to do so he can take the next watch. Noah, get some rest. Two o'clock comes awfully early."

Noah took his bedroll over to the side out of the way, but still close enough he could see the campfire and hear some of the conversation. One of the men pulled a rectangular solid metal piece, about the size of a whetstone used to sharpen knives from his shirt pocket. He called it a mouth organ but another man called it a harmonica and when he put it to his mouth and blew it created a screechy sounding music. The man could play several different tunes from a sad sounding tune to a lively tune that made Noah's foot move back and forth.

It made Noah think of the cedar flute some of the men in his tribe would play. The main difference being the flute had a soothing, pleasant sound. He had been gone less than a week but tonight he missed being with his tribe.

He noticed two of the men sitting on the far side of the campfire whispering. One of the men had a round face while the other, an older guy, looked like he could use a good meal or two. They both had short, scruffy beards and were dirty from the cattle drive. One man was chewing something that must not have tasted too good because he then spitting its dark juice off to the side. They weren't friendly to any of the other cowboys and Noah took a mental note to keep an eye on them.

Chapter 9

GONE FISHING

His early morning duty of watching the herd went without any problems. Chad picked up the little clangor and rang the sound for morning breakfast. The cook served up some mush-like stuff that smelled bad and looked like something children fixed along with mud pies. Chad had called it oatmeal and when Noah tried a bite he found that it tasted of oats and heated milk. Actually, it was pretty good and Noah liked it.

After breakfast, Noah rode along the side of the herd to keep the steers from wandering off on their own. At first he had trouble because when a steer wandered off away from the others Noah rode up behind it. That would cause it to break from the herd and take off heading entirely in the wrong direction. It didn't take Noah long to learn he had to ride in front of the steer and turn it back toward the others.

Noah spotted the birds flying up from a near-by tree again and knew Dayton was flanking them on the left side. Soon he saw a bunch of crows fly out of the trees on the right side. This could mean Dayton had a very fast horse and had crossed to the other side, or it more likely meant there was someone else flanking them on the right side. He wasn't sure now which side Dayton was riding.

Bart, the trail boss, rode up beside Noah and said, "The cook wants to have a word with you. Go on over to the chuck wagon and see what's up."

Noah rode up to Chad and asked, "You wanted to see me?"

"Yessir, we are coming up on a river later today. The men are tired of eating potato soup. Take this here cane pole and go ahead to the river and catch enough fish for supper tonight. It'll take about three skillets full. You'll have to dig your own worms. Can you handle that?" Chad handed Noah a cane pole with a string and hook attached.

Noah didn't know what Chad meant about digging his own worms but he did know about fishing. "I'll be happy to get us some fish." He took off riding ahead of the herd.

Once he was at the river, Noah looked at the cane pole. This wouldn't make a very good spear. It wasn't even sharp on either end, and the string with the small, bent, metal piece with a sharp point would just get in the way.

He looked around until he found the right size limb. He chopped it off the tree and sharpened one end. Noah took his boots off and sat them near the water's edge. He rolled up his pant legs and waded out into the cool water and walked down to where a log had fallen in the water alongside the bank.

He stood real still holding the spear. He could see the bottom clearly. He saw movement as a fish followed the log looking for bugs. Noah waited until the fish was near enough and jabbed the spear into the water. The fish fought and made a splash. When the water settled down, Noah had a nice size fish that would fill half a skillet by itself. Soon Noah had three nice fish and a couple smaller ones lying on the bank near his boots.

He heard a noise and turned around to find a man standing in a rocky place on the bank just above him. The man was scary looking because he was missing the top part of his right ear. It was the man Dayton had talked about. The man was holding a rifle pointed at Noah. The man said, "Drop the spear and your gun then come over here."

"Who are you and what do you want?" Noah asked.

"Just do what I asked," the man said.

Noah dropped the spear and took off his gun belt and threw it up on the bank. He walked up toward the man. "That's close enough. Now say your prayers and get ready to die."

"Please, one favor. I don't want to die without my boots on," Noah said.

The man looked Noah over and Noah saw the man had an evil grin on his face. "I guess that's reasonable. Just hurry because I don't have all day. And don't think about going for that gun over there or I'll drop you where you are, boots or no boots."

"No, don't worry. I wouldn't think of going for that gun."

Noah walked over and sat with his feet pointing toward the man with the rifle. He lifted the first boot to put it on. The bottom of the boot was pointing toward the stranger as he lifted the boot and slid his foot inside. Noah quickly slid his hand inside the boot.

Bam!

The stranger went flying backward and was dead before he hit the ground. Noah saw smoke coming from a hole in the bottom of his boot. He ran over to check on the man. The man didn't move and wasn't breathing. He had a rather large hole in the middle of his chest.

Noah heard a horse galloping toward him. He grabbed the man's rifle and went to get his handgun. The horse was closing fast and Noah figured the dead man had a partner. When the rider came around a tree and into sight, Noah was ready to fire the rifle.

"Wait, Two Wolves," Dayton yelled.

"Oh, it's you. I'm called Noah now. I made a little mess here. What'll I do?" Noah asked. "The cattle drive will be here later today." He was glad to see Dayton.

"We have time. They're still an hour or so away. Find out any information?" Dayton asked.

"Nothing, really. We're headed to Fort Wallace is all I know. I did see where the herd was being flanked by you and another rider."

"Yep, I ran across his tracks as I was coming to join up with you and was hoping I wouldn't get here too late. I see you handled yourself pretty good." Dayton looked down at the one boot Noah had on his foot. "Don't step in any water puddles or cow plops with that boot. I think it'll leak now. And how did you come up with your new name, anyway?"

"It kind of just happened." He grinned then asked, "What'll we do with this guy?"

"Who is your friend laying there anyway?" Dayton asked.

"I don't know. I thought he was your friend with only half an ear. He didn't stick around long enough for any introductions."

"Don't worry. I'll take care of this guy, his rifle and his horse. Just act like nothing happened. Throw me that biggest fish you caught and you go back to getting some more."

"Okay, just try not to stir up so many birds as you ride beside us."

"And you keep from chasing the steers away from the herd. You're supposed to keep them all together."

Noah had a frown on his face and he heard Dayton chuckle.

Dayton tied the man across the man's horse. Dayton took the rifle and mounted his horse. He led the other horse and went into the water and headed down stream so when the cattle drive arrived they wouldn't find strange tracks in the area.

Noah reloaded his derringer and returned it to his boot. He picked up the four fish he had left and moved up stream to a new fishing sight.

It wasn't long before he heard the bellowing of cattle off in the distance. He walked up the bank to take a look.

The herd wasn't far away and a rider was coming his way. He recognized the trail boss as he rode up to Noah and stopped.

"I thought I heard a shot a while ago," he said.

"Yep, just a rattlesnake."

"Where is it?"

"Um . . . I missed."

"How's the fishing?" Bart asked.

"Very good. Cover these swimmers with a little flour and throw them in hot oil and we'll eat good tonight."

"We'll make camp on the other side of the river. Take the fresh fish to Chad then help slow the herd and allow them to walk across the river and drink as they cross."

Noah gathered up his things and took the fish to the chuck wagon. The chuck wagon was leading the way. Noah helped lead the wagon team across the river then went back to help with the steers.

Once all the cattle were across the river the cowboys stopped the herd and settled them in for the night. The cowboys were in a better mood dining on fish instead of potato soup, again. The trail boss told two others to take the night watch. This made Noah happy because he was very tired from all he had done the last several days.

No one seemed to notice but Noah didn't talk much that evening. He was quieter than he had been since he joined the cattle drive. He was numb but could feel a wave of emotions just under his skin. He had killed his first bad white man. He was now a true warrior but it felt strange not being able to tell anyone or let his tribe back home know.

Noah was glad he killed the man before the man could kill him. The training with Dayton Colt was paying off and he was grateful for that. He simply thought he would feel excited or happy he got to kill a bad white man but he was just numb. Maybe he at least saved someone else from losing their mother or father. Maybe this bad man was someone's father. There were many thoughts going through his mind.

Noah found that his thoughts were running away from his task at hand. He had to bring them back and focus and remember why he was there. He knew he had a bad habit of over thinking things too much. He had experienced fear when the man's rifle was pointed at him.

Something was different, though. Killing didn't feel like he thought it would. It didn't make him happy like he thought he should be. He couldn't even kill as Two Wolves; he'd done it as Noah. Maybe that was the strange feeling inside him.

"Clayton, do you think it's okay to be afraid of something?" Noah asked as he and Clayton sat eating supper over next to where everyone tied their horses.

"I think everyone is afraid of something or other."

"What are you afraid of?"

"Ghosts," Clayton said. "You?"

"I think I would be a bit scared if someone was pointing a gun at me and I thought I was going to be shot."

"I guess. But that kind of fear you can do something about."

"What do you mean?" Noah asked.

"Well, you could run or you could point a gun at them or if nothing else you could pee your britches." Clayton giggled. "But with ghosts, there isn't much you can do but shake. Ma says fear is nature's way of warning you of danger. When you feel fear it's time to check and see what you are doing or what's going on around you that you need to be aware of. She says fear can't hurt you and actually helps us if we figure out why it's there. She says it's the Lord's safety rail."

"True 'nuff, I guess. Clayton, you are way smarter than you look."

"And these fish taste better than they smell," Clayton said as he put a finger in his mouth and pulled out a tiny fish bone.

After dinner Noah saw Clayton chewing on the palm of his hand. "Didn't you get enough to eat?"

"Ya, I'm just trying to get rid of the seed wart that growed on my hand. Pa cut it off once but it came back."

"I know how to fix that for you. Run over to the chuck wagon and ask for a small potato and bring it back. Then I'll show you what to do."

Clayton returned with the small potato and handed it to Noah. He then pulled out his knife from its sheath and Clayton watched as he cut it in two pieces. He ate one half then he took the other half of the potato and rubbed it over the wart. He handed that half to Clayton and told him what to say.

Clayton repeated the words, "Moon increase, wart decrease. Now what do I do?"

"Now you turn around and throw it over your shoulder as far as you can throw it."

Clayton turned completely around three times before Noah put his hand out and stopped him. "You only need to turn once."

Clayton spent a few seconds winding up then threw the half potato over his shoulder as far as he could throw it. "This actually works? When will the wart be gone?"

"Give it a day or two and it'll be gone. Just don't look at the wart until then and you'll find it has disappeared."

A couple hours before nightfall, Noah spotted four men riding on a ridge above the camp. He went over and pointed them out to Bart.

"Indians?" Bart asked.

"Nope, if it was Indians they would bargain for a steer or just steal one. They would try to trade for it first. I think these men have been following us for a spell," Noah replied.

"How do you know that?"

"I've seen tracks and other signs."

"I better put a guard here in camp tonight and let all the others know what's up. This doesn't look good. I want to believe they are some cowboys just passing through," Bart said. "But it's better to be ready just in case."

Chapter 10

RUSTLERS

The next week seemed to go by quickly. The cattle drive didn't have any problems and they were now only a few days from Fort Wallace. It had been several days since Noah had seen any sign of Dayton and wondered if he was still riding beside the herd.

Noah had made friends with most of the cowboys. Maybe there was more than one good white man. He had felt cheated by his vision quest but now it was making sense.

The breakfast triangle rang and all the cowboys headed for the chuck wagon. Chad had visited a ranch yesterday and did some trading. Today, he was fixing eggs and bacon for everyone. There was a fresh pot of coffee on the campfire too.

Noah had hated coffee. Some of the cowboys called it Texas mud. However, over the last few weeks he'd gotten used to it, and it did wake him up in the morning and made the day start off just a little easier.

Noah and the cowboys were in a good mood. They were laughing and talking about a prank one of them had played on another one the day before. Someone had slipped over and unbuckled one of the saddles and when that rider went to get on his horse the saddle slid off and he fell to the ground.

"Okay, men, we only have a few more days before we get to Fort Wallace. We'll take it slow the rest of the way and let the cattle eat and gain some of their weight back so we can get full price when we sell them," Bart said as he walked through camp heading for his horse.

The cowboy who'd had the prank pulled on him asked, "What difference does that make to me?"

"Well, you'll get a couple extra days pay out of the deal 'cause it'll take longer. And it'll be easier to let them mosey in from here instead of riding the hell out of them. Okay, men, saddle up. It's been daylight for almost an hour."

As the first man put his foot in the stirrup and mounted his horse a shot rang out off from the left side. A loud moan shrieked through the air as the man getting on his horse fell to the ground. The rest of the men ran to their horses and were mounting up and grabbing their rifles. Another shot rang out and another man hit the dirt face down.

A third shot rang out this time from the right side and another of the cowboys was hit and fell to the ground, he wasn't moving. The rustlers had them in a crossfire situation.

Noah ran to his horse and pulled his rifle from the sleeve on the saddle. He didn't think it a good idea to climb up and give the shooters a better target to shoot at.

Bart yelled, "Ambush! We have a shooter on both sides of us. Take cover."

More shots rang out as the cowboys started returning fire. From under the chuck wagon, Noah saw that there were a couple of shooters on each side but there could be more. He then heard a loud shot that sounded further back from the ridge. He saw one of the rustlers fall over the rock he was hiding behind. Noah recognized the sound as Dayton's Kentucky long rifle.

The cattle started running from all the noise of the shootout. "Stampede! You three ride off with the herd and we'll keep you covered." Bart was pointing to three cowboys still sitting on horseback.

The three men rode with the stampeding cattle and the rest were still pinned down and firing back toward the rocks that provided cover for the rustlers.

It was hard to see with all the dust from the stampede. One of the cowboys ran for his horse and was hit before he could get there. He inched his way over and slid down into a furrow not far from the chuck wagon.

Some of the cattle were running beside the chuck wagon and Noah saw this as his chance to make it to the rocks off to the side. He ran into the steers and was trying not to get run over as he made his way over to find cover.

He couldn't get out of the way of one steer with very long horns and he jumped over its head and onto its back. He rode the steer sitting backwards for several yards before he could slide off and get to his feet. Stumbling, he ran for some rocks at the side of all this action and found cover.

After the cattle had moved on through it was easier to see, but that worked for and against them. Noah saw Bart take a hit to his leg and watched as he hobbled back to the chuck wagon for cover. A couple of shots ricocheted off the front of the rock Noah was kneeling down behind. They had spotted him.

For a moment, the shooting seemed to stop. Four horses were riding fast toward the camp. Noah saw Chad standing in the back of the chuck wagon with a gun. He raised his shotgun and fired. He hit one of the riders. One of the other riders shot Chad and he fell off the back of the wagon.

Again the sound of the Kentucky long rifle could be heard in the distance and one of the three men jumped like he was shot in the back and fell from his horse.

There was an exchange of fire as one of the riders rode into the camp and another cowboy fell over holding his gut. There were only two outlaws left and not many of the cowboys left. One of the outlaws was shooting at the young boy who was hiding under the wagon by the rear wheel.

Noah aimed his rifle at that man and fired. Two more cowboys were firing at the same man. The rustler was hit from both sides and fell to the ground. The last outlaw turned his horse and was riding away when the Kentucky long rifle fired again. The man slumped down in his saddle and rode for a short distance before he finally slid off the side of his saddle and landed on the ground.

Noah ran back to camp to see whom he could help. He saw Bart still under the wagon with the boy, Clayton. Another cowboy, the one with the harmonica, came running over to see who was all right.

Bart said, "Someone helped us out or we all would have been killed. Who's left?"

After looking around Noah said, "Just us and Clayton and this harmonica guy."

Bart looked at the man and said, "Mount up and follow the herd. Those three I sent after the cattle will need help. Just try to get the herd stopped for now and then we'll have to gather the strays. We'll take care of everything here."

"Do you need me to go with them?" Noah asked.

"No, you're not experienced enough to do any good. You'll be more help here."

Noah saw a rider off in the distance. "Rider," he yelled.

Bart hollered, "Is that one of them?"

"Hold on. Don't shoot. That's my friend." Noah waved to Dayton to let him know it was okay to ride on into camp.

By the time Dayton got to the rest of the cowboys, Bart was standing and using his rifle as a crutch to help him walk.

"Bart, this is Dayton Colt. He's my partner. He's the one that helped us out with that Kentucky long rifle of his."

"Do you need a job? Looks like we could use a few new hands if you're looking for work."

"No thanks. My work is done. I'll gather up the outlaw's bodies and take them to Fort Wallace. Two Wol . . . umm . . . Noah, what're you going to do? Stay here or go with me?"

"These are your bounties. I'm needed here for now. Thanks for all your help, Dayton. We're even now?"

"What do you mean, even?"

"I mean the guns you gave me. They're paid for now?"

"Yep, you're on yur own."

Dayton proceeded to tie the dead outlaws' hands and feet and throw them over their horses. On one body he took out his knife and stabbed the man in the stomach.

"Why'd you do that? Wasn't he dead?" Noah asked.

"This guy was shot in the head. He was dead all right, but in the summer, unless they're gut shot you have to stab them or the body will bloat and swell. Stabbing prevents that from happening."

"Oh, good to know, I guess."

"Well men, let's get this mess cleaned up. Gather all the supplies and put them in the wagon, then we have some graves to dig. Take the bodies over to those rocks off to the side. We'll bury them over there. It's just not right to put them here in the middle of where more cattle drives will come through," Bart said. "I can't believe we were hit so hard so fast and we're the only men left."

Noah was kneeling beside one of the cowboys lying on the ground. "Well, here's one more we are lucky to have. This cowboy here made it into this ditch for cover but he's shot and I could use some help getting him back to the wagon."

Clayton ran over and helped walk the man back to the wagon and helped get him inside. He made sure the man was as comfortable as he could be sitting inside a chuck wagon full of food and pots and pans and other assorted supplies.

Noah looked at Bart limping around with the rifle as his crutch and asked, "Is your leg okay?"

"Yessir, just a flesh wound. It'll heal. I won't be riding for a few days so I'll drive the wagon and be the cook." He then pulled out a leather bag with bandages and started attending to the wound of the other cowboy.

When Dayton was ready to leave he went over to where Noah was digging a grave. "Well, this is where I came in so this is where I'll leave out."

"What do you mean?" Noah asked.

"Well when I first met you, you were burying people and you are doing the same now. Keep practicing with focus on your draw. Be fast but more important shoot to kill. You've come a long way and are doing very well. Learn how to wait when that is the best thing to do and then anticipate what's coming next."

"I know. How I practice is how I'll do in a situation. I'm seeing that now. Ya think I'll see you again sometime?" Noah asked.

"I sure hope so. I'd like that. Take care of yerself and good luck."

"Thanks, I will. You keep safe, my friend," Noah said. He never thought he would say that to a white man. He thought it sounded strange echoing inside his head.

After Dayton was gone and the graves were done, he and Clayton went back to the wagon. Bart said, "Clayton, ride ahead and tell the others we're on our way. Just stay with the cattle until we get there."

Clayton nodded, kicked his horse in the flanks and rode on. Noah watched until he was out of sight.

Noah walked around not saying much. His heart was heavy over some of the others that had died. He was confused about feeling this way. He didn't like white men much and sure didn't know why he was sorry about losing some of the cowboys.

He knew the sadness came from being with these men and talking and working with them. He knew one of them had a couple children and another had a wife. He had gotten to know them as people and now they were gone.

He realized his stirred up feelings were hard to think about and deal with. He knew these men and now the cowboys were dead. That was different from the sadness of someone not being around here at the present. Noah had felt both kinds of sadness and knew which was which.

Noah was riding along side of the wagon and he could tell Bart was in some pain from the grunts he made at times. The look on Bart's face also told him Bart was sad about what had happened.

"Are you okay?" Noah asked.

"Yep, I'll be alright. I knew most of those cowboys you and Clayton buried back there. I'll have to go back and tell their families what happened. That's never any fun. I'll give their families the money they earned and maybe a little extra if I have it."

Noah adjusted his hat and nodded.

They rode for a couple of hours and tried to continue with some small talk but it was strained at best. The evening sun was nearing the mountaintops in the distance behind them.

Two riders were coming toward them. They were riding fast. Noah soon recognized one of the riders was Clayton.

When they were within earshot Clayton yelled, "We have more problems ahead."

Chapter 11

THE AMBUSH

Clayton and the other cowboy rode up to the wagon and stopped. Clayton said, "The three riders that went with the herd when it was stampeded were ambushed. Joe, here, is the only one that's still alive. The other two are dead."

"How did that happen?" Bart asked.

"We were trying to ride to the front of the stampede to slow the herd down when we were shot at. They killed the other two and I just barely got away," Joe said.

"How many of them were there?" Bart asked.

"Only two but we weren't expecting them so they got the drop on us. When Clayton met me I was on my way back here. But then we thought it best to turn around and follow the herd to see where those two men were taking the cattle. They turned the herd into a dead end canyon. I figure that way the herd would stop at the end and they would be hidden at the same time."

"Okay, those two will be waiting for the five that ambushed us." Bart scratched his head and took his handkerchief and wiped off his forehead. "We don't have enough men left to flush those guys out of that canyon without getting more of us killed. And I doubt we have enough time to go on into Fort Wallace to get help. I'm not sure what to do."

"I do. I'll go in after them tonight. You all camp outside the entrance to the canyon and wait there for my return," Noah said. "Let's go. Show us where they took the cattle."

They took the wagon down the trail until Joe pointed out where the canyon entrance was. They set up camp off the main trail over in a thicket of trees for protection. It was a spot where they were out of sight yet they could keep an eye on the comings and goings of the canyon opening.

At dusk, Noah was ready. "I'm going in," he said.

Joe asked, "Don't you need help?"

"No, it'll be better if I go alone. I'm pretty good at this. As a child we played a game where the others hid and we took turns sneaking up and surprising each other. I should be back by daybreak."

Noah left his horse and headed up one of the inclines to get on top of the ridge that went into the canyon. He followed the ridge down a couple miles. Because of the thick cloud cover not allowing the moon to be seen, it was getting very dark.

He spotted a campfire out in the middle of the canyon flat land but there was only one man sitting there. He couldn't see the second man and he had to find where the other man was before he could plan any kind of attack.

Noah stopped for several minutes and held his hands over his eyes. This allowed his eyes to adjust to the dark and helped him see better once he removed his hands. He'd learned this trick as a child playing at night with his cousin Dawn.

On the darkest night, the night of no moon, Noah and Dawn went to this narrow trail where they would set traps for each other. The traps were nothing more than a stick that would snap or a string that went across the trail where they had to walk that would shake a bush if stepped on. Once he'd even stepped in a buffalo patty she had hidden under some leaves.

Dawn always beat him at this game. He never made it the entire length of the path without hitting one of her traps. It was years later before she told him of the secret of holding her hands over her eyes and then being able to see better in the dark.

He could hear the cattle crying out in the valley below. He also smelled sulfur from a nearby sulfur spring and heard the water trickling down the rocks to a creek at the bottom.

Noah found it was still hard traveling around the ridge of this canyon in the dark. Several times he had to back track to find a different route due to a cliff or drop off he came upon. He went further down the canyon until he could hear the cattle clearly. He moved down the ridge and at the bottom, the land was flat so he could move easily toward the steers. He stayed near the rocks on the side as he looked for the second outlaw.

He was thinking about checking out the far side of the valley to see if the outlaw was over there. He started to walk out to head toward the middle of the herd and use them for cover until he got to the other side. That would be much faster and safer than him traveling all the way around on the top of the ridge. He heard a soft sound that made him freeze as soon as he stepped out into the open.

Noah was good at hearing noises. His mother, Gentle Breeze, had taught him how to listen to sounds in the forest. She made him be quiet and then tell her what he heard. His mother always asked him about another noise he didn't hear. It was amazing how he could hear the small sound once he was made aware of it.

Right now Noah was grateful his mother's teachings were with him. He sensed her presence as if she were still looking over him, even though she had crossed over the bridge to be with the ancestors on the other side of life.

In front of him was the flat canyon bed. He heard footsteps coming toward him from the side where the flat land met the rocky cliffs. He turned and drew his gun. He squatted down to make for a smaller target as he faced the unknown shadow. His heart pounded in his chest. This time he wasn't playing a child's game. This time it was for real and could mean his death.

From around a large boulder only a few feet from where Noah hid crunched down a mountain lion walked out. It stopped surprised to see Noah and first it hissed as it raised the hair on its back and neck. It nervously walked sideways toward the boulder and let out a growl then a loud squalling sound.

Noah didn't move. If this cat attacked it would ruin any chance of him getting the drop on the second outlaw he searched for and, of course, there was the danger of fighting with this mountain lion.

The cat gave out another squall. A horse could be heard riding toward them. It wasn't in sight but still sounded close. Noah jumped up and dove for a group of small bushes. The cat jumped up on top of the boulder just as the horse and rider came around into view. The mountain lion turned to face the horse and growled again.

"Oh, it's a cat. Well, mister wildcat, you can't have any of my cows tonight. Now go on and get." The outlaw then took his hat off and waved it through the air to chase the cat away. The cat jumped off the backside of the boulder and disappeared into the night.

At last Noah knew where the second outlaw was. He was only a couple yards from where Noah was hiding. The horse faced the bushes and it looked like the man was looking right at him. Noah didn't move. Any movement would be seen. He watched, hoping the rider would pass by him and he could then jump out and pull the rider from his horse.

He waited.

Noah was afraid the horse would smell him or maybe hear his breathing. He breathed hard as he tried his best to remain calm forcing his breath into even intakes and exhales. He sat there so long his leg started cramping. He knew he couldn't move so he had to endure the pain.

Noah remembered watching a fox after a rabbit when he was young. The rabbit was hid well in some weeds. The fox searched and searched for the rabbit but as long as the rabbit didn't move the fox couldn't find it. When the fox got too close and the rabbit got scared, it moved just a little bit, pulling its head back out of sight. That's when the fox spotted the movement and went after the rabbit.

The muscle in Noah's leg started to twitch. His leg muscle jerked and the pain from the cramp almost doubled him over. If he had to sit in that position much longer he would be spotted. He had to try something.

Very slowly he moved his hand along the ground until he found a small stone. He didn't want to throw the stone hard because the movement of his arm would be seen so he used his thumb and flipped the stone just hard enough for it to hit behind the horse. The sound of the stone hitting other rocks caused the horse to shy sideways.

The rider pulled his gun and turned his horse to face the sound. All was quiet again. The man stood in his stirrups and looked in the other direction for what had made the sound. An owl gave out a hoot from a tree higher up on the ridge. The man settled back into his saddle and put his gun back in his holster.

Noah could at least now stretch out his leg and that helped relieve the cramp. He rubbed his leg for a second or two. He wanted to be ready for his next move. He slowly moved his body then, at the right time, he got up and ran up behind the horse and jumped and grabbed the man by the shoulders pulling him off the horse backwards.

The man hit the ground flat on his back with Noah kneeling beside him. Noah picked up a large rock and struck the man in the head. The man let out a moan then relaxed and didn't move.

His horse had jumped and trotted away from the action. It didn't go far and Noah went and brought the horse back. He used the outlaw's rope to tie the man's hands and feet. He couldn't lift the man up on the horse so he tied the horse near a bolder. Noah dragged the man up onto the bolder then he could slide the man over the saddle. He tied him so he wouldn't fall off if he came to.

He took the bridle strap and started walking back to the campfire he'd spotted nearer the entrance. Soon the fire could be seen as he continued to walk the horse closer to the other man's camp.

He saw the other outlaw stand and look at him. "Big Charlie, is that you?"

Noah took his hat off and waved it at the other man but he didn't answer. Noah continued to get closer leading the horse.

"Charlie? You want some coffee?"

Noah was close enough to make out the features of the other man. He let go of the bridle strap but kept walking closer to the other outlaw.

"Hey, you're not Charlie." The man went for his gun.

Noah was thinking, "Go for the kill." He drew and fired first. He hit the man just as the other man fired his gun. The bullet hit the dirt in front of Noah. Noah watched as the outlaw grabbed his stomach, turned to the side and fell to the ground.

From the ground the man raised his gun and pointed it at Noah. Noah fired again and this time the man jerked, gave out a strained breath and he remained very still.

Noah tied this man and draped him over his horse. The first sign of daylight was starting to show. No light could be seen in the sky yet but images were starting to take shape and things were becoming clearer. Noah walked the two horses back out of the canyon. By the time light could be seen in the sky Noah wasn't far from the wagon and he could see Clayton running out to meet him.

"You got breakfast ready yet?" Noah asked.

He heard Clayton chuckle and he handed him one of the bridle straps. "You okay?" Clayton asked.

"Yep, didn't get much sleep last night though," Noah said.

"Me either."

"Why not?"

"Joe snores." Clayton started laughing out loud. Noah got tickled at the young man's humor and he laughed also.

"Look!" Clayton put his hands in front of Noah's face and rubbed his palms together. "That trick really worked. My wart's gone."

"Good, but it isn't a trick. It's something I learned from an Indian medicine man a long time ago and it only works right before the full moon."

After a couple of hours sleep, Bart woke everyone up. "We have work to do. We need to go and check the herd and see how many are missing. Then we'll have to go out and round those steers up, the ones we can find, anyway."

Noah said, "Joe and Clayton can handle that. I'm going to take these outlaws on into Fort Wallace. You all just camp at the opening of the canyon to keep the cattle safe and I'll get us a few more hands to help bring in the rest of the herd."

"Okay, that's a right smart idea, son," Bart said.

Chapter 12

FORT WALLACE

Noah started perspiring as he rode into Fort Wallace with one guy tied across his horse and the other guy bound and being led. He had never been in any large town before and this town had a fort at the far end of the street. He looked at everyone he passed wondering if anyone knew he was an Indian.

As he rode into town, he observed the square shape of the houses the white men and their families lived in. Noah shook his head. For one thing, if someone died, their spirit could get lost and not find its way out. The spirit could get trapped in a corner. At least in a teepee the spirit would find the edge of the room and be able to follow that around and come to the door and be free. Some spirits may even rise and find the hole at the very top of the teepee that let the smoke out from the fire and be able to leave and find the bridge to the other world that way.

The town had many stores and people were walking down a wooden path that went along the front of the buildings going from store to store. As he rode past some of the men would nod their head and Noah found himself nodding back. He guessed it was some sort of greeting.

He stopped outside the sheriff's office and escorted his captured outlaw inside. He was wary that this would back fire and he would be the one put behind bars.

Inside the door on a table Noah saw a wooden bucket full of clear water. He wanted a drink but that could wait for a minute or two.

"Good afternoon," the sheriff said. "How can I help you?"

"Are you the law for these parts?" Noah asked.

"Yep, Sheriff Stone, at your service."

"Well, Sheriff, I caught this guy and another one, rustling the cattle from a herd on its way to Fort Wallace. The other one is dead and strapped to a horse outside. I'm just wondering what to do with them."

"Let me put this guy in a cell and then we can take a look at the one outside." The sheriff untied the man and marched him into the back and Noah heard the iron bar door close with a bang.

The sheriff and Noah walked outside to the horse with the dead man draped over its back. The sheriff then motioned for them to go back inside.

"I don't know the guy out there. I'll have the undertaker come and get him. He'll put him in a coffin and lean the coffin up against his storefront for others to see and maybe we'll find someone that knows him. As for the guy we locked up, I know of him. I have a wanted poster on him. He's one of the members of the Hole-in-the-Wall gang and you'll get a reward."

"Umm, what exactly is the Hole-in-the-Wall gang?"

"That's an outlaw gang that has anywhere between twenty and forty outlaws and they have a massive hideout that no one can seem to locate. Some people call them the Wild Bunch. What's your name so I can get you the hundred dollar reward?"

"Oh, the Wild Bunch. I have heard them called that. I'm called Noah."

"Hold on a second." The sheriff checked some paper work on his desk and asked, "Did you ride some with Dayton Colt?"

Nervously Noah replied, "Yes, I guess I did."

"He was in town a few days ago with a dead man that only had half an ear on one side of his head. That guy was from the Wild Bunch and Dayton Colt left you half the reward. He said you might come here." The sheriff then handed him an envelope with two hundred dollars inside. "That's about a year's wages for most people in these parts."

"Thanks, Sheriff. Do you know where I might find some cowboys to help bring in the herd we have not too far from here? We need a few hands for a couple days."

"Sure, you can check over at the saloon. There should be a few fellows over there that could use some pay." The sheriff went over to the bucket of water and took a dried gourd dipper and scooped up some of the water and took a drink.

"Thanks, I'll do that. Mind if I get a drink?"

The sheriff handed Noah the dipper and waved his hand toward the bucket. He was glad the sheriff got a drink first because he was just about to get a drink by dipping his cupped hands into the bucket to retrieve the water.

"Come back later today and I'll have that hundred dollar reward ready for you."

Noah nodded just to see if that indeed was a greeting and the sheriff nodded back. He went outside and walked down the street following the wooden path to the saloon.

Noah pushed open the swinging doors to the saloon and entered. He notice there were several cowboys sitting at some tables and a man sitting on a bench and playing music from a rather large wooden box on legs at the far end of the room. He watched as the man's fingers hit some flat, white, rectangular pieces all laid out in a row across the front of this large box to make the sounds.

He walked across the room where there was a horseshoe shaped table with a man standing behind it.

"What would you like, a beer?" the man asked.

"The sheriff said I could find a few cowboys here to help bring in a small herd of cattle to Fort Wallace. The herd is a day or two ride west of here. We need five or six men for a few days' work. Know where I might find someone?"

The barkeeper hollered past Noah, "Boys, you heard this lad. Any of you need a couple day's work?"

Three men at one of the tables stood up. "We do."

Another man standing at the end of the bar walked over and said, "I could use a few dollars. I'll be glad to go with you and help."

Noah turned to the barkeeper and asked, "Could you bring us some beers over to the table by the window? Oh, and bring me a buttermilk, if you would, please. Come on, men, join me and I'll give you all the details."

Noah and Clayton rode into the town of Wallace. He promised the kid he would help him look for his father.

The cattle had been delivered to the fort and everyone had been paid. The few that were left headed back home with the trail boss and the four new cowboys were already back at the saloon spending the few dollars they had made.

Noah had not seen any signs of Dayton and figured he had left without saying so long. Noah still watched out of the corner of his eye hoping to run into Dayton, someday. He didn't know how to go after any more bad guys. He wasn't sure of how to find any or where they might be. He did remember the sheriff had posters in his office so he would stop by on his way out of town and ask the sheriff for his help.

Noah and Clayton looked in the saloon and several places that served food for Clayton's father but didn't see him. They stopped and got a bite to eat then rented a room for the night at the hotel on the edge of town.

They put the horses and the donkey in the livery to be fed and cared for. As they were walking back to the hotel music filled the air.

"What in the thundering blazes is that?" Noah asked.

"Sounds like a banjo and a fiddle. Come on, it's this way. Let's go have a look. This might be fun."

They followed the sound to the end of town where they saw a big red barn and went inside. The barn wasn't used to keep livestock. It had a small wooden platform in the back where four guys stood and made the music sounds.

The barn didn't have stalls or feed bins. There were seats and a few tables for people to sit at. In front of the stage was a dirt floor with many couples dancing. They would lock arms and turn in circles then let go and hold hands and walk around each other. One man called out the steps for the dancers to do with their dancing partner. This man was singing out what he wanted others to do so no one would bump into each other. Behind that man were four men playing the music. There was a fiddle, a banjo, an accordion, and a guitar.

"What's everyone here doing?" Noah asked Clayton.

"Haven't you ever been to a barn dance before? Where have you lived all your life?"

Noah had no intention of answering the last question. "No, I haven't been to a barn dance yet." He stood off to the side and watched.

It wasn't long before a young lady walked up to Noah and asked, "I haven't seen you before. Are you new here?"

"Yes, I'm just passing through," he replied.

"Oh, that's too bad. Will I get to see you dance later?" she asked.

"No, this is my first time at one of these and I don't know how to dance like this."

"What a shame," the young lady said and then walked away. She stopped half way across the room and looked back at him, smiled then turned and finished walking to the other side to be with four other young ladies.

Noah watched her the whole time. "Clayton, is there something wrong with that lady that was just here?"

"No, why? What do you mean?"

"Well, it's the way she walked. Every time she took a step she twisted at the waist. Didn't you notice that? Maybe she fell off a horse and was injured as a child or something."

Clayton laughed. "No, nothing is wrong with her. Women swing their hips when they walk to show off their lovely gowns and to get your attention. I see it worked too." Clayton had a big grin on his face.

"Yes, her walking funny did catch my eye."

Clayton pushed his hat back on his forehead to get it out of his eyes. "What is wrong with you? That lady was interested in meeting you. You didn't even take your hat off when talking with her. You could have asked her to dance or at the very least got her name and asked her to dinner tomorrow, or something," Clayton said.

Without thinking how it sounded Noah said, "But she's white." His heart dropped a beat after hearing his own voice say that.

"You mean pale? Yes, maybe she is but that just means she isn't a cowgirl. She's a real lady and stays indoors a lot. Her family probably has old money. Good looking pale girls dressed in nice clothes are the ones city gentlemen try to catch."

"I guess I still have a lot to learn. Are you going to ask that girl over there in that fluffy yellow dress to dance? I see you eyeing her."

"That dress is called a gown, for your information. A dress just hangs on a lady. A gown has lots of ruffles and lace. They have petticoats under them to make them balloon out and look full and pretty."

"Ah, that's why the entire group of lady's over there looks a bit porky below their waist. I had to scratch my head over that already." Pointing with his head, Noah then said, "Look, the girl in yellow is looking at you again. Go on over and talk to her."

"I can't. Her momma would skin a boy like me for walking over and saying hello. She is awful purdy though, ain't she?"

Noah and Clayton stood around and enjoyed the music. They watched as people strolled by arm in arm and the gentleman would nod which Noah returned. The ladies without a man on their arm would all gather together on the far side talking to one another. Noah noticed that a man would walk up to one of the girls and bow. She would put her hand out for him to take and he would lead her out into the middle of the dance area to dance. When the dance was over the man would bow and the lady would hold the edge of her dress and squat down just a little and then the young lady would return to her friends.

Noah thought he saw someone he knew. From the back he looked just like Chief Black Jacket. He was puzzled as to why the chief would be there. The man turned around and Noah saw it wasn't the chief after all. This man wore a dark coat with smooth material that hung down to his knees. In the back the coat was cut in the middle and the cut went clear up almost to the man's waist. He had a stiff looking hat with a short brim and the hat had what looked like a short stovepipe that was flat on top.

The older gentleman had a gray beard and wore something circling his eyes that hung off his ears and rested on his large nose. It had what looked like flat glass covering his eyes. Noah had seen men wearing these before but thought that was something white men wore in battle to protect their eyes. He didn't know some of them wore them all the time.

Noah liked this man even though he wasn't the chief. This man had a very small black peace pipe and was smoking it. He had to be one of the good white men Noah's vision talked about.

A young lady and an older woman walked in and stood not far from where Noah and Clayton were standing and watching the dance.

"Lucy, the Brown girls are across the way. Make your way over and stand with them. I will be there in a minute but first I must speak with the banker's wife," the older lady said. She walked away waving a little white cloth she held in her hand.

Noah looked over at all the young ladies on the other side but he didn't see any girls that were brown.

He saw Lucy looking at him. She walked over and said, "Good evening. Would you be so kind as to walk me across to my friends? I do so hate to not have an escort."

Noah looked around to see if she was talking to someone else but there wasn't any one near except for Clayton. He watched as Lucy held out her hand, palm down, and left it hanging there in front of him.

Clayton used his elbow and poked Noah in the ribs. Softly he said, "Take your hat off and say hello. It's like you are from some other nation. I swear."

"Maybe I am." Noah took off his hat and said hello.

Lucy smiled and wiggled her fingers on the hand that was still hanging in the air in front of him.

Clayton again poked Noah in the ribs with his elbow. "Take the lady's hand."

Noah took hold of Lucy's hand. Lucy's face twitched.

Clayton moved his elbow toward Noah's ribs but Noah saw it coming and stepped out of arm's reach. "Stop poking me in the ribs."

"You gently hold a lady's hand. You don't squeeze it like it was an axe handle."

Noah eased up on his grip and saw Lucy smile. They just stood there looking at each other until Clayton said in a firm voice, "Lucy, this is Noah. Noah meet Lucy. Now that you two have been introduced, Noah, you may walk her over to her friends."

Noah walked Lucy over to her friends. She started introducing them but Noah never did see any brown girls. Lucy came to the last two girls of the group. She pointed to one girl with a wave of her hand and said, "This is Noah and Noah this is Lilly Brown and her sister beside her is Sarah Brown. Their father is the governor's right hand man."

He nodded at each lady being introduced until he saw Sarah Brown. This was the woman that spoke with him earlier that evening. And no, she wasn't brown at all but rather a pale white like Clayton had said.

White people were so strange at times. Why would they have a name that didn't have anything to do with the way they looked or some great event from their life?

Noah smiled at Sarah and said hello. She smiled back and touched his shoulder as she straightened his collar. He didn't know what to say or do next, even though he felt he wanted to say something and that he should say something.

The older lady that came in with Lucy returned and went straight up to Noah and looked him over from head to toe. She stepped back and gasped. "No, no, he will never do. Now go away. Shoo," she said as she waved her handkerchief like she would wave away a fly or gnat.

Noah nodded at the ladies and turned and walked back to where Clayton was standing watching the action. He heard the girls giggling as he left.

He walked up to where Clayton stood and Clayton asked, "How did it go over there?"

"The older lady with Lucy chased me off but I think the girls all like me," Noah said.

"How do you figure that?"

"They all giggled as I left. Girls giggle when they like something."

"I don't want to be the one that puts dirt in your rainwater but they were laughing at you. Next time we come we'll take a bath first and dress up in fancy dude clothes. I bet they won't laugh then. Come on, we'd better git."

Noah walked out with Clayton. The whole time he was leaving he kept looking back and watching as the ladies as they followed him with their eyes and were whispering to each other while giggling. Sarah gave a short, quick wave with the small white cloth she held in her hand. Her mother spotted her waving and pulled her arm down.

Still, Noah felt there was more to it than them making fun of him. People were angry and mean when they made fun of someone, not giggling. The spark he felt had to have hit some kindling that could start a fire.

Chapter 13

DON'T LOSE
YOUR MARBLES

Noah and Clayton walked down the hall and entered their room at the hotel. The room had two single beds with a pillow at the head and blanket folded at the foot. They saw one cloth covered sitting chair and one wood framed straw chair. The room had one dresser with a pitcher of water sitting on top and a large bowl used for washing. A single candle stood in a metal cup that had a ring on the side to carry it if someone needed to carry the light around during the night. There were two hooks on the back of the door to hang things up.

Clayton ran to the first bed and sat with a bounce. He bounced a few more times then said, "I've never stayed at a hotel before. This is nice and soft."

"I've never stayed at a hotel either." Noah walked over to the bed by the window and pulled the blanket down on the floor and started making a place to sleep.

"What are you doing?" Clayton asked.

"I'm making me a place to sleep."

"On the floor?"

"Yes, I'm going to sleep down here. Where are you sleeping?"

"Well, I'm sleeping on the bed. Didn't you have beds in your house growing up?"

Noah thought a minute before he said, "No, not this kind of bed. I guess I could try it once to see what it feels like." He watched as Clayton got undressed down to his long underwear and crawled into bed under the top sheet and laid his head on the pillow.

Noah put his blanket back on the bed, got undressed and did like Clayton. The soft bed took him by surprise. He had never laid on anything as comfortable as this and that included the times he slept on the ram hide.

After having a breakfast of eggs and a biscuit with honey they went out to search for Clayton's father. They walked almost all the way from one end of town to the other end. They checked the saloon and the hardware store. They looked in the dining halls but without success.

Noah and Clayton walked out of a feed and grain store and followed the wooden path that went down to the next store when Noah felt a hand on his shoulder and was spun around. His hand went to his gun.

The young man standing before him wasn't wearing a gun so he didn't draw. He remembered what Dayton had taught him. He knew he had to prove anyone he shot and killed was a wanted man or else he could be the one going to jail.

The man, a couple of years older than Noah, had a clean shaven face and wore dark colored pants with a light colored shirt that had ruffles across the front and collar. The man seemed angry as he held up both fists in front of his face with his elbows in front of his body for protection. He moved very carefully in front of Noah ready to fight.

Noah grinned to himself at how this young man looked. He had never seen anyone stand that way in order to tangle with another person before.

He didn't want any trouble and wasn't sure what the young man had in mind. "What's this all about?" he asked.

"You stay away from my girl," the man said with determination in his voice.

"You've made a mistake. I don't know your girl," Noah said.

The man didn't swing his fist at Noah. Instead he shot his fist straight out from his body and caught Noah by surprise. The punch landed against Noah's jaw and sent him tumbling backward.

Noah faced the man ready this time. The man moved his feet quickly and shot two more punches, very fast, straight out from his body. A left punch hit Noah in the stomach and a right punch landed in Noah's face below his left eye.

Noah plummeted backward, off the wooded pathway and he fell over the rail where horses were tied. He landed between two horses and before he could stand up the young man was standing over him.

"Now be a good lad and leave Sarah alone. Don't ever bother her again," the man said. The young man stood back and looked at Noah.

Noah held his jaw and nodded his head. The young man nodded, lowered his fists, straightened his shirt and walked away.

Clayton hurried over to where Noah sat on the ground beside one of the horses. "Are you okay?" Clayton asked.

"I didn't see him swing at me until there was his fist only inches from of my face. I didn't even have time to duck."

"I wondered why you just stood there and let him hit you like that."

"I didn't have much of a choice. What was that all about anyway?" Noah asked as Clayton helped him to his feet and took his hand and dusted him off.

Clayton chuckled. "That, my friend, was what all the giggling was about at the dance last night."

"What do you mean?"

"Those girls were using you to make a boyfriend jealous. And from the look of things it worked."

"Well that's a fine how-do-you-do." Noah got tickled at himself for trying to talk how he had heard some other white men talk back at the clothing store.

He stood still for a moment as he remembered Sarah's smile and the look on her face when their eyes met. He still believed she would go to dinner with him if he were but to ask her. And he thought if he got the chance he might do just that.

Clayton grabbed his arm and pointed to four riders coming their way. "The lead man is Billy. He's one of Pa's friends. Be careful around him; he's real mean."

The four cowboys stopped when they got to Clayton. "Hello, Clayton. Who's that you're with?" Billy asked.

"Hi, Billy. This is a guy from the cattle drive, his name's Noah. Have you seen my pa? He was supposed to meet me here."

"Sorry, kid, I haven't seen him. We just now got into town and we're looking for him ourselves. I'm sure he'll show up soon. You take care now and we'll talk later." The four riders rode on down to the saloon, dismounted and went inside.

Noah and Clayton continued their search for Clayton's pa. They walked past the sheriff's office and found the sheriff sitting outside on a bench. "Mornin, Sheriff," Noah said.

The sheriff motioned for Noah to come over closer. "You see those cowboys that stopped and talked to you? They're part of the Wild Bunch gang. They'll be unhappy when they learn you brought one of them in the other day. You best take the boy and leave town."

"If they're wanted men, can't you arrest them?" Noah asked.

"Not as long as they behave. They aren't wanted here in Kansas. It would take a U. S. Marshall or a bounty hunter to bring them in. And by bounty hunter I mean a seasoned professional bounty hunter." The sheriff gave him a stern and serious look to show he meant business.

"Sheriff," Clayton said. "We are looking for my pa. He's easy to remember if you ever saw him. He only has half an ear on one side. It was shot off by an Injun."

Noah gasped slightly. He stared at Clayton. This suddenly became a very awkward situation. He didn't realize the man he had shot and killed was this boy's father.

"Son, I've seen your pa but he's dead. He was brought in more than a week ago. I'm very sorry."

Noah said, "Thank you, Sheriff." He quickly took a hold of Clayton's arm and led him away. He wasn't ready for the boy to know that he was the one who had shot and killed his father.

"Clayton, are you okay? I'm sorry about the bad news from the sheriff. What are you going to do now?" Noah asked out of concern for the boy.

"It's okay. My father was corrupt. I've wanted to kill him myself a few times. He didn't treat Ma or me very nice, especially when he was partaking of the spirits. I guess I'll miss him some. He was my pa. So," Clayton sighed, "let's see, I guess I'll just go back home."

"Spirits?"

"Drinking moonshine."

Noah patted the boy on the back and saw Clayton had watery eyes.

Noah wanted to go after the four riders, the four bad whites, that came into town but he felt a responsibility toward Clayton. "Come on. Let's go get our horses and we'll head back to Wyoming. I'll make sure you get home safe. We need to let your ma know."

They walked into the Golden Checker General Store for some supplies before heading out. Inside, they saw a bunch of barrels with chairs pulled up to them and each had a board with black and red squares on the top. A few men were playing checkers at two of the barrels.

"Clayton, you should get your ma something nice to take back to her. She's all you have now."

Clayton spent a few minutes looking around. "I'll get her this blue bonnet. She'll like that. She always wanted one. I do have an adopted sister that's part Injun. Should I get her something too?"

"You hold onto your money and I'll get her this child's bow and arrow set. Do you think she'll like that?"

Clayton shrugged his shoulders. "I guess so. I don't know her too well because she can't speak. She hasn't talked since Pa brought her into the family several years back. We just call her Girl because we don't even know her name."

The clerk put the blue bonnet with embroidered white flowers into a small, round hatbox. They paid for the supplies and gathered them up and walked outside.

Noah and Clayton stopped to watch some other boys playing a game in the alley beside the store. The boys drew a circle in the dirt with a stick and each put small round, what looked to be colored rocks in the circle and took turns trying to knock them out of the circle using a bigger round stone.

"How old are you Clayton?" Noah asked.

"I'm twelve, but I can ride and shoot with the best of 'em."

"I know you can, partner. You want to try your luck at that game with the other boys?"

"Sure, but I don't have any clay marbles."

"Wait right here." Noah went back into the store and came out with the marbles in a small cloth bag that had a drawstring and handed them to Clayton.

"Here ya go. You forgot to get yourself something. Now go on over there and see how you do at that game. Just don't lose your marbles and I'll take the supplies on down to the livery stable and tie them on the donkey and bring our horses back around."

Noah took his time. He felt Clayton should spend some time playing with boys his age. A little over an hour later he walked the two horses and the donkey back to pick up Clayton when he saw Clayton walking toward him.

"Game over?" Noah asked.

"Yah, their pa came by in a wagon and they had to go."

"How did you do?"

"Well, the first round I lost about ten but then I caught on how to do it. When the game finished I think I came out ahead." Clayton opened his bag and counted his clay marbles. "Yes! I won seventeen!"

"Good job, so, you had fun then?"

"Sure did. Those boys were nice. They asked me if I would be going to their school. I sure would like to go to school someday."

"Well, maybe someday you can do just that. Okay, let's mount up and head out. We have some riding to do," he said as he handed Clayton the bridle strap to his horse.

They rode hard the rest of that first day. Noah wanted to put some distance between them and those four gunslingers back in Wallace. Maybe he could return and track them down once he had Clayton safely home.

The second day as they rode northwest they didn't push as hard. Noah thought they were safe. He showed Clayton how to spot and track down a rabbit. He was going to let Clayton take the shot. Just as Clayton got the rabbit in his sites the rabbit got spooked and took off running in a zigzag pattern.

"Get ready," Noah said.

He then gave out a very loud whistle. The rabbit stopped and sat up to look and Clayton fired. That evening they camped early to give the horses a rest and had the rabbit for supper.

Around noon the following day Noah led them off the main trail and into a wooded area. They stopped under a shade tree. He took out his canteen and got a drink of water.

"Are we stopping to fix a bite to eat?" Clayton asked.

"Not exactly. We're being followed."

"How can you tell? Did you see someone?"

"No, but the birds in the trees behind us keep flying up like something is disturbing them."

"Maybe a bear is scaring them."

"If it is a bear he's been keeping up with us all morning. So my guess is this bear is riding a horse and carrying a gun."

Noah looked around and then rode over to a tree with a low hanging limb and stopped. He grabbed the limb and pulled himself up into the tree. "Hand me your hunting knife. Then, you take the horses and ride on over this ridge. Go about a mile then find a place out of sight and wait for me there."

Clayton took the horses and rode out of sight. Noah climbed higher up the tree and found a spot with lots of leaves for cover. It wasn't too long before Noah saw a horse and rider leaving the main trail and following their horse tracks up and into the woods.

The rider approached the tree where Noah hid and he recognized the rider as one of the four gunmen he saw back in Wallace.

The man took his time walking his horse up to the tree where Noah sat. The man made his horse walk as he searched the ground to follow the tracks just left by Noah and Clayton's horses.

Noah waited.

When the rider was under the tree he stopped and looked around. He took his bandana from around his neck and wiped his brow.

Noah took a deep breath in preparing to jump. The man heard Noah move and looked up. He spotted Noah and drew his gun and fired.

Chapter 14

THE REWARD MONEY

Noah saw the gun come out and he leaned back behind a thick branch just in time and the bullet hissed through the leaves very near his head. Noah launched himself from his perch and his feet hit the gunslinger's head and knocked him from his horse. Noah landed on his side and he jumped up and dove on top of the man and tried to cut him with the knife. The man blocked the knife and being much stronger than Noah rolled him off and was now sitting on top of him.

Noah struggled as the man used his fist to hit Noah in the face with several hard blows. Blood poured from Noah's nose. The man hit him again and again. Noah thought he was going to be beaten to death.

He raised his right leg and managed to hook his foot in front of the man's face and kicked him away. They both stood up but the man had his handgun and pointed it at Noah.

There was a loud whistle.

The gunman stopped and looked in the direction of the noise.

Blam!

A shot was fired and the gunman staggered back and fell. He rolled several times down the hill before coming to a stop next to a large rock.

Noah being dazed squatted down thinking the shot was at him. He looked at the kid standing beside a tree with his rifle smoking not far from where the fight took place.

Noah yelled at the boy, "I thought I told you to take the horses and stay out of sight."

"Ya, my pa always said I never listened very good. But you have to admit I'm a fast learner. And you're lucky I knew how to whistle," Clayton said with a smile on his face.

"But why did you do that? Doesn't it bother you that you shot someone?"

"Pa always said when it's him or me I'll take me every time. And, well, you said we were partners, didn't you?"

"Yes, but killing is my job."

"Well, you're not as good at it as you think you are."

"You have a smart mouth, too," Noah said.

"Pa used to say that about me, too. What do we do now?"

They walked down to check the body. It lay lifeless curled up beside the rock. Clayton went back and brought the horses around.

Noah asked, "Did you know this guy?"

"Yep, he's one of the Wild Bunch; same as the other three that rode into Wallace with him the other day. They are all friends of my pa. This one's name is Pete. He was a tracker for the army a few years ago. There's a reward for him, too, if we wanna turn him in."

"Well, that's up to you. You'll get the reward."

"Okay, let's tie him to his horse and take him on into Lincoln. Mom could use the extra money."

"How do you know so many of these outlaws? Is it because of your pa?"

"Yep, he rode with them and many others of the Wild Bunch stayed at our house sometimes. Let me ask you something. Why does that whistle thing work?"

"It's an unexpected distraction. It confuses them and they can't help but to look and see what's going on. I didn't know it worked on people as well as animals. Oh, and by the way, thanks."

Noah could see a lot of himself in Clayton. He understood this boy didn't have much of a childhood and was already a man. He was now wondering if he would have to shoot his way into the boy's house to return him home.

Noah and Clayton rode into Lincoln a day and a half later. They stopped by the sheriff's office and turned in the body. The deputy took the information and said, "You all will have to wait until the sheriff gets back into town the day after next before you get the reward. He had to take a prisoner to Dodge City."

"How much is the bounty on this fellow?" Clayton asked.

"Six hundred dollars. You're a very rich man," the deputy said.

"Okay, we'll be back then but in the mean time we'll get a room at the hotel across the street and just make ourselves at home," Noah answered.

Noon the following day Noah went alone into Miss May's Restaurant for a bite to eat. Clayton had grabbed his bag of clay marbles and went off to make some friends to play with.

As soon as Noah walked inside an older, plump lady with her white hair pulled back in a bun walked up to him and said, "Hello, I'm Miss May. Welcome, please come on in and I will find you a table. Are you new in town? I haven't seen you around."

"Yes, I'm Noah. Just got here yesterday." He followed the jolly lady over to a table that had one other man sitting.

"I'm going to put you at this table with Luther. No one should eat alone. How are you doing Luther? Your food is almost ready."

Luther was an older man with a mustache that curled up at the ends. "And who am I having the honor of eating with today?" he asked.

"This here is Noah. He's new in town. Noah, I'll bring you a steak and biscuit and some coffee. How's that sound?"

"I was just going to order some ham and potatoes. Could I have milk instead of coffee?" Noah replied.

"Nope, I'll bring you a steak and I'll add a potato and milk. A strapping young man like you needs more than just a slice of ham." Miss May walked away and headed for the kitchen.

Luther chuckled. "She's one fine lady. Best person in the world you would ever want to meet. But she does have to have everything her way. She's usually right, though. What brings you to town?"

"I'm just passing through. I'm taking a young'un back to his ma in Wyoming after he lost his father."

"Is he a relative?"

"No, we were on a cattle drive and his pa got shot and died so I'm just taking him home."

"That's mighty good of you. So, you're a cowboy?"

"No, I was just a cowboy for that one cattle drive. I'm not sure what I am yet. What do you do, Luther?"

"Nothing." Luther started laughing. "I've done about everything there is to do, I guess. My last job was with the railroad. I guarded the payroll car. That was a couple of years ago."

"That can be a dangerous job," Noah said.

"Yes sir, that's why I settled down; quit while I was ahead."

Miss May brought the food and placed it on the table. "Now, if there's anything else you need just give me a wave and I'll come running."

"Thank you, Miss May," Luther said.

"Yes, thank you, ma'am," Noah said.

Noah noticed Luther eyeing him through most of the meal. As they were just about done eating Luther leaned toward Noah and said in a soft voice, "You best be careful tracking down outlaws."

"What do you mean?" Noah asked, startled at the remark.

"Outlaws are mean. They know every dirty trick in the book. You're still a greenhorn. They can sense that about you. They'll kill you in a heartbeat if they can. And believe you me, they can. I don't know why you're doing what you're doing but let whatever happened go. Find a job you like. Find someone that makes you happy and live life. All this killing business will change you. You'll become what you're fighting against. You'll become your own worst enemy."

"How do you know all this about me?"

"Look, I like you. I can read people pretty good. That black eye and those bruises on your face give you away. Just heed what I'm telling you, son. You aren't like those people. Quit before it's too late."

"I'll give it some thought but I can't quit just yet."

"The longer you do this type work, the deeper you get sucked in. I know."

"Thanks for the advice." Noah finished eating and nodded at Luther then left the table and walked outside.

The next day Noah and Clayton were going through some of the shops in town; killing time until the sheriff got back. They walked over and sat on a bench in front of the shop that had a pole with red and white stripes curling down from the top to the bottom with a red ball on the top. Men were going inside and getting their hair cut off. Noah figured they didn't want to get scalped either.

Noah and Clayton went and got their horses and donkey and tied them to a rail in front of the hotel next door. They were just waiting to get the reward money then go.

Three riders came slowly down the street looking all around when they spotted Clayton and came to a stop in front of where Noah and Clayton were sitting.

"Hello, again, Clayton. You seen Pete?" one of the riders said.

"Why, Billy? Did you lose him?" Clayton asked in a nervous voice.

Noah stood up and said, "Clayton, you best go back over to the hotel and check our room to see if we left anything behind." Clayton stood back but didn't leave. Noah then turned his attention to the three riders. "Leave the boy out of this. If you have unfinished business, then finish it with me."

Billy dismounted and walked toward Noah. Noah heard a jingle sound as Billy walked. He looked down and saw that Billy had a silver wish boned shape piece coming from the heel of each boot. At the end of this silver piece was a tiny silver star with sharp points that jingled when he walked.

This bothered Noah. Warriors from his tribe wore bells around their ankles sometimes to protect them from evil spirits coming out of the earth. He knew Billy had protection and it would be harder for him to take Billy down if it came to that.

Billy walked up to within a few inches of Noah's face but Noah didn't back away.

The other two riders dismounted and walked their horses over and tied them to a hitching post. They walked out into the middle of the street and stood, waiting. Noah looked over and saw the men pull out their handguns and check them to make sure they were loaded. He saw them return their guns to their holsters. They were ready.

"So you think it'll take three of you to kill me? That don't seem exactly fair," Noah said.

"You have it all wrong. It'll only take one of us to kill you, but you see, the one that shoots closest to your heart wins your horse and gun."

"And what if I don't fight?"

"If you don't come out here and face us we'll kill you and the boy," the outlaw said. Billy turned and walked out and stood with the other two men.

Noah walked out and stood before the three gunmen. People cleared the street and high tailed it out of the way. The showdown was set.

He stared at the three men and he could tell they were ready to draw their guns.

Noah yelled, "Wait! I'm not ready."

Chapter 15

THE GUN FIGHT

Noah carefully unbuckled his gun belt and took it off. He walked over to the donkey and got something from the supplies. He took off his pants and put on his buckskin britches. He took his boots off and put on his moccasins. He handed his cowboy hat to Clayton and noticed how big Clayton's eyes got. He took the child's bow and arrow set and put the quiver full of arrows over his shoulder. He hung his gun belt over the donkey.

As he changed clothes he saw a man leaned up against a storefront that was wearing those silver wishbones on his boots. Noah asked the man if he could borrow those for his moccasins. He told the man he wanted to jingle as he walked out to the gunfight.

The man obliged and even helped put them on Noah's moccasins. They didn't fit the soft shoes he was now wearing but the leather strap held them in place. The spurs flopped around as he moved but Noah jingled as he walked out to face the three outlaws. He now felt protected and he walked back out into the street carrying the small child's bow. If he was going to die, he was going to die an Indian.

Noah faced the three gunmen again. He saw them smile then actually heard a laugh from one of the men and heard the other two chuckling. Someone walked up beside him. He glanced over and saw it was Clayton wearing the blue bonnet he had gotten for his ma.

Noah could hear people standing on the edge of the street talking about what he'd done and the way he was dressed. He could see men pointing at him. He had caused quite a distraction.

Noah started to send Clayton away when another man walked up and stood on the other side of him. It was Luther. The smiles were gone from the gunslingers and the situation got serious, really fast.

Luther whispered, "Get ready. I'll start."

Luther was holding a derringer in his left hand. The derringer wouldn't be of any use this far away. He pointed it at the ground and fired it, dropped the derringer and drew his gun.

Everyone jumped and went for their guns. Noah jerked his hand up to grab at the quiver but instead of an arrow he pulled out his Colt revolver, pointed it, and fired.

Clayton dove to the ground to make a smaller target and pulled a handgun from his belt and fired. A bullet landed in the dirt beside Clayton's face and he had to spit the dirt from his mouth.

The three outlaws were moving backward and were firing. Noah was shooting to kill as Dayton had taught him to do. Billy, the one in the middle across form Noah, fell straight back and didn't move. More shots were fired. Noah heard the whizzing sound of a bullet as it passed his left ear.

The man across from Luther yelped, turned, and went down. Luther dropped to his knees and was bleeding from a wound in his thigh on his right leg.

A stray bullet broke a window of a store behind the last outlaw standing. More shots rang out. The last gunman flinched from pain, dropped his gun and was holding his wrist. Clayton was still firing and the dirt in front of the last man standing exploded in dust balls.

"Hold up! Shoot him if he moves," Noah yelled. "Clayton, are you okay?"

"I'm good."

Noah ran over to check on Luther. "I'm okay. I was just grazed. Help me get to the doctor and I'll be fine," Luther said. "You are one crazy cowpoke, Noah. I've never seen anything like this in my entire life. This will be talked of for years to come and I just had to be a part of it."

"Ya, I'm crazy. I think it was the loco weed someone put in my oatmeal this morning." He then smiled and helped Luther to his feet.

"I can hear the story now of how one man with a kid's bow and arrow took down three desperados," Luther remarked.

The deputy ran up the street toward the gunfight with his gun drawn. There was a cloud of smoke still in the air and the smell of gunpowder lingered. He went over and arrested the man holding his wrist. The guy on the ground was moaning.

"Call for the doctor," the deputy yelled at the crowd of people watching.

Noah looked up hearing the noise of the afternoon stagecoach coming into view at the end of the street. He saw a large wagon type box pulled by six horses. It looked somewhat like a small wooden house on wooden spoke wheels with windows that had curtains and a door. A man sat on a bench near the roof holding the reigns and he had a shotgun resting beside him. It pulled up to all the commotion and stopped. The door flew open and the sheriff stepped out.

"I go out of town for a couple days and all hell breaks loose. Who started this?" he asked.

No one could say where the first shot came from. All the people questioned never saw the first shot. When that shot was fired everyone still had their guns in their holsters as best they could tell. The sheriff did learn that the three riders had called Noah out and threatened to kill him and the boy.

The sheriff walked over and was looking at the three men. "Deputy, put the two wounded men in jail and have the doc look 'em over after he's done with Luther. You guys are in luck. The two wounded men only had a reward if they were taken alive. I think it's about $200 each. The dead man was wanted dead or alive and is worth $500. Come over to my office later and we'll settle up."

"Split mine between Luther and Clayton. I wouldn't have been here to even say this if it weren't for them," Noah said.

The sheriff looked at Noah. "Are you Indian?"

Luther spoke up. "He's okay. He's with me. I'll tell you all about it when I come to get the reward money. I do declare he's a bit odd but he's one of the good guys. Sheriff, you're in for one strange tale."

A man carrying a small black leather bag dashed over to Luther. Noah took notice that this man was dressed in one of those cloth jackets. It was old and worn and had patches sewed onto the elbows. He had white hair above his top lip and short gray whiskers on the lower part of his face. He had a gold chain that went from his belt to a small pocket in his pants.

"Luther, what on God's good earth where you trying to do? You're getting too old to carry on like this." The man said.

"Hello, Doc. You got here pretty fast," Luther said.

"I heard all the shooting and grabbed my medicine kit and headed this way. I knew something was going on and I'd be needed. Sure didn't think it would be you out here acting like a fool."

Noah watched as this white medicine man tore Luther's pants and took a look. He opened his satchel and pulled out a bottle and poured something on the wound that made Luther wrench in pain.

"Whoa, Doc, take it easy, that burns," Luther said.

"Maybe that'll remind you to stop this tom-foolery."

The sheriff said, "Doc, when you're done here come on over to the jail. I have two more for you to look at."

The doctor took hold of the tiny chain on his belt and pulled a small round gold piece with a white face on one side that had little black lines pointing to some numbers out from his pocket and looked at it. "I'll be over in fifteen or twenty minutes, Sheriff."

Noah thought about his vision quest. It had come true. He had become the enemy and he did find a few good white men he didn't know existed before.

He looked over and watched Clayton. Clayton's mouth didn't stop moving telling Luther about diving to the ground to make himself a smaller target. He seemed to be excited about the shootout but he was still a kid. Noah knew he would have to have a talk with Clayton to let him know how close he came to dying and that there was more in life to get excited about than a gunfight.

Noah wondered if the man he had killed had a family. When he shot and killed Clayton's pa he didn't know the man as the father of this new friend, Clayton. He hated the thought that maybe he was doing to them what had been done to him but like Clayton's pa had said, if it was them or me, I'll take me every time. As best Noah could figure out was they had brought it on themselves and it was their choice to be the evil person they were.

"Choices," he mumbled to himself. "I better take stock of some of my choices."

Noah took his time getting back into his Levi's and boots. He handed the man back his spurs and thanked him. It had felt good to be dressed as an Indian again. It had been a long time and made him homesick for the way things used to be.

He missed his tribe and the friends he had that were still stuck back on the reservation. He missed his mother, Gentle Breeze.

He wondered when killing white men would make his sadness and his anger toward the white men go away. So far, it had only made him numb.

At least he wasn't stuck on the reservation. He was doing something about the bad white men. He was getting back at them. Maybe he was preventing other Indian families from suffering the cruelty the white men imposed upon him and his tribe. He was no longer a victim of being Indian. He was fighting back.

Noah and Clayton had been on the road for over a week and had made it to Wyoming. They had crossed the Platte River and were heading west toward Fort Laramie. The land of rolling hills with fields of tall grass made riding easier.

Noah and Clayton heard shots off in the distance. They stopped their horses to see what was going on. At the bottom of one of the rolling hills were three small Conestoga wagons. The bandits were smart. They waited until the teams of horses would be pulling the wagons up hill and would be slower. The bandits could then overtake the travelers easily.

"Injuns! Come on we have to help," Clayton said. He kicked his horse and raced off.

"Wait," Noah yelled. "We can't fight Indians." But it was too late. Clayton headed toward the wagons at a gallop.

At first Noah thought it was just more bad white men and he wanted to help. He had to look a few seconds before he realized it was Indians. "Ah, cow pies," he said in disgust. Noah dropped the lead strap to his donkey and took off after Clayton.

He didn't know what he was going to do. He had almost caught up with Clayton and they were closing in on the wagons. He could hear the yells of the Indians on horseback as they fired guns and continued to chase after the wagons.

He drew his Colt revolver and fired two shots up into the air. Clayton slowed down and allowed Noah to catch up to him.

"Why did you do that? Now our element of surprise is gone," Clayton said.

Noah fired into the air once more then he yelled, "Ee-nahzjee, ee-nahzjee!"

One of the Indians stopped his horse and looked back at Noah and Clayton. He raised the hand with his rifle and yelled something to the others. The others stopped their chase and brought their horses up alongside of the Indian with his rifle held up in the air.

Noah and Clayton slowed their horses to a walk. "What's going on here? What did you say? How'd you know Injun talk?" Clayton asked.

"I told them to stop," Noah replied. "Now, let me do all the talking." Noah was hoping these Indians were friends with his tribe, the Lakota.

He and Clayton rode up to within about twenty or thirty yards of the Indians and stopped.

The Indian leader spoke, "I am Crazy Elk, of the Crow Nation. Who are you? Why did you want us to stop?"

Noah knew the Crow weren't exactly friends with his people. The two nations had fought against each other in years past. He would have to think of some good reason or he would become their next kill.

Noah looked Crazy Elk over for several minutes. Crazy Elk wore a tan buckskin shirt with fringe down both arms. His long, black hair was pulled back with a headband made from a leather strap and it had an eagle feather hanging on one side of his head. He, and the others, had red and yellow war paint across their faces.

"I am Two Wolves, now called Noah, of the Lakota nation," Noah said as he heard a grunt coming from Clayton.

"Lakota, huh?" Crazy Elk responded. "Lakota is just a fancy word for Sioux and we aren't friends with the Sioux. Maybe it's a good day for you to cross the bridge to the afterlife." He raised his rifle and pointed it at Noah. The others of the war party did the same.

Chapter 16

CAPTURED

Noah had seen some of the elders from his tribe barter with whites and Indians from other tribes before but he had never traded with anyone for supplies or weapons. He had to find out what they would trade and what they needed in exchange for his life.

"Are you attacking the wagons because your people are hungry?" he asked.

"What do you think? You are Indian or have you been away from your home too long and forget how it is?" Crazy Elk asked.

"Let us trade for something you need."

"We have captured you and the boy. You want to trade the boy? We can take him and your horses and guns already."

"No, the boy is not for trade. We can give you food for your people."

The donkey brayed not far from where they were sitting on their horses.

Crazy Elk smirked and looked around at the other warriors. "We do not want to eat donkey, if that is the food you are talking of."

"I can give you money."

"My people can't eat frog skins and we can't very well go into a town somewhere and buy food."

"I can bring you steers. How many steers do you want to let us go and to not attack the wagons?" Noah asked.

There was a pause. Noah wondered why he was trading for the lives of the white families in the wagons. What he wanted was for all the whites to go away and never return. He knew this to be just a dream of the elders and life would never be that way again.

Crazy Elk talked in a low voice to some of the other warriors getting ideas and letting them have a say on what he should ask for. After several minutes they seemed to agree and nodded their heads. They all faced Noah and would look back and forth between Noah and Crazy Elk as the two spoke to each other.

"Twenty cows and ten rifles," Crazy Elk said.

"No, five cows is more than you would get from the wagons."

"You are forgetting, we can shoot you and leave you here."

"Then you would only get a couple guns and two horses and you would have to eat the donkey."

An angry look came across Crazy Elk's face. He walked his horse over beside Clayton and raised a tomahawk. Clayton flinched and ducked his head down beside his horse's neck.

"Eight cows, no guns," Noah said.

Crazy Elk lowered his tomahawk. "Fifteen cows and ten canteens of firewater."

"Ten cows and ten blankets. No firewater."

"No deal. We have got blankets before. They are poison and kill our people."

"We will give you the blankets white people use, no poison ones." Noah knew they were getting down to where they could strike a deal. He also knew the leader would have the last say to save face.

"Ten cows, ten blankets, and ten leather bags," Crazy Elk said after much thought.

Noah accepted the terms but knew it had to be formally agreed upon. "You make it extremely hard on me. You are very skilled in trading. Now we must smoke on it."

"Okay. Come with us. We will ride over to those trees on the side of that far hill," Crazy Elk said.

Noah told Clayton to go and get the donkey and meet them. Noah followed the warriors over to a tree line at the far side of the grassland. Everyone dismounted and formed a circle and sat down.

One of the warriors brought out a long wooden pipe rolled up in a piece of buffalo hide. The warrior had to use both hands to hold the pipe. The pipe had carvings on the side of buffalos and an eagle head bowl that stood on top of the pipe at one end. Another warrior took a pouch and opened it. Tobacco was sacred to the Indians but was hard for Indians to buy or obtain. So, the warrior pulled out some wild life everlasting plant, also known as rabbit tobacco, and filled the bowl.

A fire was built in the middle of the circle by putting some small sticks and leaves together and striking a flint on the metal edge on someone's knife until a small blaze formed from the sparks and started burning. Crazy Elk took a burning stem then lit the pipe and passed it around.

It was custom to only tell the truth as the pipe was being smoked. Each Indian, in turn, repeated the proclamation of the deal and took a draw of the smoke then passed it on to the next person.

Once the ceremony was over everyone stood and the pipe was taken and cleaned then rolled up in its protective leather sheath.

"Where are my steers? When do I get them?" Crazy Elk asked.

"Where's the nearest town?" Noah asked.

"Fort Laramie is less than a day's ride to the west," Crazy Elk said.

"Good, Clayton and I will ride into Fort Laramie and get the steers and blankets and be back here in a couple days."

"Ten steers, ten blankets, and ten leather bags. You will stay here with us. Send the boy. He has three days to return or you die."

"It will take six days to get everything and bring the steers back; maybe longer if the boy has to go alone."

"Then he has until the sunset of the fourth day."

Clayton rode up leading the donkey and dismounted. Noah walked over to Clayton and put his arm on Clayton's shoulder. He walked him over to his horse and got some money from his saddle bag and handed it to Clayton.

"Sorry you had to find out I was an Indian the way you did. I wouldn't blame you if you just kept riding once you leave here," Noah said.

"Nope, I'm not like that. We're partners and that's the way it is. Tell me what you need me to do and I'll do it."

"You have your work cut out for you. I made a deal and you'll have to go alone into Fort Laramie and buy ten blankets and ten leather bags and twelve steers. We only need ten but get twelve in case one or two wander off because you won't have time to go and round them up. Then bring them back within four days. First, go to the fort and get a fresh horse. Then get the blankets and bags. Head back this way and stop at the first ranch you came by going into town and buy the twelve steers. That way you won't have as far to bring the small herd back here to us. Drive them slowly at night but keep them moving. Do you think you can you handle all that?" Noah asked.

"Sure enough, you ain't talking to some ole cowpoke. I'm a real cowboy," Clayton said.

Noah then whispered something in Clayton's ear.

"No tricks, no soldiers, no gunmen," Crazy Elk said.

"No, no tricks, no soldiers or gunmen. You have my word," Noah answered.

Clayton put his foot in his stirrup, mounted up and pointed his horse west and rode off.

In the afternoon of the fourth day, a cavalry patrol went along the road below the trees where the war party was hiding. They stopped when they got even with the Indian camp. Two riders broke formation and headed up the hill toward the camp.

Crazy Elk started getting ready to attack the two riders. Noah jumped up and said, "Let me go talk to them. I can get them to leave."

Crazy Elk held up his hand to his men and nodded at Noah. Noah ran and jumped on the first horse he came to and headed toward the two riders as both the war party and the patrol watched.

When the horses came together the three of them stopped. "I'm Private Davis. Are those Indians up near the trees? Are you in need of help?" one of the cavalry men asked.

"I'm Noah. Why do you think those are Indians?"

"Some wagons came into the fort a couple of days ago and said they had been chased by Indians somewhere around this area. We're just out looking for them. Aren't those Indians up there looking down at us?" Private Davis stood in the stirrups to get a better look.

"Those men up there are just the same as me. Don't you think if they were Indians they would be running away? Those men are just waking up. They had a wild war party last night if you know what I mean. They ended up dressing and acting like Indians for laughs. You should have been here. It was quite a sight. They'll head out later today once they can walk straight enough to get to their horses to go back home."

"You don't seem drunk," Private Davis said. Noah saw a wide grin on his face.

"Oh, no sir. I don't drink. I was just along for the ride."

"Okay, so you haven't seen our Indians then?"

"No sir. I haven't seen your Indians."

The private saluted Noah and the two soldiers turned their horses around and headed back down to the cavalry patrol. Noah watched a few minutes then rode back to the war party.

The Indians watched as the cavalry patrol rode down the trail and out of sight.

"Thank you," Crazy Elk said to Noah. "You probably saved many of my men. You are free to go. We are even."

"Well, hold on a minute. I have a bunch of cows coming here later today. They are still yours. We smoked on it. And your people are still hungry."

The pleased expression on Crazy Elk's face showed Noah that the Indian leader liked what Noah had said. His action, on the other hand, was still stern; he had to save face in front of his men. "Then we must give you something in return for what you did for us. What do you want?"

"I want us to be friends," Noah said.

"We cannot be friends," Crazy Elk said. The Indian leader's eyes showed a different demure.

Faint cow bellows drifted through the air from the other side of the hill. Everyone stood and came over to Crazy Elk. "What do you want us to do? The cows are coming," one of the warriors said.

"Get your horses and go meet them. Bring them here."

"We will settle up later. Right now, you must take your cattle and leave this area before the cavalry returns," Noah said.

It wasn't long before cows came over the top of the hill into sight. The Indians along with Clayton moved them down onto the grasslands and held them there. Crazy Elk and Noah rode side by side down to where they were.

As Clayton rode up beside Noah he seemed tired but excited to have accomplished his mission. "I made it with eleven steers. One managed to escape during the night. You okay?" Clayton asked.

"Yes, everything here is good. You did a great job," Noah said.

Clayton got off his horse and untied the bundle of blankets from the back of his horse. "These blankets made my saddle feel more like a soft sitting room chair." He took the blankets over and handed then to Crazy Elk.

Clayton walked over to one of the cows and untied a bundle made from one of the blankets and opened it on the ground. When he unrolled it, ten women's pocketbooks fell out. Noah broke out laughing. "That's not exactly what I had in mind when I told you ten leather bags," Crazy Elk said.

Crazy Elk looked at the lady handbags and got an angry look on his face. Noah could tell he was insulted and wasn't sure what he was going to do as he raised his tomahawk high in the air as if he was going to throw it at him.

Chapter 17

THE SADDLE BAGS

Noah and Clayton froze at the sight of the tomahawk. Crazy Elk rode his horse closer. Several of his men joined him with puzzled looks on their faces. One of his men realizing what the leather bags were started laughing at the pocketbooks. Another man cracked a big grin and the others started snickering.

Crazy Elk threw his tomahawk and it stuck in the ground beside the leather bags. He then broke out into a loud horselaugh. Everyone laughed intensely for a few minutes. Finally Crazy Elk spoke, "These will have to do. Next time I will mention that the bags I want are saddle bags."

"Did you get that other thing I asked for?" Noah said to Clayton.

"Yes sir, right here."

Clayton went over to a large bag tied around his horse's neck and took it from the horse. He walked over to Crazy Elk, opened the bag, and offered some to the Indian leader.

Crazy Elk looked inside the sack. He had a bewildered look on his face. "What is this, a bag full of funny looking beetles?"

Clayton took one out and showed it to the others. He put one in his mouth and said, "Here, try one."

Crazy Elk looked over at Noah. "It's okay. They're good. I bet you have never had anything like this before."

Crazy Elk took one and looked it over. He smelled the little white ball with red stripes on it several times. He touched it to his tongue. He tasted the candy and his face had an unusual delightful expression on it. The others took one and tried it. They all made sounds as they smacked their lips while eating the peppermint balls.

"I didn't ask for these in our agreement," Crazy Elk said.

"That's because you didn't know about them or you would have asked," Noah replied. "This is what friends do for each other."

"Two Wolves Noah, you are a strange man," Crazy Elk said. "May the Great Spirit ride with you and keep you safe because I may not be around to save your ugly butt next time you get into trouble."

"Nor I you," Noah said.

Crazy Elk took the sack from Clayton and with a long sweeping motion of his hand he turned his horse toward the cattle and the war band headed the cattle north.

Noah and Clayton rode with the Indians for several days and helped with the cattle. Watching the interaction of the other Indians gave Noah a good feeling. He enjoyed being with them even though they were from a tribe that the Lakota used to be at war with.

The war between tribes of other nations had come to an end. They had to stop killing each other when a bigger threat, the white man, came along. Noah thought he might be the only one still after the white man.

He and Clayton went hunting with the Crow warriors for food while they were on this small cattle drive. He got to show Clayton some of the Indian ways and customs. The Crow did things just a little different than the Lakota but their love for Mother Earth was the same.

At night, they all listened to the stories the other men told: stories of when they were young and on hunting trips or stories about some of their gatherings at powwows. He learned the Crow had lost many people in the Indian Wars the same as the Lakota did.

Noah noticed the men hardly ever talked about the massacres. While sitting one night with one of the older men named Blue Feather he had to ask, "Some of your tribe were at the battle of Greasy Grass River weren't they?" Noah asked.

"Yes, I was there. There were Indians from all over that came to fight this battle against Yellow Hair. We stopped him too. Killed every last one of them. But there are so many whites that the battle to end all violence against the Red people was just another battle to them. You are too young to have been there so why do you ask?"

"I was there."

"No, that had to be before your time. Many warriors say they were there and they weren't. They just want to be part of the greatest battle the Indians fought. Don't be like the dreamers."

"But I was there. I was born during the battle."

"Oh, you are the one born there? You are Gentle Breeze's son?"

"Yes, how do you know of Gentle Breeze?"

"She is a hero among all the nations. She saved many lives by killing the flagman that directed the army that day. Once he was dead, the army was lost as to what to do and where to go to do the most damage. That was one of the main reasons we won the battle. Noah Two Wolves, I didn't know you by the name Noah."

Noah felt proud to hear that so many people were saved by what his mother did. He had no idea her actions were remembered by the people of so many nations. He had heard the stories from his tribe but had not realized she had hero status from tribes all over. It meant a great deal for him to hear this.

"Yes, I go by Noah now. I had to change my name in order to be accepted by white men as I hunt for Gentle

Breeze's murderer. She was slaughtered not long ago and now I'm hunting the killers down."

"I wish you great success. Somehow I knew the son of Gentle Breeze would be a great warrior and I see that you are. It is an honor to be talking with you," Blue Feather said.

The following day when the sun rose to its highest point Clayton told Noah they must head west to get to his home.

"I can't believe you're Indian, Noah. I can't believe I am riding with Indians either, but here's where we need to change direction. My home is that way," Clayton said as he pointed toward the west.

Noah rode over to Crazy Elk and said, "We must go now. I have to take Clayton to his home."

"I understand. We will meet again," Crazy Elk said.

"You be safe, my friend."

"Good-bye, Chief," Clayton said.

"I like that. I'm now Chief Crazy Elk."

Chief Crazy Elk took his fist and placed it on his heart. Noah and Clayton did the same then the two of them rode off.

They rode northwest several days. They went across grasslands and through mountain passes. They finally came to a ridge and high on top of this ridge they stopped to look out and see the magnificent view.

"How much further?" Noah asked.

"See those lines of hills that shoot up into mountain ranges as they go further along? That is the start of the Devil's Horns. Devil's Horns create a canyon in the middle and down that canyon is where Ma lives. It's out of sight and no one bothers us there. The only way in and back out is through the Devil's Horns," Clayton said. "The mountains are on both sides of the canyon and are impassable. We live about half way up that canyon. At the end is another canyon called the Hole-in-the-Wall. In there is another ranch, the

Wild Ranch, but anyone that goes up to that ranch never comes back. They never return because they are killed. The men at that ranch don't like strangers."

"Sounds like some seriously bad dudes you have for neighbors."

"Yah, they watch over Ma and me and my adopted sis. Come on, we only have a couple hours ride from here."

They rode down and followed the trail into the Devil's Horns. The mountains on both sides grew larger and higher as they followed the road. The rocks were jagged and couldn't be climbed except by mountain goats.

"There's the house." Clayton pointed to a small cabin off to the left about a half mile ahead.

Noah saw a young lady run into the house as they approached. It looked like she had been at the well drawing water.

The old log house had a small front porch with a seat hanging down held with chains and another chair that had rounded runners instead of legs. As Noah looked at the chair he thought that the chair wouldn't sit very still if someone sat in it. It looked to him as though it would rock back and forth not letting the person rest as they should while sitting.

There was a small barn off to the right of the cabin with the barn door open. Several chickens ran through the yard and there was one old hound dog in the shade at the side of the porch.

They got off the horses and walked them up to a hitching rail in front of the porch over to the left. An older woman walked out pointing a double barrel shotgun at them. The younger woman stood in the doorway looking out to watch what was going on; not the greeting Noah expected.

"Ma, I'm home. I made it," Clayton yelled. He ran up on the porch and gave the woman a hug.

"Where's yer pa?" she asked. "And who's this?"

"Pa's dead. He got his self shot and killed. This is Noah. He was on the cattle drive with me and looked out fer me until I made it back."

"Well, that don't surprise me none about yur pa. I've been expecting Pa to git his self kilt for a long time now."

Ma had on a homemade dress of pale blue that went down to her ankles and was dirty near the bottom edge. It had a white lace collar with white cuffs on the long sleeves. On her feet were old worn brown leather button shoes. She wore a dirty, white apron that covered most of the dress. She wore her silver and black hair pulled back in a tight bun at the back of her head held by some kind of hair comb.

Noah waved and took the horses and donkey and tied them to the hitching rail. He walked over and picked up the water bucket sitting beside the well still full of water and brought it back over to the porch and set it down.

"May as well bring that there water on in the house. I have a few biscuits and some gravy and left over fried chicken if y'all is hungry. Girl, go fetch the milk bucket and go get us'uns fresh milk and feed the cow while you're in there," Ma said.

"Ma, I got you something in town." Clayton ran over and got the bonnet he bought and carried it over and handed it to Ma.

"Well, that there's right purty. Thank you, Clayton. Yer such a good boy thinking of yur ma that a way." She put the bonnet on and said, "Look, it matches my dress."

"And your eyes," Clayton added.

Ma smiled and Noah could see the blue in her eyes as they twinkled.

The young woman started for the barn when Clayton said, "Girl, hold on a second. Noah here brought you something too." He ran over and got the child's bow and arrow set from Noah's horse and took it over and gave it to the young woman.

She looked at Noah with a perplexed look in her eyes. Noah turned red in the face and said, "I'm sorry. The way Clayton talked I thought you were his younger sister. I didn't mean any disrespect."

She dropped the child's bow and arrow set on the ground and walked on across the yard and disappeared into the barn.

"Well, you'uns come on in and set yerself down and I'll fix ya that grub," Ma said.

"Is it okay if I take the horses into the barn and give them some water?" Noah asked.

"Sure, since it's so late ya may want to give them some hay while yer at it. I guess ya be spending the night." Ma said.

"Thank you kindly, ma'am," Noah said. He walked over and untied the horses. He made a clicking sound with his mouth as he led them across the yard and into the barn.

Inside the barn he saw the young woman at a stall milking the one and only cow. She looked about his age and had high cheekbones and long shiny hair. She looked almost Indian except her hair was dark brown with a light red tint. She had dark tan skin and had an ample figure. Noah had never seen anyone as beautiful as her. He walked over to her and said, "I am sorry. I didn't know you were a young lady when I bought that gift for you."

She stopped milking and pulled out a butcher knife and pointed it at Noah. He held up his hands and walked away. He wondered if maybe she didn't hear him. He took the saddles off the horses and took the supplies off the donkey and got the animals some water from the well and fed them some hay from a haystack just outside the barn door. When he finished he looked around but the young lady had left and gone back to the house.

The door to the cabin was open but Noah knocked before going inside. Ma and Clayton were sitting at a small homemade wooden table. On the table sat another plate with food on it. Ma motioned for Noah to sit down and eat.

Noah looked around but didn't see the young lady. "Thank you. Clayton, tell me about your sister," Noah said.

"Sister, humph," Ma said.

Clayton, with a mouth full of food, spoke, "We call her Girl. She can't talk so she's never said her real name. Pa brought her here several years ago to help Ma with all the chores. He said she was being beat by the people that owned her so he took her and brought her here to save her life."

"That was good of your pa," Noah said.

"He had a good streak once in a while. But I knew his mean streak would do him in sooner or later," Ma said.

While they ate, Girl fixed a fire in the rock fireplace at one end of the front room. When they were finished eating, Ma motioned for them to come and sit by the fire. "Gets a might cool up here at night even in the summer. Yer welcome to sleep in here tonight if ya wanna. It's better than the barn."

Girl took the dishes and moved them from the table and washed them in a large tin container then put them away on a shelf covered with a curtain.

Clayton told his ma all about the cattle drive and the reward money he got.

That evening, Noah went out to the barn and retrieved his bedroll. He didn't see the child's bow and arrow set on the ground. He took his bedroll and brought it inside. Noah looked for but didn't see Girl. Ma and Clayton went back to the bedrooms.

He unrolled his blanket and settled down in front of the fire. He stared at the fire and watched the flames dance across the logs. He listened to the crackle of the burning wood as he became comfortable and relaxed. A loud pop made some sparks jump out of the fireplace and landed near him. He rose up and using his fingernail he flicked it back toward the fire. As he watched the red-hot coals glowing he felt completely safe.

He was almost asleep when he detected movement in the doorway going back to the bedrooms. Without moving, he opened one eye. He could see the shadow of the young lady watching him.

Chapter 18

CHEWING TOBACCO

The morning light had just begun filtering its way into the cabin. Noah woke but remained still for the first few minutes. He smelled coffee. There beside him on a small table was a cup of fresh hot coffee. He didn't really like the taste of coffee but he had become accustomed to the effects of how it woke him up in the mornings.

He sat up half startled. How could anyone have brought him coffee without him waking to notice? After all he was Indian. The door opened and Girl walked in carrying an armload of firewood.

"Good Morning," he said very loud. Still holding the wood she nodded to his cup of coffee. "Yes, thank you. Do you need help with the wood?" he asked, again using a loud voice.

She shook her head no and walked over and threw some wood onto the red coals from the fire the night before. Within a few minutes she had another fire burning.

Noah noticed she wore a different dress, which looked much nicer than the one she had worn when they first met. The dress she wore now was much shorter. This yellow dress showed the top of her ankles. She had her hair fixed in two ponytails, one down each side of her face at her temples, and they were tied with red ribbon.

"Can you talk with your hands using sign language like I have seen Indians do?" Noah asked Girl. Noah wanted to find a way to talk with Girl.

She studied his face. She rolled her eyes, sighed and walked into the other room and started fixing some eggs for breakfast. She mixed some corn meal with water in a bowl and threw the mixture in a large cast iron skillet and put it over the wood burning stove. Noah watched as she took the half done bread and turned it over without using a fork or spoon. She just flipped it into the air and caught it with the skillet.

He got up and folded his bedroll and laid it over in the corner. He took a minute to think of what to say before going in and trying again to communicate with Girl. When Ma came walking into the main room, she carried her shotgun with her.

Ma said, "Your loud voice woke me up. You don't have to talk so loud to Girl, she ain't deaf."

"Oh, sorry about that," Noah said as his face turned red.

Ma slid a lever on the gun and the barrel broke down and hung from the butt of the gun. She looked in both barrels to make sure they had a shell in each chamber. She snapped the double barrel back in place and set it beside the front door.

"You ate yet?" she asked.

"No, ma'am," he replied.

"Girl, what's the hold up?" she asked as she made her way to the stove. "Clayton, time to rise, son," she yelled back at the bedrooms.

Two feet were heard hitting the floor in the other room. It wasn't long before Clayton came in slowly, rubbing his eyes, and sat at the table. "Mornin' all," he said.

"Clayton, as soon as ya eat, I need ya to go and fetch us a couple squirrels for supper. And, Girl, you best get started chopping more wood for tonight."

The hound dog barked and two horses were heard riding up to the yard. Ma was the first one to the door and when she opened it she had her shotgun pointed at the riders as she walked outside. Noah watched from the window beside the table.

"Whoa," the older rider said as he brought his horse to a halt. "Your husband back yet?"

"He ain't never comin' back. He's dead. My boy come home yesterday and told me."

"Ah, that there's a shame. Sorry to hear that. I guess you'll be needing some money to help you out now that your man is gone," the younger man said.

Ma turned her head and spit tobacco juice out in front of the two horses. "Jesse, I don't need no help from the likes of either of you two."

Girl went outside and went behind Ma and hopped off the porch and went to the barn. The younger man, Jesse, watched her every move. "I'll pay a pretty penny for Girl. You may need money to survive once cold weather sets in and when that happens my price will go down. Best if we make a deal now while I'm in a generous mood."

"Mark my words, if you so much as touch that child I'll make a girl out of you with this here shotgun."

"Now don't be like that. She's not a child and right now is when you will get the most for her," Jesse said.

"I'm done talkin' atcha. Now go and git out of gun range before my trigger finger starts ta itchin."

"Well, you give it some thought, old woman."

"The only thing I'll be thinking of is whare to bury you when this here gun makes a loud sound and you go flyin' off the back of yer horse."

The two men, tipped their hats, turned the horses and headed on up the canyon toward the ranch at the far end.

Noah had finished eating and walked out onto the porch in time to see the riders disappear behind a wall of rocks.

"What was that all about?" Noah asked.

"Oh, that young feller, Jesse, has a fancy for Girl. I don't want nothin' to do with that bunch of riff-raff that lives up the holler." Ma then turned her head and spit again.

"Do you have a lot of trouble from those men at the other ranch?"

"They're a crude bunch. Sometimes Pa would let a few of 'em stay here when they were getting ready to ride off the next mornin' to rob a stage or bank or something. We had a fight or two break out. I guess the worst that happened was when Pa had a gunfight with one guy.

"The man got drunk and grabbed Girl and was going to take her back to a bedroom. Pa grabbed him and threw him out of the house. The man walked out in the yard and he called Pa out. As soon as Pa walked out the door onto the porch the man drew down on Pa. Pa was faster and shot him twice, once in each leg.

"Pa tied the man on his horse and sent the horse back out of the canyon away from the ranch. No one ever saw the man again so we don't know what ever happened to him.

"Pa was bad but he never let anyone hurt any of us, even Girl." Ma spit again.

"What's that you are eating that's so bad you have to spit it out?" Noah asked.

"Chawin' tobaccy. Ya don't eat it. Ya just chew it and spit it out. Want to try a chaw?"

"I can chew anything you can chew," Noah replied taking the statement as more of a challenge than a question.

He looked over at the barn and saw Girl standing in the doorway holding an axe. She saw Noah looking at her. She ran her free hand through her hair and walked around the corner. A minute later sounds of chopping echoed off the canyon wall.

Ma put her hand into the pocket of her apron and pulled out a twist of tobacco. "Here, take a bite of this."

Noah held the twist up to his nose, made a face at the smell, and then took a big bite. He started chewing but before he could even spit he felt dizzy. He took one step toward the post holding up the porch roof to lean against it to steady himself.

The next thing he could remember was waking up with a soaking wet head. He was on the ground beside the porch. He could hear Clayton running around him and laughing. He looked up and saw Ma sitting in the chair with round runners rocking back and forth laughing. Clayton was yelling, "He even fell off the porch!"

Girl stood over him with an empty bucket in her hands. She helped him to his feet. He had something in his mouth so he swallowed. His stomach started churning and burning. He ran in a zigzag pattern across the yard and he just barely made it over to the weed patch at the end of the yard before heaving his guts out. Ma and Clayton laughed even harder.

Another bucket of cold water poured over his head. Girl had gone to the well and drew another bucket only this time it was to clean him up. He was really sick. Girl had to help him back into the house where he could lay down until he felt better. He walked wobbly because the room wouldn't stop spinning around.

He went over to his bedroll to rest. He didn't even trust himself sitting in a chair in his condition.

Ma came over several hours later and said, "Do you want some milk to settle yer stomach or another chaw?"

"Milk, please," Noah said. "How can you chew that stuff?"

"It takes a bit of getting used to. I think ya better stay here another night or maybe two in the shape yer in." Ma laughed then added, "Now ya know why ya have ta spit."

"Don't worry. I've learned my lesson as far as tobacco goes."

"Supper's almost ready."

"Not for me. I'm not ready to eat anything right now."

"Too bad. Girl's frying up the squirrel Clayton shot this afternoon. Squirrel makes a nice red sop gravy to go with the bread."

Noah got up and sat in a chair beside the front window and welcomed the fresh air.

A bunch of riders went by heading for the far ranch. Ma grabbed her shotgun and looked out the door.

"Trouble?" Noah asked.

"Naw, just a bunch of those scatter-brained cowboys from the other ranch heading back. That thare looked like Butch Cassidy and on the other side looks like the Sundance Kid. Pa used to ride with those heathens. That's what got him kilt."

"What kind of ranch is on up the road anyway?"

"Ya better stay away from there. They'd just as soon kill ya as look at ya. Nothin' but a bunch of outlaws up there. They have a fortress at the end of that box canyon. No one can get to them. They guard the pass and don't let anyone in."

"I was also wondering why you allowed Clayton, a twelve year old boy, to go on that cattle drive."

"I didn't like the ide'er but Pa insisted. He said it would be good for Clayton and he was almost a man and could handle it. Pa wanted Clayton to find work other than the kind of work Pa did."

This made Noah feel a little guilty about what had happened even though he didn't bring it on and wasn't at fault. He had no choice. He wanted to change the subject and get to the main point of why he was talking with Ma in the first place.

"May I ask about Girl?"

A smirk came across Ma's face. "She's sumpin, ain't she? Thar ain't much to tell though. Pa got her when she was jest a child from one of those cowboys up the holler, paid handsome fer her too. Before ya git all interested in her ya should know, I think she's Indian."

"Has she ever talked?"

"When she first came here I could hear her balling her eyes out at night so I think she has a voice but she ain't never said a word."

"Mind if I stay for a while and help you all get ready for winter? I can bring in some meat and help with cutting some wood; whatever you need me to do."

"Stay as long as ya feel like it. Clayton thinks a lot of ya so yer welcome here. And good luck trying to get to know Girl." Ma chuckled and walked out the door.

The next day Noah had been out hunting and came riding back to the house with a deer across his horse. Ma was at the door with her shotgun but saw him and set the gun down. Girl came running over with a large pan and her butcher knife. As soon as Noah dropped the deer to the ground Girl started dragging it off to the side. Girl went to the well and drew a bucket of water and took it over to the deer. She started in skinning the animal.

It surprised Noah at how well Girl did at skinning and cleaning the meat. It seemed natural to her. She stood and looked at Ma. When she saw Ma looking her way she turned her hand upside down and shook it.

"Ah, right. We need salt to cure the meat. I'll send Clayton up to the ranch to get a bag of salt," Ma said.

"Ah, Ma, do I have to go right now?" Clayton asked.

"Yes, you ain't doin' nothin'. You sure have fussy britches sometimes."

"I'll go with him," Noah replied.

"Not a good ide'er," Ma said. "But ya can do what ya like."

Noah and Clayton saddled their horses and mounted. Noah saw Girl looking at them with her brow wrinkled. She took a step toward Noah then stopped and turned to look at the deer. She then looked at Noah again and took several steps toward him and again stopped and went back to where she was working.

"It's okay," he said to Girl. "I'll be back."

They rode about a mile toward the box canyon. The trail narrowed and that is where Clayton stopped and said, "We have to wait here."

A shot rang out from the cliff above them. The bullet ricocheted off the rock beside Noah.

Chapter 19

A PINK SHOOTING STAR

Another shot rang out and this time the bullet hit in the dirt in front of Noah's horse. The horse gave a long, loud neigh sound and reared its front feet high in the air. Noah had to lean forward and hold onto the horse's mane to keep from falling off.

Clayton yelled, "It's me, Clayton."

The armed guard stood and yelled back down, "Okay, you can pass but your friend has to wait there. You know the rules, Clayton."

Clayton leaned forward on his saddle with one arm across the saddle horn. "That man ain't worth a plugged nickel."

"What's a plugged nickel?" Noah wanted to know.

"That's a nickel used in target practice. You set the nickel on a post and shoot it. If you hit the nickel in the middle the lead bullet will stick to the nickel because the edges will roll up around the nickel to hold the bullet. When that happens you can't spend it because it's not worth nothing any longer because it's plugged with lead."

"Would you shoot the lady on the coin or the teepee on the back of the nickel?" Noah asked.

"What teepee on the nickel? There ain't no teepee on it?

"Well, there is something that looks like a teepee."

"Oh, you mean the V on the back. That ain't no teepee. The V just means its five cents. That there is just Roman talk for five," Clayton said.

"I guess I'd shoot the V then."

Clayton grinned and said, "Me too. I don't have anything against the lady on the other side of the nickel."

Clayton straightened up and looked at Noah and nodded. He rode on up the trail and out of sight. The guard stood in sight but had his rifle pointed at Noah. Noah couldn't relax while he waited. This would be more like how Indians would protect their camp but why would whites need to protect their ranch? Something at the ranch must be a secret and Noah wanted to find out what it was. He had been stopped today but he knew if he got the chance he would return at a better time.

Noah sat nervously on his horse waiting for Clayton. He was looking around to get a feel for the rock formations and to see any paths or a way to get by the guard. He saw none. He did see an old wooden signpost with a sign that read: *Welcome to Wild Ranch—Keep Out*. The sign had several bullet holes in it.

Clayton returned and waved to the guard. He had a large cloth sack of salt behind his saddle. Noah and Clayton headed back home. They had meat to preserve for winter.

"What is so important at that ranch that they need armed guards to protect it?" Noah asked.

"They just don't let anyone in. They don't want the law sneaking up on them without warning is all. Most of the cowboys up there have a price on their head."

"What's the ranch like?"

"Oh, it's a big place. There's the main house and two bunk houses, several barns and some kind of house made from thick logs with bars on the windows like a bank or maybe a jail. I'm not allowed to see what's inside that building. It always has a guard at the door. On up the road

146

are three smaller cabins where some families live. You ain't thinking of visiting there are you?"

"Not today," Noah said then chuckled so Clayton would think he was just curious.

They rode back home and tied the horses at the hitching rail. Noah was surprised the deer was already dressed out and Girl was cutting the last of the meat into small chunks so it could be packed in salt and hung to cure. The salt would keep the meat from drying out and keep it safe from mice or insects and give it a good flavor when cooked later on.

Noah helped Girl carry the meat into the barn and into a special room called a smoke house. They used seagrass cord to tie the meat and let it hang free from the rafters keeping it safe from critters and vermin.

As Noah and Girl were leaving the smoke house they both went to push the door open at the same time. Noah's hand was on top of Girl's hand and he could tell she tensed up and froze. He stopped for a second then pushed her hand so the door would open.

She looked up at Noah and smiled. He returned the smile but she dropped her head and walked out. Noah followed and touched Girl gently on the shoulder to say something. She jerked away and looked at him. Noah raised his hand in the air to show that he wasn't going to harm her and said, "I just wanted to say thanks. You did a great job of cleaning that deer."

He wanted to touch her hair. He had never seen hair the color of hers. It was a dark brown, almost black but in the sunlight it had a red glow to it. He couldn't keep his eyes away from her.

She looked into his eyes then made a motion with her hand for him to follow her. Noah was in high hopes and excited she wanted to meet with him. She led him over to where the deerskin was laying out on the ground. She pointed to the end of the cabin and picked up one end of the skin and started dragging it over to the cabin wall. Noah grabbed the other end and helped Girl move the skin to the side of the cabin. Noah helped her hang the skin on the side of the wall to dry and she nodded at him then went to work scraping the extra fat from the skin. Not exactly what he thought she wanted but was glad to help just the same.

Noah found Ma sitting in the chair that moved back and forth on the porch. He went over and sat in the floating chair with chains holding it in the air. He sat slowly and tested the seat to make sure it would hold him. It moved as he sat down. "This chair is like having someone swing me around back when I was a kid. We would throw a rope over a limb of a tree then tie it. We would sit in the loop of the rope and swing back and forth and sometimes spin around twisting the rope and let it go. It would spin one direction until it was all twisted out and then it would twist in the other direction. Boy, were we dizzy when it was done. The swing part was my favorite though. I would hold on and tilt my head back and look at the tops of trees as I went back and forth."

"This is called a swing. And I want to say thank ya for the meat you gots us today."

"Ma, where is the nearest town that has a sheriff?"

"Why? You going to have that guard arrested for shootin' at'cha earlier? Clayton told me what happened." Ma laughed then said. "The nearest town that has a lawman is Casper. Head south across the Powder River then y'all will come to the North Platte River where Casper is. It's a good day's ride from these here Big Horn Mountains."

"I was born in the northern part of the Big Horn Mountains during the battle of Greasy Grass . . . umm, I mean, the battle of Little Big Horn."

"Look, Son, I've been to the store and back a few times in my life. I knowed ya was Injun the first time I seed ya. But that's okay. When ya live up here ya make friends when ya can git 'em. Ya never know who may be the one to save your leathery hide."

The next morning Noah wanted to wake early before anyone else. He didn't have anything special to do; he just wanted to be up when Girl came in to make the coffee. But when he woke he could smell the coffee and feel the warmth from the fire. Girl had thrown some wood on the fireplace and got the fire going again and the morning chill in the air was beginning to feel warmer. She did all that without making a single sound.

He sat up and daylight was just now turning shadows into images. He picked up his cup and saw a biscuit with honey on a tin plate beside his cup. He smiled. Girl had to be Indian to be able to move around so freely and not disturb him.

He was wondering what Indian nation she was from. He was thinking of her beautiful hair and remembering the reddish glow it had in the sunlight. He had seen many people from a lot of tribes but never saw anyone with hair like hers.

He took a sip of the coffee and was trying to think of just the right words to say when he greeted Girl this morning. He wanted to say something special that had meaning yet needed no reply. He wanted it to be brilliant not just a compliment on how she looked or how nice the morning was.

Maybe he should go out and pick some wild flowers to give her to put on the table and maybe she would let him put one of them in her hair. That could work. That wouldn't need a reply and it was a nice gesture. It sure sounded better than the embarrassing gift he brought her when he first came there.

He stood up and folded his bedroll and laid it over in the corner. He took another sip of his coffee and grabbed the biscuit and went outside. He walked down the road looking for any flowers he could find. He remembered passing a small stream on his way in.

He found the stream beside the road not far from the house. It still had a little water running. He followed the stream a little way until it came to a pool of water not much bigger than a horse-watering trough. Growing nearby were several different flowers to choose from.

He gathered a couple yellow lilies and blue flags. He picked a handful of purple fireweeds with its tiny flowers all bunched up on one stalk. Then he saw one pink shooting star. It was the only one left. All the others of this flower had bloomed and were now gone. This would be the one he would put in Girl's hair.

After following the stream further down he then gathered some scarlet fairy trumpets and a few white cut leaf primroses. He took the bandana from around his neck and dipped it in the water. He used it to wrap around the stems of all the flowers so they would still be fresh when he returned.

Pleased with his find he hurried back toward the house to put them in water before they wilted. He remembered how much his mother loved wild flowers. She showed him how to find them and what they were called. She told him that no other warrior would learn this and how it would make a big difference in his life someday. He wasn't sure back then what she was talking about but today it made perfect sense.

He felt sad thinking about his mother. He remembered why he was hunting down and killing bad white men. How could he expect Girl to want a life like the one he had chosen? He thought about just throwing the flowers away but something inside him still wanted Girl to have them.

For the first time Noah felt some confusion about what he thought was his mission in life. What could be a better purpose than killing whites like the ones that caused him so much pain and anger? At the same time his mind went to thinking of Girl.

The cabin came into view but something was wrong. He saw eight mounted riders in the front yard. He could tell they all had their guns drawn. He could see Ma pointing her shotgun at the men. He looked but didn't see Clayton or Girl anywhere.

One rider got off his horse and yelled, "Noah, come on out here. We know you're in there."

Noah crouched down behind a large boulder to see what was going on.

"He's not here. He's gone," Ma yelled back. "What'd ya want with Noah any hows?" Ma spit tobacco juice at the man.

"Noah's the one that killed your man and he killed a couple more of our guys too so now he is going to pay," the guy hollered.

"You'uns have ate loco weed. And even if Noah did what y'all say he musta had good reason," Ma replied.

"Men, go in the house and drag him out here."

"The first man to take a step this way will be the bravest, deadest man I ever met."

"Now Ma, give him up and you won't have to die."

"Ain't gonna do it. This is my place. You'uns have no right bein' here."

Noah dropped the flowers and drew his gun. He knew his Colt revolver didn't have the range to shoot anyone from where he was and if he tried to get closer they would spot him.

"Now Ma, you know me and you know when I mean business. This ain't got nothing to do with you. Now step aside."

Another man dismounted and walked toward the front porch.

"Don't come another step closer," Ma yelled.

The man didn't stop and when he got to the first step there was a flash from the double-barreled shotgun and then the loud BOOM. The guy flew through the air and landed on his back out in the middle of the yard.

Chapter 20

GIRL IS GONE

The men on horseback opened fire. Another loud boom rang out from the shotgun and one of the riders flew backward off his horse. More shots from handguns echoed off the canyon walls. Ma fell to the floor of the porch and hit her head against the rocking chair making it rock.

Noah stood and started to run toward the men but Clayton came up from beside the road and grabbed him around the waist and pulled him down behind a boulder.

"Ma's gone and we have to save Girl," Clayton said with tears streaming down his face.

Noah's eyes got watery when he saw the tears in Clayton's eyes and he felt the boy's pain as if it were his own. He wanted to hold Clayton in his arms but there wasn't time.

"Where is Girl?" Noah asked.

"She was gone this morning."

"What do you mean she's gone?"

"Sometimes she leaves before we get up and is gone all day. I don't know where she goes. All I know is that we can never find her when she does this but she always comes back before dark."

"Okay, keep your head down."

Noah and Clayton watched as the men entered the house and came back out. One of the men picked up the shotgun and then a couple of the men headed for the barn. They came out leading all the horses and the cow.

"No one's here. They couldn't have gone far though because we have their horses," a man yelled from the barn.

The hound dog started barking at the men and one man raised his gun and shot at the dog. The dog yelped and ran into the weeds disappearing out of sight.

"Alright, Jesse, you and Matt drag the old lady into the house out of sight. A couple of you men will have to drag these other two bodies off into the brush across the road. Then, Matt, you go and stay in the house and, Jesse, you wait in the barn for them to return. The rest of you men take the horses and cow back to our ranch. We'll come back this afternoon and check on you. We'll get 'em."

Noah and Clayton watched as the riders left with the livestock. The two men pulled Ma through the doorway into the house dragging her by her arms. Noah saw one man run to the barn and disappear out of sight.

"What are we going to do?" Clayton asked.

"I'm not sure. We need to take care of those two before the others return and before Girl comes back. If only there was a way back to the house where we wouldn't be seen," Noah said.

"There is. It's the path I just came down looking for you. Ma sent me away when she saw that there was going to be trouble. I climbed out the back window. The path leads up into the back yard behind the garden. She told me to find you but I didn't find you in time."

"Okay, that's a good start. But listen, it's not your fault. Things happened too fast for anyone to help Ma."

Noah and Clayton headed up the path toward the house. It wasn't really much of a path but more like just knowing which rock to go around and which tree to turn beside so Clayton led the way. After jumping over a log and climbing over several rocks and sucking in his gut to fit between two boulders that were close together Noah could see a clearing ahead. Noah could see the garden, the house, and the barn from where he stood at the edge of the forest.

Clayton motioned for them to move through the underbrush to be closer to the back of the house. The barn was now out of sight and Noah could see the back bedroom window still had the shudders open where Clayton had jumped through to escape.

Clayton started looking around for something. He picked up a long skinny stick and a large dead limb and handed the limb to Noah. "If we just shoot the gunman the outlaws from the ranch will hear it and come running so I'll get the man inside to stick his head out the window and you knock his head off with this club," Clayton said in a low voice.

"Okay, but how in tarnation are you going to get that man to stick his head out the window without him shooting at you?"

"That'll be the fun part."

"Fun part?"

Clayton winked then crawled over to the end of the backside of the house. He put his arm around the corner and brought back a dried skin of a raccoon. He attached the skin to the end of his stick and walked to the open window. He peeped in.

"Now, get ready and when you see a head poke out of this window you knock it off as hard as you can," Clayton said.

Noah took his club and raised it above the window with both hands and nodded he was ready. Clayton stuck the raccoon pelt inside the window and then took his other hand and knocked the glass washbowl off the table. He ducked down as soon as the bowl hit and broke on the wooden floor.

Footsteps could be heard coming fast down the hallway. The door opened and Clayton waved the raccoon pelt around a few times then brought it back outside. The footsteps came to the window and the man stuck his head out the window looking for the raccoon.

Noah brought the club down on the man's head as hard as he could. The club broke in two as it hit the man so hard he nearly fell clear out of the window. His chin hit the bottom of the windowsill and he hung, lifelessly, half out of the opening.

"See, nothing to it," Clayton said. Clayton tried to pull the man outside but had trouble getting the dead weight of the man to move. Noah pushed the man's shoulders until the outlaw fell back inside and lay dead on the floor.

For the first time he felt good about killing another man. His feelings scared him for a moment but he had another problem to take care of and didn't give his feelings another thought.

Noah peeked around the corner at the barn. He got a glimpse of weeds moving and saw some reddish hair in the weeds as it disappeared behind the barn. His first thought was of Girl. He had been thinking a lot about Girl recently but knew this was no time to allow his mind to wander. He had been seeing Girl everywhere he looked lately but it was always something else. This time it was probably just a red fox or the hound dog.

Clayton sighed and commented, "I remember when Ma was teaching me to read and I didn't want to learn. She wrote a word down on the paper and asked me what it was. I shrugged my shoulders because I had no idea. She told me that our old red tiger tailed cat could even read this word and she asked me if I was dumber than the cat. I said no and there was no way the cat could read that word. She laughed and held the paper down in front of the cat. The cat looked at the paper and said 'Meow.'

"Ma started laughing. I asked her what the word was and she told me the cat read it correctly and the word was meow. I couldn't help but get tickled. From that moment on

I wanted to learn so I could be smarter than the cat. Ma had a way of doing things like that to get me motivated."

Noah knew what Clayton was going through. He pulled Clayton to him and put both arms around him and gave him a tight hug. "I didn't know your ma long but I really liked her. I would love for you to tell me all the stories about her when we get out of this mess. Deal?"

"You have a deal," Clayton answered.

Noah knew they had to think of something. They didn't have all day. He sat with his back against the cabin as he pondered his next move. Clayton was beside him on all fours, peeping around the corner at the barn.

"Maybe if we start a fire back here we could draw the man out of the barn. He should run over here to see what is going on," Noah suggested.

"That'll work. Let's do it," Clayton said.

"Wait, that might bring the others from the ranch if they see the smoke. Let me think a minute."

"I know, you can change clothes with the dead man inside then go out on the porch and motion for the man in the barn to join you. That might work," Clayton said.

Noah stood and went to the window and peered in at the dead man on the floor. He was lying in a pool of his own blood and his shirt was all bloody. Noah cringed at the thought of wearing those clothes and figured the man in the barn would see the blood and know something was wrong.

After thinking some more, Noah knew he couldn't stall any longer. If he did, the closer to danger they would come. This plan was the best one they could come up with so Noah put both hands on the windowsill and pulled his body up and into the room. Clayton followed him in.

Clayton ran through the cabin before Noah could stop him. Noah caught up with him in the main sitting room. Clayton kneeled down over his ma with tears running down his face. He took his hand and placed it on his ma's cheek. She had tobacco juice streaked down her chin. He took his sleeve and wiped her chin. Noah gave him a minute then put his hand on the boy's shoulder.

"Do you think she was in a lot of pain?" Clayton asked.

"No, it happened too fast. She just knew she had to save you and Girl and that's what she did."

"Ma, you sleep now and Noah and I will take it from here and save Girl." Clayton leaned over and gave Ma a kiss on the forehead.

"Come on, I need your help getting this guy undressed," Noah said.

A tear came to Noah's eye as he remembered how he felt when his mother had died not long before.

Noah led Clayton away and into the back bedroom. They took off the man's boots and pants. Next they removed the blood soaked shirt. Noah got undressed and into the dead man's pants and boots. He held the shirt up and with an agitated look on his face started putting it on. Clayton handed Noah one of his pa's old shirts that was the same color as the dead man's. Noah put the clean shirt on instead. Noah cringed at wearing this shirt too because of what had happened with Clayton's pa but he didn't let on that it made him uncomfortable. He was looking around for the man's hat.

There was a loud commotion coming from the barn. Noah looked out the window and saw the chickens flying and running out the barn door making clucking and squawking sounds and fleeing for their lives.

"I think I saw a fox go around the barn a minute ago. I bet it is after the chickens. You stay inside," Noah said.

He retrieved the hat and put on his own gun belt and walked out onto the porch. He watched the opening of the barn for any signs of the man hid inside. In the shadows he thought he could see two people. One was smaller than the other and had long hair.

"Girl!" he hollered.

He jumped off the porch and ran as fast as he could to the barn. Clayton was right behind him. When he got to the barn he saw the man lying face down and blood coming from his back. Girl was kneeling beside the body holding her butcher knife. The knife had blood dripping from the blade. She pulled his head up by the hair and cut his throat. She dropped the man's head and looked up at Noah.

Noah stood there speechless. She could really use that knife she had pulled on him just a few days ago. And her skill of being able to slip around very silently had paid off. Noah took a deep breath and sighed. Girl had taken care of the immediate danger.

Clayton looked down at the bleeding man on the ground and said, "That was Jesse."

Noah looked at Girl. "Are you okay?"

She nodded yes.

"What do we do now? The others took these two men's horses back with them," Clayton remarked.

"First I am going to change back into my own clothes. Then we best bury Ma," Noah replied as he started walking back to the house.

Clayton grabbed the shovel from a tool rack inside the barn door and they walked back to the house.

Noah changed clothes and with the help of the other two they carried Ma outside. Noah held her by the shoulders while Girl and Clayton each carried her by one of her legs.

"Ma would want to be buried beside her garden. She looked forward to spring each year so she could plant her beans and potatoes and other vegetables. Ma even had a few flowers. She loved spending time out here pulling weeds and taking care of all her plants." Clayton's voice cracked as he talked.

Noah took his anger out by using the shovel to dig the grave. He glanced over and saw Clayton turn his head away and hide his face into Girl's shoulder. Girl held Clayton close and had her hand on the back of Clayton's hair. He finished digging the grave beside the garden and they laid Ma carefully in it.

Girl went into the house and brought out Ma's favorite blanket and covered her in it. When Clayton saw Girl bringing the blanket he ran inside and brought out the new blue bonnet and put it on Ma's head.

Noah took the shovel and threw dirt in the grave to cover Ma. Clayton and Girl stood next to each other with their arms linked together; their shoulders were slumped and their heads hung low. Clayton leaned his head over and tilted his head until it rested on Girl's shoulder. They watched until the body was completely covered.

After Noah said a few words and a prayer to the Great Spirit by the graveside Girl leaned over and plucked a pink shooting star flower from the cuff of Noah's pants.

"I found that this morning and was going to give it to you for a surprise. What are you going to do with it now?" Noah said.

Girl shrugged her shoulders and took the flower over and laid it on top of Ma's grave.

"Let's go inside and get some food and whatever else we need to hike out of here," Noah said.

Clayton grabbed Noah's arm. "Riders! The outlaws are returning!" Clayton pointed to the road where a dozen or so men were coming from the Wild Ranch.

They were caught out in the open. They didn't have time to make it into the house or the barn without being seen. Girl grabbed both Noah's and Clayton's arm and gave a hard tug as she shouted, "Dinna let 'em see us. Quickly, this wye. Run for the epple tree!"

Chapter 21

BONNIE BRAI

Noah and Clayton stopped and just stared at Girl. Girl could talk? Now Noah couldn't talk, he was speechless. He knew at that moment he could be pushed over by the wing flap of a butterfly. He and Clayton looked at each other with their mouths fully opened. Noah looked into Clayton's eyes which were big as a boiled new potato. Girl pulled on their arms once again.

"Scoot. Ye don't want to die do ye nou?" Girl said as she turned and ran toward a path back behind the barn.

Noah and Clayton looked at each other with wide eyes then ran after Girl but she was too fast to catch. She was already past the apple tree and at the line of trees in the back and disappearing. They made it out of sight and ducked behind some rocks just as the horses rode into the yard.

Noah watched as men ran into the house and then the barn. The lead rider waved his rifle and the men spread out and were looking everywhere. Three riders rode on down the trail and another one rode back to the ranch.

He looked around for Girl but didn't see her. He drew his gun and got ready to defend his position. Clayton had grabbed a gun from the man in the barn and now had it out and was ready. Noah found a tree big enough to provide cover yet allowed him to see what was going on in front of him back toward the farm.

Girl tapped him on the shoulder. "Come on. What ye be waitin' fur?"

Noah jumped. "How do you do that?"

Girl put one finger up to her mouth. "Shush. This wye if ye please unless this be the spot ye wish to take ye last breath."

Noah and Clayton followed Girl down a twisting and rocky trail. The trail went over the backside of the mountain and they had to climb in steep places. Noah held onto some saplings for balance as he made his way down the path. It followed the edge of the mountain and was narrow in places. He looked over the side and saw the tops of trees below. The drop off was maybe fifty or sixty feet down.

Noah saw that Girl had stopped up ahead and was waiting for them to catch up to her. She waved her arm for them to hurry up. The trail had ended. "What now?" he asked.

Girl removed a dead bush in front of some rocks by picking it up and throwing it to the side out of the way. He watched as Girl got down on all fours and crawled beside a thicket and to an opening in the rocks. Noah and Clayton did the same. Ahead he watched Girl disappear down a dark tunnel inside the mountain. He followed.

Noah lost sight of Girl once again as he crawled through this small cave. He saw a light glowing just a little way in front of him. When he got to the light in the cave, it opened up into a larger room and Girl stood in the middle holding a lit coal oil lantern.

He stood and looked around. The cave was very clean and it had a fire pit in the center. Sitting beside the fire pit was one small pot used for cooking. Nearby was a stack of wood. There was a bed on the floor with a blanket and even some dream catchers and a medicine wheel hanging on the wall.

"Welcome to me secret hidin' place," Girl said.

"Well bust my britches," Clayton said as he looked around.

"Girl, you did all this?" Noah asked.

"Aye, Ah did, nou, ye must stop callin' me Girl. Ah have a name. It's Bonnie Brai."

"Well, it's good to meet you Miss Bonnie. Or are you married?" Noah playfully asked.

"Nae, me not be joined with any man. And it is not Bonnie, Ah said me name is Bonnie Brai. We can stay here tonight and maybe tomorrow we can get away from these parts, if the good Lord be willin'."

Noah was hypnotized by the way Bonnie Brai talked. He loved the funny sounding words she used and how her face lit up as she spoke. He wanted her to talk more just so he could hear her voice.

"Why haven't you ever talked before?" Clayton asked.

She put her hand on Clayton's head and rubbed his hair. She gave him a hug and then leaned forward and looked him in the eyes and said, "In case ye didn't notice, Ah talk different and Ah didn't want to be made fun of. Besides, most of the time Ah didn't have nothin' Ah wanted to say."

Clayton asked, "Why do you talk the way you do? It is so funny sounding."

"That be a long story, Laddie. Me mither was born in a place across the ocean called Scotland. She met an Indian on her visit here and then when Ah was born she taught me to talk the same wye she talked. My faither taught me his wye, huntin' and stayin' out of sight when the need be but then thay were both killed by some white men and Ah was sold to yer faither six years ago when Ah was but twelve and ye know the rest from thare. Nou scoot and get the fire started and Ah will fix us a wee bite to eat."

"I'm sorry you lost your parents. I know what that's like. I lost my father the day I was born and lost my mother not long ago."

"It twas awful. Some riders ambushed us while we were busy dressin' out an antelope me faither had killed on his huntin' trip. Thay rode in fast and were shootin'. Me faither drew a gun but thay shot him first. Me mither lay on top of me to protect me and thay shot her in the back. Thay went over to me faither and cut his hair from the top of his head. Thay were goin' to do the same to me mither but she had bright red hair and one man said leave her because thay wouldn't get a reward for her scalp.

"One man picked me up and carried me across the front of his saddle until we got to the Wild Ranch. When we got thare he gave me to another man that took me down to whaur Ma and Clayton lived. Thay took me in and treated me good so Ah stayed and became a part of thair family. Ah could have run away at any time but Ah had nowhere else to go." Bonnie Brai looked at Noah for a minute. He nodded and Bonnie Brai turned away and went over and picked up the pot. She took down some salt pork she had hanging from a jagged rock over at the side of her camp area.

Noah saw Clayton was walking around exploring the cave so he put some sticks into the fire pit and started a fire. As the flames grew he added some of the short logs and limbs and in no time he had a nice and warm fire going. Bonnie Brai took the pot and added some water from a brown jug she had and added some of the dried salt pork and a few potatoes and wild onions.

Bonnie Brai gave Noah some food in a tin cup she had and she and Clayton ate out of the pot. "Noah, Ah gather ye are a cowboy. Ah overheard Clayton tellin' Ma ye two met on the cattle drive. Do ye like that work?"

"It's okay, I guess. I think Clayton liked it more than I did." Noah didn't want to say what he really did. He didn't think Bonnie Brai would like him if she knew how he lived his life and his job was killing people.

"He's a bounty hunter. He kills wanted white men and gets a lot of money for it," Clayton blurted out.

The conversation got quiet after that last remark and Noah kept glancing over at Bonnie Brai to see if he could tell what she was thinking. Their eyes met a couple times and he tried to smile but he couldn't get a read on how Bonnie Brai felt about him being a bounty hunter.

After dinner, Noah said, "We should get some rest. We have a hard day tomorrow. It's going to be a long and tricky walk to get away from this place alive." He went over and put more wood on the fire to keep the chill of the cave at bay.

"Ye are welcome to share these leaves and moss Ah call a bed but Ah wasn't expectin' company so we'll have to share the one blanket. Noah, ye can keep the fire goin' and that'll be yer job. Clayton, ye can be in the middle if ye don't mind."

Noah woke in the night and got up to put more wood on the fire. The fire had died down and only coals were burning. Once the fire was blazing again he looked over and his heart sank. Bonnie Brai was gone.

He knew if she found out he killed people she wouldn't want to be around him. He figured she was afraid of him now and left.

He heard a noise and turned toward the tunnel leading to the outside. He saw Bonnie Brai was coming back in a hurry. "Good, ye be up. Ah think we have trouble. Come outside and see," she said.

Noah followed her back through the cave to the entrance. He stood and listened. "Do ye hear that?" Bonnie Brai asked. "It's those dogs from the Wild Ranch; the ones that are short to the ground and have those big floppy ears and run with their noses to the ground. Ah have seen 'em track before and thay do a right good job at it."

It was dawn and light was breaking over the mountains. Dogs could be heard barking and heading their way along the ridge. "Dogs have a certain way they bark when they find the scent of whatever they are hunting for. They howl.

These dogs have our scent and are heading toward us. We have to get out of here now. Get Clayton," Noah said.

"Follow me back inside. Ah know the wye out." Bonnie Brai turned and hurried back into the cave.

By the time Noah joined her she had already woke Clayton. She grabbed the lantern and hurried around the fire pit to a tunnel. "Come on, this wye."

Bonnie Brai led the way with Clayton next and Noah bringing up the rear. The tunnel was small compared to the rest of the cave but Noah could walk through the opening without having to bend down.

The path started going down and it was slow walking. It wasn't long before they were doing more climbing down at a steep grade than walking. The dogs could now be heard again and the barking echoed off the cave walls. Men's voices were heard from behind them.

The path got even slower to follow and the small opening shrank and all of them had to bend over to walk. Bonnie Brai handed Clayton the lantern so everyone could share the little light they had as the path got even steeper.

Noah stopped for a minute and put his palms over his eyes and held them there blocking all light. When he removed them a moment later his eyes could see a bit better in the almost dark cave. His eyes had adjusted to the pitch black from being covered with his hands.

After a long and hard climb down the path leveled out and was now straight. Bonnie Brai and Clayton were bent over and squatted down to walk but Noah had to crawl to get through the narrow tunnel. The path was now full of mud and in places it had water a couple of inches deep.

Noah could see a spot of light ahead. The tunnel was so small now he had to straighten his legs out and use his elbows and scoot to get through the opening. The water soaked his clothes and it felt cold. He could see that Bonnie Brai went out the small opening that allowed the sun to shine into the cave. Clayton followed. When Noah got to the opening they helped pull him through to the outside.

He stood wiping some of the mud from his clothes. The others just had a little mud on their hands, knees and feet. Noah had to stretch from being bent over for so long. The climb through the cave had taken well over an hour.

"I'm glad to be out of that cave," Clayton said. "It was colder than a witch's . . ."

"Don't talk about a witch," Noah interrupted.

"Nou ye don't believe in witches do ye?" Bonnie Brai asked.

"I don't know. I've never met one and don't want to. Besides that is no way for the boy to talk," Noah said.

He looked around to get his bearings. The daylight hurt his eyes for a few minutes as they adjusted to being in the bright outside. The sun did feel good and warn. They were all standing at the bottom of the high ridge and next to some rocky cliffs. In front of them were some rolling hills and a few giant granite boulders. Off to the right were some trees about a hundred yards from them.

Noah started for the cluster of trees. Bonnie Brai grabbed his arm and said, "That wye is a dead end. It goes into another canyon and we'll be trapped. We have to go to the left to get away."

"Are you sure? By going that way we'll be in the open and spotted as soon as they come out of the tunnel," Noah said.

Before they could go in any direction Noah spotted riders about a mile away off to the left and they were coming fast.

"Okay, ye win. Head for the trees," Bonnie Brai said.

They turned and started to run toward the trees when a large dog came through the cave opening and was growling. It ran and jumped at Noah and he turned to face snapping teeth as the dog lunged at his face and knocked him down.

Chapter 22

THE STAND OFF

Noah grabbed the dog's head. He had a hand on each side of its face and pushed it away from his own throat as it slobbered and snapped its sharp teeth trying to bite a chunk out of him. Noah, on his back, wrestled with the dog on top of him. The dog yelped, jumped to the side and fell over. Noah's heart beat hard and fast.

Bonnie Brai was standing over them with her butcher knife out and the blade was red with fresh blood once again. She extended her hand to help Noah to his feet. Their eyes met and Noah couldn't help but smile, just the touch of her hand as she helped him up sent chills down his spine. At that moment he wanted the world to stop so he could talk with Bonnie Brai and get to know her, but right now they had no time for that.

Noah stood, still holding her hand for as long as she held it out for him to take. He started to speak but he heard the hammer of a handgun being cocked. He quickly pushed Bonnie Brai to the side out of danger. She fell to the ground as Noah drew his gun and fired. His bullet hit dead center in the chest of a man that had just crawled out of the tunnel. The man dropped face down in the dirt and laid still. Noah saw a rifle barrel poking out of the opening and he fired a couple more shots into the tunnel.

A man yelled and the rifle dropped. Noah ran over to the opening and emptied his gun into the small passageway. Another man yelled and Noah heard a splash.

Noah looked inside but couldn't see anything. He grabbed the handgun and the rifle. He could reach one man so he pulled him through to the outside. Clayton took the man's gun belt and found another handgun. Clayton put his ear to the small hole and said, "I hear more coming. Want me to go in after them?"

Noah looked over at the riders to see how close they were.

"No, they'll be able to see you and you'll not see them. Grab any guns and ammo you find and let's head for the trees before the riders get any closer. If we hurry we can make it there and get hidden before we have to fight it out."

They made it to the first tree when a gunshot was heard. The bullet ricocheted off some nearby rocks. They could now hear the sound of horses' hooves hitting the ground.

Noah pointed to some large rocks up beside a small cliff wall next to the trees and the three ran to find cover and a good place to fight back as the posse closed in on them.

They found a group of boulders that would provide protection. The boulders were large enough to hide behind yet they could see over. The far side was open so they could flee if they had to and the other side had boulders they could use for defense. Behind them was the cliff so no one could sneak up on them without them knowing.

Noah glanced over at his two associates with concern. He worried over what was about to happen and hoped they would all come through this without getting hurt. He realized he cared and that made his job harder.

Noah showed Clayton were to stand and watch. "Bonnie Brai, you can help by loading the guns until we run out of ammo. Clayton, you take the front side and I'll take the side toward the trees. Make every shot count. I figure they will try and make us run out of bullets. How many do you think are out there?"

"I counted over two dozen. What do we do if we run out of ammo?" Clayton asked.

"When we get low on ammo, you take Bonnie Brai out the back and I'll use what shots we have left to cover you from here. Maybe I can make it to a few of the dead ones and get their guns."

"This is just like the Alamo, don't you think?"

"This is nothing like the Alamo."

"Why isn't it? We are pinned down with a bunch of guys attacking us."

"Because all the men fighting for their freedom at the Alamo died. Watch out for that man coming from the tunnel. He's heading this way."

Clayton steadied his rifle on a rock and took aim. Clayton fired the rifle. He hit the man covered in mud running toward them.

"Okay, keep your heads down. Lead is going to be flying all around here soon," Noah said.

The posse got to the trees. The men dismounted and took cover. They were running in and out of the trees trying to get as close as they could to the three hiding behind the boulders. Everything got quiet. Then one of the outlaws yelled, "Now."

All the outlaws started firing at once. Bullets were bouncing off the rocks all around where Noah, Bonnie Brai, and Clayton were buried in. It was hard for any of them to even look over the boulder to see who to shoot at.

There was a loud blast. One of the outlaws fired a shotgun. The tiny pellets flew through their hiding place and were bouncing off the rocks all around them. Bonnie Brai made a hissing sound. She used her fingernail to pull one of the pellets out of her leg just above her right knee. She looked at it then flipped it away.

"Mean little buggers aren't thay?" she said.

Noah found a crack between two boulders and could see a small section of the trees though it. He fired and one man fell backward to the ground.

Noah saw a canteen being raised for a man to take a drink of water. He couldn't see the man behind the tree but wanted to scare the bejeebers out of him. He took aim and fired and hit the canteen and sent it flying.

Behind another tree he saw only the toe of a boot sticking out. He steadied the rifle and fired hitting just under the man's toe. The man scooted back behind the tree so fast he lost his footing and had to lean forward into view to keep from falling. Noah was ready and shot again hitting the man in the arm.

Noah took a second to wipe the sweat from his forehead with the sleeve of his shirt. With a worried look he glanced over at Clayton and Bonnie Brai to make sure they were safe and out of the line of fire.

Noah watched as several men moved from tree to tree inching their way toward them. He noticed that the men didn't run at them but took time to make sure they could make it to cover. He fired a couple more shots to keep the outlaws from moving any closer.

"I think they are trying to move in closer to pick us off. I did manage to slow them down some," Noah said as he looked around to check on Clayton and Bonnie Brai again but Bonnie Brai was gone. "Dab burn it. Where'd she go?"

Clayton looked around and answered, "She'll be okay. Remember she does this from time to time."

"Fresh cow pies! Now is not a good time to be doing this."

A bullet hit close to Noah and exploded against the boulder. A piece of the rock flew off and hit Noah in the face making his cheek bleed. Noah and Clayton fired back taking the best shots they could to do the most damage. They usually hit the man they were aiming at.

"Ouch!" Clayton yelled. He turned around and sat down beside the large boulder he was hiding behind. He rolled up his sleeve. There was a little bit of blood coming from his shoulder. "I'm okay. The bullet almost missed me."

"What do you mean almost missed? Are you hit or not?"

"It's nothing. It's just a tiny scratch." Clayton looked around and found a rock. He turned the rock over and got a handful of the moist dirt and packed it on the wound then rolled his sleeve back down.

The fighting went on for almost an hour. The outlaws had them pinned down and were slowly moving closer and closer toward them. Noah and Clayton's ammo was getting low but they were holding out so far.

There was another blaze of bullets being fired. Clayton and Noah ducked down but this time none of the bullets were hitting the rocks they were hiding behind. Noah fired a couple shots trying to hit some of the Wild Bunch but saw they were shooting at something else.

Two horses were coming in the back open area of their small rock stronghold.

Noah turned and almost fired. It was Bonnie Brai. She rode one of the horses with the heel of her foot over the back part of the saddle and the other foot still in the stirrup. She hung on the side of the horse and had one arm holding the mane to stay on the horse and the other hand holding the lead strap of the second horse she was bringing back with her. Noah knew at once that is how she got through the gun fire without getting shot but the horse she was leading wasn't as lucky. It had four places in its side with blood oozing out.

As Bonnie Brai dropped to the ground with a couple of handguns stuck inside the cord she used as a belt, the wounded horse whinnied and dropped to its knees then rolled onto its side. Its nostrils were flaring. It raised its head, gave out a sigh and laid its head down. Its eyes closed and it was gone.

Bonnie Brai handed the extra guns to Noah and said, "This'll help should we need it, and more likely than not we will need 'em."

Noah spotted several more riders off in the distance heading to join the other outlaws. This gave him an idea and he could use this minor distraction to put his idea into play.

The new riders arrived and were getting off their horses and heading for cover. Noah called to Clayton, "Take your gun and you and Bonnie Brai get on the horse and get out of here. I'll cover you until you're safe then I'll join you later on when this is over. Mount up and get Bonnie Brai to safety now."

"Aren't ye comin' with us?" Bonnie Brai asked.

"Yes, sure, I'll be right behind you as soon as I can."

"How?"

"Go!"

Clayton made Bonnie Brai get on first. He got on behind her. He spurred the horse and they took off riding as fast as the horse would go. Noah watched as they rode with Bonnie Brai's head down on the horse's neck and Clayton with his head leaning on Bonnie Brai's back to make the smallest target possible.

Noah started firing with a gun in both hands to ensure the outlaws couldn't get a shot off towards the escaping horse.

Three gunmen ran to their horses but when they put their foot in the stirrup to mount their horses the saddles slipped off and onto the ground. One man fell backward and his saddle landed on top of him.

From the commotion several other horses trotted away where they had been untied. Noah heard one of the men yell, "Our horses."

Noah was thinking, "How does she do all this without ever being seen?"

Noah remembered seeing someone holding out a white flag once. He remembered when the man did this the others walked out into the open. He didn't know what it meant but thought that if he did this it would draw some of them out.

Noah quickly looked around for something that would work. He didn't see any white cloth. He ran over to the dead horse and looked in the saddlebag. There he found a wanted poster on a yellowish piece of paper. He took the poster and stuck it on a stick and waved it above the rock he was hiding behind.

The shooting stopped. Noah watched as he waved the paper and saw a couple of guys stand and slowly start walking toward him with their guns still drawn. Noah dropped the stick, took aim and fired.

He wounded a couple of the gang but then his gun made a clicking sound. The men all took cover again. He couldn't fire so he scrambled around and checked the rest of the guns to see which ones had bullets. He only found one gun with three bullets left in the chamber.

He sat for long time just peeking out from behind a rock watching to see what was going to happen next. He heard one man yell, "He's out of ammo."

One man stood slowly and after not being shot at he started walking toward where Noah hid. Two others went to their horses and mounted up to ride after Clayton and Bonnie Brai. Noah took aim and fired two shots and both men fell from their horses to the ground.

The shooting started again as the one man ran back and took cover. Without Noah returning fire it soon got quiet again and Noah just waited. He picked up the stick again and this time he put his hat on the end of it and waved it around to draw more fire to keep the outlaw gang occupied. His cowboy hat had several holes in it within a few seconds.

But at least he had bought Clayton and Bonnie Brai more time to get away.

Noah sat and feared what was going to happen in the very near future. He had accomplished one thing; he got the brother and sister away. They should be okay. They would make it.

He doubted his choice to be a bounty hunter was the best move he ever made. He thought of his mother. His main regret wasn't killing white men but that he didn't get to face the one that killed his mother.

The joy of killing had now faded. There wasn't that much joy in killing from the start. It wasn't like what he thought it would be when he was so sad and so angry. The first man he killed was more of a shock. He did get used to it some later but the fact he had killed Clayton's father had never left his mind. He almost got Clayton and Bonnie Brai killed. He just never liked what he did. But it didn't look like all that would matter much longer.

Noah felt pleased in getting Bonnie Brai out of harm's way though. He remembered the look in her eyes when she got the child's bow and arrow set and how embarrassed he felt. He knew he liked her from the first day they had met but it wasn't easy getting to know her. He knew nothing of how to talk to a woman, one that he liked so much. Feelings made everything harder. Feelings got in the way of the things he did and the way he thought about other things.

His thoughts now went to when his father met his mother and he wondered if the two of them had the same feelings toward each other when they first met as he did with Bonnie Brai in the short time he knew her.

The thing that bothered him the most was the fact that he stood here thinking about Bonnie Brai while he was in the middle of a gunfight.

Noah said out loud, "Great Spirit, thank you for protecting Bonnie Brai and Clayton and allowing them to escape. Keep them safe and watch over them until we all meet on the other side of the bridge to the afterlife. I don't mean today exactly. I can wait awhile if it's your wish. But allow them to live a long time and find happiness regardless of what happens to me here today."

Noah was now ready to meet whatever fate was in store for him next.

He snapped his attention back to the situation at hand because of a noise he heard just around the corner of this rock he was hiding behind. He raised his gun and when the outlaw showed himself to Noah, he fired his last bullet and the man fell backward out of sight.

Noah looked out and saw several more men walking his way. They ducked down as low as they could when they heard the shot but ran toward Noah. There was nothing left for him to do but face them. He stood, threw down his gun and the first man came around the corner with a rifle pointed right at his head.

The men standing and facing Noah cocked the gun he held and said, "I'm going to kill you on the count of three just so I can watch you sweat. One . . . Two . . ."

Chapter 23

THE DEATH WAGON

The man had a smile on his face that could barely be seen underneath all the hair on his upper lip. The mustache was thick and curled up into a ring on each side of his mouth. There was no mistake though. The evil grin could be seen through his mustache, and also in his eyes. He took a couple of steps closer to Noah as he counted. He had the stock of the rifle in his left hand and planted the butt of the rifle against shoulder and eased his index finger onto the trigger.

Noah raised his hands over his head, not to surrender but with his palms toward the heavens. "Great Spirit, I strive to be the best person I know how to be. Hear my prayer . . ."

Noah heard a choking sound and looked over at the man with the gun. The man dropped the rifle and staggered forward. The man held his chest and blood was running across his hands. He grasped the arrowhead sticking out from his chest. He doubled over and fell forward to the ground, curled up in a ball. When he fell, another long arrow was protruding out of his back.

Shots were fired and men ran to their horses. Noah grabbed the rifle and peered out over the rock that he used as cover. More shots were being fired as the outlaw gang mounted horses and were riding away.

Loud war whoops filled the air and Indians scurried everywhere. The outlaw gang couldn't get away fast enough. It looked like they were heading for the safety of Wild

Ranch where the canyon walls would provide the shelter of their fortress.

Noah stepped out into the opening and watched as the Indians drove the gang off chasing them a short distance. One man on the ground with an arrow sticking out of his leg took aim at one of the Indians. Noah quickly raised the rifle and fired. The man sat backward and then his head dropped to his chest as he dropped his gun.

Three horses with riders came up to Noah and stopped.

"Greetings, Chief Crazy Elk, of the Crow Nation,"

"You owe me ten more cows," Chief Crazy Elk replied.

"I owe you a lot more than that."

"No, you are only worth ten cows, no more." Chief Crazy Elk waved his arm toward the other warriors. "Men, we will camp here tonight. These trees and rock formations will keep us hid. This is a good place to rest."

"Aren't you afraid that Wild Bunch will be back?"

"No, they will be awake all night wondering if we are going to attack them so we are safe here."

After some of the dust settled the warriors went around and collected any guns and ammo they could find. They took any horses that were left behind and tied them with their own. One warrior brought one horse down and handed it over to Noah. "Here, you may need this," he said.

"You're right, thank you," Noah replied then nodded his head at the warrior.

Guards were posted and scouts were sent out in both directions to secure the camp. Several campfires were lit as some of the warriors returned with wood. Food was being prepared and Chief Crazy Elk motioned for Noah to join him and some of his warriors at his fire.

Noah took a canteen of water when it was offered and stretched out to relax from what he thought moments ago was his last day, even last moment, on this world known to him as Turtle Island from the legends of his ancestors.

Off in the distance he heard a whooping sound. He sat up and looked in the direction the Indian had yelled. He saw a buckboard wagon being pulled by two mules heading their way. There were two people on the wooden seat and a horse tied to the back of the wagon. He watched as the two in the wagon bounced around when the buckboard went over rocks and fallen tree limbs making its own path toward where everyone was standing by the fire.

Noah watched as the wagon drew closer and the two passengers bounced almost off the seat as it wove its way around some rocks. It pulled up to the camp and stopped. Noah stood as Clayton jumped off the wagon and held out his hand to help Bonnie Brai step down.

"Where'd you learn to drive a wagon like that?"

"Oh, I can drive a wagon alright. It's these darn mules. They want to go where they want. They aren't as smart as horses," Clayton answered.

Bonnie Brai ran over to Chief Crazy Elk and gave him a tight hug. "It's so good to see ye again, Grand-faither," she said. "Ah see ye have met Noah, and thank ye so much for helping us."

"Chief Crazy Elk is your grandfather?" Noah asked.

"Aye, me faither was his eldest son. We rode straight into him only a few miles down the trail. Clayton rode on to the next ranch and bought us this wagon and mules. It cost him all the money he had too, it did. He said we would need 'em to take the wanted men back to town for the rewards."

Clayton went over to Noah and punched him in the arm. "I'm glad to see you're okay. I wasn't sure what I'd find when we returned. I didn't know if we could get back in time."

"I'm just glad you're here." Noah smiled. "I'm glad you and Bonnie Brai are alive and well."

"Do you want to load up the dead men now or later?"

Chief Crazy Elk pointed with his left hand to some of the warriors. "Drag all the dead outlaws over and put them on the wagon. Looks like there are a bunch of them here so, Noah, you and Clayton did pretty well. You got a few of them before my men came and killed the rest for you. We would have gotten all of them too if you hadn't scared them off."

Noah furrowed his brow at the remark until he saw the smirk on Chief Crazy Elk's face. He then nodded his head in agreement.

Some of the warriors and Clayton set out to gather all the dead outlaws. A shot rang out. Noah grabbed the rifle and jumped to his feet. He looked over to where the sound came from.

One warrior with smoke coming from the barrel of his gun said, "This one was still breathing but he is not breathing now."

"Thirteen," Clayton yelled after the last one was loaded.

"Are you sure? Count them again. Maybe there are only twelve or maybe there are fourteen," Noah said.

Clayton recounted and said, "Thirteen, why is there a problem?"

"Thirteen is a bad sign. No good comes from the number thirteen."

"Yes, I agree. We must be ready because something else is getting ready to happen," Chief Crazy Elk said.

"Unhitch the mules and let them eat and rest. We'll take the bodies to town at first light after we all get some rest," Noah said.

The next morning Noah got Clayton up and they were getting ready to take the wagon into town. Clayton brought the mules over and was putting the harnesses on them to hitch them to the wagon. Bonnie Brai was walking with her grandfather.

"Sis, are you going with us to town?" Clayton asked.

She turned and looked over at Clayton then at Noah. "Aye, Ah will be goin. That is if it's alright with Noah."

"I was hoping you would go with us. I'd like that a lot. I want to show you all the things you can see and do in town." Noah looked over at Chief Crazy Elk to see his expression.

The chief nodded his approval and said, "I can trust you. You have kept your word before. Bring the ten cows to our village. We are returning there and Bonnie Brai knows where to find us."

After eating some fry bread for breakfast they said goodbye and climbed onto the wagon. They had three horses tied to the back to take with them. The chief let everyone know that the big dark gray stallion belonged to Bonnie Brai. Clayton took the reins and snapped the leather straps across the mules' back. The mules jumped and started pulling the wagon over the bumpy land. Clayton turned them to head down the hill to where the ground was smoother. It wasn't too far before they found the road headed toward town.

Midafternoon on the third day they pulled up to the sheriff's office and stopped. They were glad to get down off the wagon. Noah went inside and brought the sheriff back out to look at the shipment of outlaw carcasses.

"We'll have a hard time telling who some of these men are. It may take a few days and then we need to get them in the ground as soon as possible. They're already getting ripe. I know a few of these guys and it looks like you may have thousands of dollars coming your way," the sheriff said.

"Some of these men were ripe before they were shot. We'll be at the hotel when you need us, Sheriff," Noah said.

"Well, you best get a room for a week or more. It'll take that long before I can get your money to ya. And one more thing . . ."

"What's that, Sheriff?" Noah asked.

"You're more than likely a dead man. When the Wild Bunch finds out about this they'll come gunnin for ya. For now I'll have someone take the wagon and horses down to the livery stable."

"I think the Wild Bunch already knows but thanks, Sheriff."

Noah, Clayton, and Bonnie Brai walked down the wooden path that followed along the front of the stores until they came to the hotel and went inside.

The lobby of the hotel was a large room with several tables and there were guests sitting on couches reading books and newspapers. At one side of the lobby was a double archway into a dining area. They walked up to a counter and Clayton picked up the bell by the wooden handle and rang it. The man behind the counter took the bell away from Clayton and said, "I'm right here. May I help you?"

"We need a large room with two beds," Noah said.

"Will you be staying long?" the clerk asked.

"About a week or so, I think," Noah answered.

"Here is the key. Room five. Your room is down this hall over here." The clerk pointed to a hallway off to the left of the desk. "Enjoy your stay."

The room had two windows and two double beds. Bonnie Brai slid her hand along a metal wash pan and then the wooden bucket filled with water. There were some wash clothes and some towels hanging at the side of the table. Clayton walked across the large woven rug at the foot of the beds and sat at a table with a lantern and two chairs. This room even had a small room off to the side. None of the three knew what this room was for. It only had a small chair that had a hole in the center of the seat and a porcelain bucket sitting under it.

"Wash up and we'll go get something to eat then go shopping for some new clothes. I don't even think washing mine will help them much," Noah said.

Clayton started pacing back and forth, looking out the window, and pacing some more.

"What is wrong with ye? Ye are actin' like a penned up turkey the day before Thanksgivin," Bonnie Brai asked.

"I'll be right back. I have to ask the desk clerk where the outhouse is," Clayton said as he left the room in a hurry.

A few minutes later the door swung open and Clayton ran into the room. "I found out what that little room is for. It's called a water closet." He quickly ran into the very small room and shut the door.

"Ah be goin' to go ask where Ah can get some fresh water. After ye two wash thare won't be any clean water for me to use. Ah will be right back," Bonnie Brai walked out the door.

Moments later Bonnie Brai raced back into the room and said, "Come here, ye have to see this. Ye won't believe what ye eyes will be tellin' ye."

She took the wooden bucket and poured the water into the wash pan and went out the door with the bucket. Noah followed her down the hall and around the corner.

She stopped and in front of them stood this strange looking thing with a long handle and a snout. Bonnie Brai put the bucket under the snout and held the long handle. She started pulling the long handle up and down. Fresh water poured from the snout and into the bucket.

"Look at this. Someone said it's a hand pump. Have ye ever seen anythin' like this before in ye life?" Bonnie Brai asked excitely.

"No, I reckon I haven't," Noah said as he watched the waterfall fill the bucket. He walked over and took hold of the pump handle and pushed it up and down until some of the water overflowed the bucket and ran onto the floor. He then picked the bucket up and took it back to the room for them to use.

When they all were ready they left the room and went into the dining area. Clayton read the menu to the other two and after explaining what flapjacks were they all ordered the flapjacks and some eggs.

After relaxing and eating lunch they went from one end of town to the next going into stores and seeing all kinds of items they had never seen before. One store had books and Bonnie Brai found one with pictures of Scotland.

"Look at this. Tis pictures of whaur me mither lived." She turned page after page enchanted with all the towns and countrysides from the land where her mother had lived. Noah paid for the book and when they went to leave Bonnie Brai had a sad look on her face and didn't want to put the book back on the shelf. She held it tight to her chest.

"The book is yours. You can bring it with you," Noah said.

Bonnie Brai looked surprised and her eyes lit up and her whole face started smiling. She hugged Noah and gave him a kiss on the cheek. He didn't know how to act. He turned a bit red in the face and looked around to see if anyone was watching.

The three walked taller than usual as they strolled down the wooden sidewalk to the next shop. Noah pointed at a wooden sign above the door with a picture of bread carved on it. Bonnie Brai nodded and they went inside.

Bonnie Brai walked over to a counter that had several large cakes sitting on top. One cake was covered with chocolate icing and had 'Happy Birthday Joyce' written across the top. Another cake, round with white icing, had little blue and silver bells covering the sides. On the top stood a tiny man dressed in black and a woman with a white gown. The miniature couple was facing each other.

"Good morning. I see you are admiring the wedding cake. Are you two looking to buy one of those? I can have one ready with only one day's notice. Have you set the date yet?" the lady behind the counter with an apron covering her dress asked.

"The date?" Bonnie Brai asked.

"Yes, the day you'll be married," she replied.

"Oh," Bonnie Brai answered in surprise. "Not at all."

The woman was a kind looking rather young woman with light colored hair and brown eyes. She had her hair pulled back in a bun and had a spot of flour on her cheek.

Noah cleared his throat; he didn't know how to answer. He looked over at Bonnie Brai. She glanced over at him then turned away.

"Ye must be makin' bread because somethin' smells so good," Bonnie Brai said.

"I sure am. Would you like a taste?"

"Aye, that would be wonderful."

The woman went in the back and returned with three slices of fresh bread. Noah, Bonnie Brai and Clayton took a piece. Clayton smacked his lips as he ate the bread. Noah made an mmm sound and Bonnie Brai took little bites.

"Oh, this be the best bread Ah have ever put in me mouth. Ah can taste the fresh yeast. It's so good," Bonnie Brai said.

"Now remember to let me know a day ahead of your wedding so I can get your cake ready," the lady said and then smiled.

"We will," Noah said.

As they were leaving the store Bonnie Brai looked at Noah with a disdained look on her face.

"What?" Noah asked.

"We will?"

"I didn't know what else to say. Besides, you never know."

"Ye never know what?"

"When we'll get married."

"Ye best wake up because ye are still dreamin."

They returned to the hotel later that evening wearing new clothes. Noah kept staring at Bonnie Brai. He had never seen a woman look as beautiful as she did wearing her new dress.

"You look mighty pretty in that pink dress, Bonnie Brai," he said at last.

"Tis lovely alright. But it makes me feel as if Ah can't move or I'll get it ruined. I'm glad ye got me some pants to wear also. And ye look and smell much better now too."

"Yes, at least now he doesn't stink to high heaven. I was wondering if maybe we were partners with a polecat. And Bonnie Brai ya do look very purty," Clayton added.

That night, Noah and Clayton took the bed by the door and Bonnie Brai took the bed by the window. They said good night and fell sound asleep.

At daylight the next morning Clayton woke Noah up by yelling, "It's Bonnie Brai. She's not here. She's gone, again!"

Chapter 24

THE NEW RANCH

"Gone? What do you mean Bonnie Brai is gone? Where is she? Did you check the water closet? Did you check the hotel dining area? Did you look for her down the hall where the hand pump is?" Noah got up and grabbed his boots. He tried putting them on but was in such a hurry he had them on the wrong feet and had to take them back off and switch them.

"Yes, I did check those places and I couldn't find her. But it's no big deal, I guess. Remember, she does this all the time," Clayton reminded Noah.

"Yes, but not in town. Where would she go? I think maybe this time it's my fault. She may not have liked what I said yesterday at the cake shop. Do you think I scared her?"

"You scared Bonnie Brai? You're foolin with me, right? I don't think she was scared of you or anyone else for that matter besides we never knew where she went before so why not in town? I'm only concerned this time because all her new clothes are gone."

"Okay, go check the livery stable for her horse and I'll check with the sheriff." Noah grabbed his hat and followed Clayton out of the hotel.

They met a few minutes later in the street half way between the sheriff's office and the stable. "Her horse is gone," Clayton said as soon as he saw Noah.

"The sheriff hasn't seen her. You take the other side of the street and we'll check every store and building from one end of this town to the other."

Noah hurried from one store to the next. Many had not even opened yet. He looked for Clayton every time he walked back outside. When he saw Clayton he would stop for a second. Clayton always just shook his head no.

By late afternoon they had looked everywhere they thought she could be and asked everyone they ran into but no one had seen Bonnie Brai. Noah was in a state of panic but wasn't sure he needed to be. Bonnie Brai did always return before night so maybe she just had one of those moments where she had to be alone.

The next morning when she wasn't back was another matter. Now it was time to worry. Noah hadn't slept all night so at the first light of the morning sun he woke Clayton and said, "Go get us some biscuits and meet me out front. I'm going to get the horses."

For days they searched every farm and ranch in the area with no sign of Bonnie Brai. On the third day Clayton nudged Noah when they returned to town and said, "We have to get out of here. I've noticed more and more members of the Wild Bunch hanging around. They could only be gathering here for one thing."

"Are you sure it's them?"

"Oh, I'm sure. I know most of the guys that went up to the Wild Ranch, ya know. Let's face it, Bonnie Brai probably went back to her grandfather," Clayton said.

"I wonder why she left. I was hoping she would stay with us."

"Me too but she didn't like the fact you killed people for money, even if they were the bad ones. She told me so once."

"You're right. If I keep on being a bounty hunter we'll both just end up dead. I'm tired of it any way, all the killing didn't bring back my mother. It's time to do something else, maybe a cattle ranch. I'll go and get our money and we'll leave in the middle of the night."

"What are you going to name our new ranch? We've been here a spell now and it's time we put up a sign," Clayton said as he and Noah carried some gear and supplies from the barn into the house.

"I've been thinking about that. Do you think the name B & B sounds okay?" Noah asked.

Clayton got a smirk on his face, "You mean for Bonnie Brai, don't you? You're going to name this place after my sister? I like it."

"Not exactly, but kind of. I was combining Bonnie with my mother's name, half of each, Bonnie and Breeze. The names don't fit together for a ranch but the first letter of each name works just fine I think."

"Yes sir, I like it. I'll get us a sign made first chance I get. Noah, can I ask you something that has been bothering me?"

"Sure, what's on your mind?"

"Well, it's about my pa. You've never told me about how he died. I guess I've been thinking about it and want to know."

"I've wanted to tell you but I never knew when would be a good time to bring it up. Looks like now is the time. I'm sorry your pa had to die and I'm sorry I was the one that killed him. At the time I didn't know he was your pa but that wouldn't have made a difference. I didn't have much of a choice. He caught me unarmed when I was fishing that day during the cattle drive and he had his gun pointed at me. He said he was going to kill me and I thought for sure I was going to die. I had to use the small gun in my boot to defend myself."

"Did he suffer?"

"No, it happened very fast, and then it was over. I just hope we're still good in spite of what I had to do." Noah waited nervously for Clayton to answer.

Clayton paused a few minutes with his head down then replied, "We're good. I just needed to know. Hey, let's get to it. We have work to do."

Noah and Clayton were moving into the new ranch house though it was only half finished. The barn had been completed not more than a month ago and they were staying there until the house was livable. They had put the reward money they earned together and bought land close to the reservation Noah was from. It was the land where Noah's mother was buried.

He had put Clayton in charge of the small herd of cattle they had bought to get them started. Clayton made a good foreman and had a way with cattle. Noah was hoping the small herd would double by next year.

Noah thought about Bonnie Brai daily but when he got too sad he took a short trip over to the reservation and visited the friends and family he had left. He didn't have a lot of time to think too hard about anything right now. The involvement with the building of the house before cold weather set in took most of his time.

They had plans for a bunkhouse for the hired hands and they hoped to finish that before Christmas. They would work on that project next.

The house sat on top of one of the rolling hills with scattered trees. It had a beautiful view from every window of hills, grasslands, and trees with the exception of the one window beside the table. Outside that window about eighty or ninety yards away was the barn.

On the front of the house was going to be a large porch. Noah wanted to put one of those swinging chairs on one end and a couple of those chairs that rocked back and forth on the other end. Just off the porch were two hitching rails and beyond that a large tree that would provide shade for the front yard in the summer and colorful leaves to look at in the fall.

Noah designed the house to be round. He wanted his spirit to find its way outside once he died like they can in a teepee. He knew what being trapped felt like. The downstairs was all open with a grand front living area that had a huge fire place made of stone in the center. Off to one side was an area to fix food with a wood burning cooking stove and table and chairs. The back door led to a spring of fresh water not far from the house. He had ordered a hand pump to be put in but it hadn't arrived yet.

The spring was close enough that the running water could be heard trickling over the rocks in the quiet hours of evening. Sometimes there were frogs trying to see which of them could be the loudest. The spring made a creek that ran down the hill a half-mile or so and into a small pond the cattle used for drinking and cooling off during the hot days of summer.

Across the other side of the room were wooden steps leading up to the bedrooms that circled the living area downstairs and was open slightly in the middle to allow heat from the fireplace to filter into the rooms. Under the stairs they built a small closet with a chair that had a hole in the seat and a porcelain bucket under it. He remained Indian but used some of the white man's modern ways for comfort. At times, though, he didn't feel right in using the water closet. It just didn't feel natural to go to the bathroom inside where he lived.

He had returned home a hero for killing so many white men. He didn't feel like a hero, after all, he didn't get the men that killed the women of his tribe or the ones that killed his mother.

Life on the reservation was still very hard. People there still lived in teepees and went hungry much of the time. They were not free to roam around and find food without the risk of being shot and killed and even scalped, so it was difficult at best to provide for their families.

He had stayed on the reservation for a short time when he and Clayton first returned but he could no longer live that way. Between the conditions his people had to endure and the way they were enslaved in camps on the reservation and forgotten was hard for Noah to accept. His people were very poor but they were good people. They deserved much better.

Noah knew he had been slightly spoiled by white customs but the main reason he couldn't stay on the reservation was how his people were still being treated. They were not free to go and find game and hunt without being thought of as a war party and killed. There were no jobs for them to earn money the way whites did; no way to provide for their families.

If he could show some of his family that they could live a useful life and earn food to take care of their families he would do that. He hoped that having a ranch would inspire others to do the same. His people were good at adapting; that is how they had survived all this time.

Noah had to leave the reservation. He had experienced the freedom his people had fought for and lost. He understood why many of his tribe, his nation, would rather die than live the way they did. It had been their land and it had been stolen from them.

Now all he wanted to do was what the chief told him during his sweat lodge ceremony. It was his duty, his honor to help and provide for those not able to feed themselves any longer. His cattle would help his family with the food problem once he got it going.

"The wagons are here with the lumber for the house. Where do you want the men to put it?" Clayton asked.

"Have one wagon unload here by the front door and we'll use that wood first. The rest of the wood can be unloaded in the barn," Noah said.

"The men want to know if we need some helpers to work for a few days."

"If any of them have experience building a house, keep them. If not let them go. I have hired several from my tribe to help but we need someone to show them what to do or this job will never get done. Teaching them how to build a house may even help them find jobs in other places later on. Are you helping today?" Noah asked.

"Can't, I'll be with the herd. A couple of cows are calving any day now."

Over the next few days two of the four bedrooms had the walls in place and it was looking more like a house on the inside with each new room being finished. The wood porch just outside the double front door was about half done.

On the outside the men had most of the cracks between the logs that formed the walls filled with clay from the creek. This would keep the winter winds from giving off a chilly breeze inside when the snows came.

One day Noah heard someone working out in the barn. He went into the barn to find Clayton replacing one of the planks along the back wall.

"What happened here?" Noah asked.

"This is the second time this board has been loose. I think someone kicks it loose to get into the barn."

"Is anything missing?"

"No, but look over here in this empty stall."

Noah walked over to the stall and looked in. Along the back wall he saw a bundle of straw flattened out and it looked like a bed.

"Has someone been sleeping in here?"

"That's what it looks like to me," Clayton answered.

"Why would they do that? We allow all of the helpers to sleep in the house."

"Maybe whoever comes in here at night is not a helper. We have another problem too. We have cattle missing, six from the other day and four from last night. I think we have some rustlers about."

"Hmm, this is a problem. Keep an eye out for whoever has been sleeping here." Noah went over and saddled his horse then saddled Clayton's horse. He was leading them out the barn door.

"Are we going somewhere?" Clayton asked.

"Yep, let's go find some tracks and go catch us some cattle thieves."

Chapter 25

ARRESTED

Noah and Clayton rode off to find the trail of the missing cattle. It didn't take very long before they saw tracks from the steers and several horses going off the ranch property heading west. The tracks were fresh and were easy to follow. Noah and Clayton could ride fast and would be able to catch up to the thieves soon.

After riding only an hour Noah said, "It won't be too long before we have them in sight. This is just like old times."

"It may seem like old times to you but you take care of the ranch and the building of the main house. For me it is just another day of work. I have to stay with these heifers all day long, every day."

"Look, there they are. Looks like they have camped for the day. I'm not sure what that's about. Wouldn't cattle rustlers move the herd into their own herd or take them to market?" Noah asked.

"How are we going to handle this?"

"Let's just ride in and see what's happening." Noah said. He saw Clayton give him a funny look with his face scrunched up. "Oh, don't worry so much. I don't think these men are really rustlers. I noticed the horse tracks and the horses didn't have iron shoes. I think our rustlers are someone else."

They rode toward the men in the camp but before they got there Noah recognized the men. He saw them at work butchering the cattle and packing the meat in salt and putting the meat in burlap sacks and loading them onto a wagon. He smiled at the sight of these men working.

They rode up to the campfire and dismounted. "Chief Crazy Elk, I haven't seen you in a coon's age. You came a long way to steel my cattle." Noah paused and watched as Chief Crazy Elk looked over at him. "It's good to see you," Noah said.

"It's good to see you also. But you are wrong. I didn't take your cattle. I took my cattle. It's the ten steers you owed me. We are even again."

"You could have walked up to my front door and I would have had my men gather the steers up to give you. You and your men are welcome in my home. How did you know where I lived?"

"Some of my relation told me, or maybe it was a little bird," Chief Crazy Elk said.

"This little bird must be a ghost that disappears in the night." Noah looked around to see if he could find the relative but she was nowhere around.

"Are you looking to find the little ghost? She isn't here. I thought she was with you but after watching your ranch for a of couple days I knew she wasn't around anywhere."

"She left without saying anything. That was before we bought the ranch. I thought she returned to you."

"She did but she came for only a short visit and I saw her once after that," Chief Crazy Elk said. "If she didn't tell you she was leaving maybe she will return or maybe she isn't gone and you just can't see her." Chief Crazy Elk grinned and Noah thought the chief knew more than what he was saying.

Noah's heart still sank. He wondered where she could be and hoped she was okay.

Noah walked over to his saddlebag and searched until he found a piece of paper and a pencil and wrote something on the paper and handed it to Chief Crazy Elk.

"What's this?" Chief Crazy Elk asked.

"It's a bill of sale. It says you bought these cows from me and you are my friend. That way if you are stopped you won't get questioned about the cows."

Chief Crazy Elk laughed. "If I'm stopped do you think we'll have time to show this paper to anyone in the midst of all the shooting?"

Noah leaned forward on his horse with his hands crossed over the saddle horn. Noah noticed Chief Crazy Elk looking at him shaking his head. "What's wrong?" he asked.

"I was seeing if you were getting pale in the face."

"My face may look pale to you because I no longer wear war paint. I have adopted some different ways but these ways will help my people. It's helping you now by helping to feed your tribe and . . ."

"Good, you still get riled up and I see the red returning to your cheeks. You are still a warrior," Chief Crazy Elk interrupted.

Noah nodded his head but he wasn't smiling. It was important to him that he be accepted by Chief Crazy Elk. They were basically doing the same thing. They just had different ways of feeding their people. He respected the chief for using the old ways but was worried the old ways would keep the chief and his men in constant danger.

Noah watched as a couple of the warriors skinned out one of the cows. They took the hide and rubbed it with salt so it would keep on the journey back home. Noah knew that Indians used every part of any animal they killed.

"Those hides will make nice covers to sleep under this winter," he said.

"We won't use them for that," the warrior said. "They aren't as warm as buffalo. They don't have enough fur. We will use them to make pouches and to cover our teepees. The leather is softer and can even be used for clothing. We'll put them to good use once we cure them."

"Well, keep your knife sharp and your eyes even sharper. Clayton, mount up and we'll head back. Chief Crazy Elk, live long and be happy."

"I've already done that."

Half way back to the ranch Noah spotted a posse of riders coming toward them. It looked like they were coming from his ranch. He turned to Clayton and said, "If these men are after Chief Crazy Elk, back me up and I'll tell them that is our men taking some cattle to market."

The posse rode up to Noah and stopped. The one wearing a star on his shirt asked, "Are you Noah?"

"Yes, is there trouble?"

"I have to take you in."

"Take him in where?" Clayton asked.

"To jail. There's a poster out on him for killing a lawman. Seems one of the men he turned in for that reward was wearing a badge."

"That's not true! If one of those men was wearing a badge maybe that is why the Wild Bunch always got away. They had a lawman working for them. I don't believe it because I loaded those men in the wagon that day and there was no badge," Clayton yelled.

"I don't like what you're suggesting, young man," the sheriff said.

"Calm down. It's just a mistake. I'll go with these men and you return to the ranch and take care of things. I'll be back in a few days," Noah said.

"It'll take more than a few days. The circuit judge will come around in two weeks for your trial. You'll be in my charge at least until then. You need to carefully hand me your gun, please."

Noah didn't like being caged up. He paced the floor most of the day only getting to see another person when he was fed or when there was another prisoner in the cell next to him.

He could see through the window bars a platform being built in the street at the corner. It had thirteen steps leading to the top where a wooden arch with a rope hung from the middle of it. Some men were on the top platform testing it out. They had a burlap sack filled with grain sitting beside them. One man slipped the noose around the grain sack and tightened it. The other man pulled a handle and the sack dropped through a trap door of the platform. It fell half way to the ground and when the grain sack came to the end of the rope the noose tightened so hard against the sack it spit open and the grain spilled out.

The door to the cells opened and the sheriff came in with another man. The man was wearing strange clothes. He had smooth looking dark pants and a white shirt. Over the shirt was a jacket with long sleeves and it was the same color and texture of the pants. His shirt had a small black ribbon tied in a bow around the collar.

The gentleman was an older man with a narrow face. He had short gray hair that stuck out in the back and wore dark rimmed glasses that made his eyes look tiny when Noah looked at them. He carried a black leather satchel full of papers and held a derby hat in the other hand.

"You go on trial tomorrow. This here is your lawyer, Mr. Henry. He arrived on the train this morning from St. Louis. I'll leave you two to talk." The sheriff walked out closing the door behind him.

Mr. Henry pulled a wood chair with a laced cane bottom up next to the bars and sat down. "Looks like you've gotten into a bit of a scrape. You are charged with the murder of a law officer. What's your side of the story?"

"It's not true. I had a shootout with the Wild Bunch gang. Clayton loaded the dead men in a wagon and we took them in and collected the reward. None of them was wearing a badge. Don't you think I would have noticed that? How did you know to come and represent me?"

"I got a telegram and some money was wired to my office. It doesn't matter from whom. The fact is without me you will hang. Ever see a man hang? It's not a pleasant sight. Now, let's get started. Tell me all about your life."

"What does my whole life have to do with anything?"

"I have to work from the assumption the jury will think you are guilty. I have to make them like you then bring in enough doubt so they feel good about letting you go. The only thing I don't want you to tell me is if you are Indian or not. Keep that to yourself. As long as the jury doesn't know you are Indian we have a chance."

"We?"

"Okay, you."

"But I am Indian. My life is about Indians against whites . . . umm, cowboys."

"Not today, it isn't. It's about a good guy against bad guys."

Noah talked with the lawyer for several hours. Mr. Henry then stood and said, "Okay, now I have to go and find what they are saying happened and compare that to what the real truth is. I'll need to find some volunteers for the jury; family people that have some values so I can show them what a good person you are. If I can do that we . . . umm, there's a good chance of you walking out of here. I'll be back later today so we can practice what will be going on during the hearing and what you will say."

"Why do I have to practice? Can't I just tell the truth?"

"It isn't all about you telling the truth. It's more about how you say it that will make a difference. If you seem nervous at all then the jury won't believe you no matter what you say. I know innocent people get nervous but if you act nervous the jury will think you are lying. That's just how it works."

"Do you think I'm guilty?"

"Who cares what I think? Who even cares what really happened? It's a matter of getting the jury to believe what we say is the truth."

"Do you think they'll let me go free?"

"That I don't know but we have a better than average chance of pulling this off. You don't happen to know your clothing size would you?"

"No, why?"

"I'll bring you a suit to wear tomorrow. We want the jury to believe you are an upright citizen. A person they would greet when they see you at church. We want them to like you. I'll send you in some bath water and someone to cut your hair, too."

"Tomorrow, do you think it'll take that long?"

"Not really but tonight may be the longest night you'll ever spend in your life."

Chapter 26

THE TRIAL

Noah was in handcuffs and led by the sheriff down the street past the gallows to the court room. They walked to the end of the street and went into a church building. Noah was brought to the front and made to sit in the first row. The sheriff sat beside him. Mr. Henry put some papers on a table in front of Noah. The table on the other side in front of the first row held papers from the prosecuting attorney. There was a chair with a table where the pulpit once stood. There was also a chair beside that table making the church resemble a courtroom.

People were coming in and sitting in the pews. The jury was brought in and they sat in a section over to one side that had song books piled up at the end of the rows.

The judge came in and sat at the table facing everyone. He picked up a small wooden hammer and rapped the table. "Good morning. Let's get started. I'll read the charges. Noah, you were arrested for the murder of a law officer. What do you have to say?"

"Not guilty, your honor."

"Okay, please come up here and sit in the chair beside my bench. Raise your right hand. Do you swear not to lie? Remember we are in a church and God can hear you."

Noah was nervous and believed the white god was listening. He only hoped this white god didn't have it in for him for killing bad white men. "I swear," he replied.

"Okay, now sit. Prosecuting attorney, we will start with you. What do you have to say?" the judge asked.

A man in a suit sitting at the other end of the front row stood and said, "Your honor, gentlemen of the jury, this is a simple case. I can't imagine this taking very long. Noah, are you a bounty hunter that gets paid for bringing in bodies and saying they are bad men to get the money?"

"No."

"No? What do you mean no? Didn't you bring in a wagon full of dead men for a reward?"

"Yes, I did. Thirteen outlaws."

"Thirteen, same as the number of steps on the gallows."

"Objection," Mr. Henry said.

"Withdrawn. You say you brought in thirteen dead men so you are a bounty hunter. You lied to the jury."

"I didn't lie. You asked if I am a bounty hunter. I am not. I was a bounty hunter. Now I'm a cattle rancher like many of the good people here."

"Who killed all those men? Wasn't it you?"

"No, I killed a few but there were others there with me. Three of us were surrounded by the Wild Bunch outlaw gang and we had a shootout."

"If that were true, wouldn't the three of you be dead right now? Didn't you, in fact, hunt those men down and kill them in cold blood one at a time?"

"No, we were surrounded and the three of us would have died that day if it wasn't for a band of Indians that came and ran the outlaws off," Noah said.

"Now why on Earth would a band of Indians come to your rescue unless you are an Indian? Are you an Indian?"

Someone from the middle of the crowd yelled, "He's an injun."

Noah's heart skipped a beat. He remembered to do what his lawyer told him to do whenever he got nervous so he slowly straightened up and took a couple deep breaths.

"Order, order in the court," the judge said as he hit the mallet down on the table.

"My name is Noah. Is that an Indian name?"

"Weren't you born on a reservation?"

"No, I was born along the Little Big Horn River," Noah said.

"But isn't that Indian country?"

"That area is still wild and free. It's God's country up there."

"So, you are saying you aren't an Indian?"

"You are the one saying I am an Indian, not me."

"Have you killed white men before?"

"Yes, as a bounty hunter I've killed bad white men, killers and robbers that had a price on their head."

"You may step down. Next I want to call the sheriff to the stand," the prosecutor said.

The sheriff walked up and took the seat. The judge asked, "Are you going to lie?"

"No," the sheriff said.

"Please, continue," the judge said.

"Do you remember who brought in a wagon full of dead men for the rewards?" the prosecuting attorney asked.

"Yes, it was Noah."

"And out of those thirteen men, how many had a wanted poster on them?"

"Eleven."

"Out of the two without a wanted poster, how was those two's death ruled at the time?"

"Self-defense at first," the sheriff said.

"You say at first. What happened to change your mind?"

"A few days later a man came to my office and asked me if I knew one of those bodies was wearing a deputy's badge," the sheriff said.

"Now why on Earth would someone spot the badge a few days later?"

"It was the day some men were taking those bodies to boot hill to bury them. I walked over to investigate and saw the body wearing the badge. I went back to my office and issued a warrant for the arrest of Noah."

"No further questions, your honor."

The sheriff stood to walk back to his seat.

"Your turn, Mr. Henry," the judge said.

"Sheriff, please remain in the witness chair. I'll start with you," Mr. Henry said.

The sheriff sat back down and Mr. Henry walked back and forth in front of the jury. He turned to face the sheriff and asked, "Has crime in this area slowed down since Noah brought those wanted men in to your office?"

"Yes, I guess it has at that."

"Would you say, since that day, have there been more killings or fewer killings in the area?"

"Fewer, I guess."

"Are you sure about that, Sheriff?"

"I never thought about it but now that you mention it I'm sure there have been fewer killings in these here parts since that day."

"Now, as a sheriff, do bounty hunters make your job harder or easier?"

"Easier, I guess for the most part."

"So, bounty hunters are not evil?"

"No, some of them are a little rough around the edges."

"Do you consider Noah one of those that are rough around the edges?"

"No, I remember having a hard time even believing he was a bounty hunter at first."

"Did anyone ever say they saw Noah kill this man?"

"No."

"Who was the man that brought your attention to the badge?"

"I don't know. Someone said he was a ranch hand just helping out," the sheriff said.

"Do you know what ranch he was from?"

"No."

"Could he have been a hand from the Wild Ranch?"

"Objection!"

"I withdraw the question. Was the dead man with the badge one of your deputies?"

"No."

"Of course not or you would have recognized him immediately and you would have known if one of your deputies was missing. Do you believe if you did have a deputy missing that all the lawmen in this area would know about it?"

"Objection. Where are we going with these questions?" the prosecutor asked.

"You honor, it's a simple question. Wouldn't you like to hear the answer?" Mr. Henry asked.

"You may answer," the judge said.

The sheriff sat up and said, "I'm sure all the officers of the law from all over would know and be on the lookout for any deputy reported missing."

"This so called dead deputy, was he reported missing from anywhere else?"

"I haven't heard of any reports of any deputies missing."

"That's good. We rely on our law enforcement men to protect us. I'm glad none are missing. Oh, by the way, what was the man's name that had the badge?"

"No one knew him so I don't know."

"Then how did you know he was a deputy?"

"He was wearing a deputy's badge."

"So, couldn't someone put a badge on a dead man? I'm sure the dead man wouldn't stop him."

Noah heard a few chuckles coming from the jury.

"You are trying to make me look stupid. The man had a badge so he was a deputy."

Mr. Henry looked to the back of the court room and said, "Billy, will you stand up and let the jury see what you have pinned to your shirt?"

The jury turned to see a small young boy about six years old stand up. He stood looking very proud. On his shirt was a tin star.

"Billy, are you a deputy?"

"No, I'm a sheriff," the little boy said.

People in the courtroom broke out laughing.

"Order, order in the court," the judge said hitting the wooden mallet on the table several times to get everyone refocused on the trial.

"Yes, let's get back to business," Mr. Henry said. "Sheriff, what was the size of the bullet hole in the dead man wearing a badge?"

"He didn't have any bullet holes in him. Well, none that would have killed him."

"What do you mean? Was he shot or not?" Mr. Henry asked.

"He didn't have any bullet holes in him but he did have several buck shots across his chest and in one arm from a shotgun. I don't think it was very many so that wouldn't have killed him."

"No bullet holes? Then how did he die?"

"He had an arrow through his chest."

"Oh, so he wasn't killed from a gun, he was killed from an arrow. Was Noah carrying a bow and arrow or a shotgun when he brought in the wagon full of dead men?"

"No, not that I saw."

"If the man was killed by an arrow wouldn't you think that maybe, just maybe, an Indian killed the guy?"

"Objection."

"I withdraw the question, your honor, but it does go to show that Noah told the truth about Indians being there. Sheriff, I only have one more thing to ask. Would you ask a cold blooded killer to be your deputy?"

"You have to be able to kill but I wouldn't ask a stone hard killer to work for me, no."

"But didn't you ask Noah if he would be interested in becoming a deputy and working for you?"

"Yes, I believe I did. But that was before all this happened."

"Thank you, Sheriff, you may step down. I recall Noah to the stand."

Noah stood and walked over to the chair beside the judge's desk and sat down.

"Remember, you are still sworn to tell the truth," the judge said.

"Noah, I need to get something straightened out about you being an Indian. Do you even own a bow and arrow?"

"No, sir."

"Have you ever shot an arrow from a bow?"

"Yes, sir, when I was a kid I did a few times."

"Do you own a shotgun?" Mr. Henry asked.

"No, but I do know how the man was hit with buck shot."

"Please tell the jury about this man the sheriff is calling a deputy without a name."

"I saw some men from the Wild Ranch shoot and kill Clayton's ma. Before she died she managed to shoot and kill two of the men that were threatening her and shooting at her. She let two of them have it from the blast of her double barrel shotgun. The man I'm on trial for killing was one of the riders that shot and killed Clayton's mother. The man was sitting on his horse right beside the one that Ma killed when she fired her shotgun. I guess he picked up a few stray pellets of buck shot."

"Why didn't you save Clayton's mother?"

"I was too far away and couldn't get there in time. When these men saw me they started chasing me and Clayton until they had us trapped and they surrounded us. That was when we had the shootout with the outlaws."

"Okay, thank you. Do you have a family and is your family white? And remember to tell the truth because we can find out easy enough."

"Yes, I have a white family. I am raising a boy about twelve years old. His parents were killed; his ma by the men from the Wild Bunch I just told you about. So I took him in. Some of you may even know Clayton. He has been to this town a few times for supplies for his ma."

"What will happen to this boy if you are convicted?"

"I don't know."

"Just why in this world did you ever want to be a bounty hunter?"

"My father was killed fighting beside General George Custer, so I grew up without him in my life. My mother was killed by some outlaws not long ago so that's when I wanted to stop bad men from killing someone else's loved ones."

"Why did you stop being a bounty hunter? I'm sure there are a few bad men still around," Mr. Henry commented.

"Yes there are. But I just couldn't kill any more people. Even bad men have children and it just wasn't in me any longer. I'm much happier on my ranch raising cattle."

"Thank you, Noah, you may step down. Your honor, I'm done here."

The judge said, "Now we will have the prosecutor give his ending argument."

The prosecuting attorney stood and faced the jury. "Like I said at the start, this is a simple case. Don't let all the hog wash hide the facts. Fact one, a deputy was killed. Fact two, Noah brought this deputy in for the reward; therefore he alone is responsible for the death of this man who gave his life to protect us. It is the least we can do to see that he gets justice for all his efforts. Thank you."

The judge said, "Now, Mr. Henry, your closing remarks if you please."

Mr. Henry stood and faced the judge. "I don't have anything to add but I would like to review what we heard here today." He cleared his throat and turned to look at Noah then over to the jury. He put one hand on the desk in front of his seat and leaned in to address them.

"We learned how much safer life is because of the work of bounty hunters. We learned that not everyone has what it takes to be a bounty hunter. We learned not everyone wearing a badge is a deputy, like Tommy back there . . ."

"It's Billy, and I'm a sheriff," a small but strong voice said from the back.

Mr. Henry took a minute and walked over to the jury section. "Billy, yes, thank you. We don't have a missing lawman that we know of and he wasn't even shot. I'm not sure of what we do know actually. I'm not even sure why we're having this trial. The only thing I am sure of is that Noah, here, has a cattle ranch and is trying to make a living like many of us. Why? Because he is raising an orphan. Wouldn't we want someone to give our child a good home if, God forbid, something happened to us? This court was held in this church. Is Noah a sinner? And if he is don't you think God will punish him? And what would God do to us if we punish an innocent man? Thank you for returning a verdict of not guilty and letting Noah return back home to care for Clayton." Mr. Henry walked slowly over to his seat and sat back down, smiling at the jury.

"Okay, men of the jury, please go over to the baptism tub and vote if he is guilty or not," the judge said. "I'll be back shortly while you are deciding." The judge then hit his hammer on the table and walked outside.

Noah watched as the twelve men stood around talking. He saw eleven of the men raise their hands in the air. They talked some more. One man was arguing but then he nodded his head. This time all twelve men raised their hand in the air. After they did that they stood around smiling and joking with one another. He saw one man point to the back toward Billy and chuckle.

Mr. Henry kept looking at his pocket watch while Noah drew in deep breaths and exhaled allowing the tension to escape. He thought things went well and was hoping not to return to his jail cell.

"How did we do?" Noah finally asked.

"I've learned a long time ago not to guess. We'll have to just wait and see."

After an hour the judge came back in and sat at his seat in the front of the church courtroom. Everyone took their seats and the room got very quiet.

The judge hit the little hammer on the table and asked, "Jury, have you agreed on the verdict?"

One of the men stood and said, "Yes, your honor, we have."

"Well, let's hear it then."

"Your honor, we find, in the case of Noah killing a deputy, that he is . . . not guilty."

"So be it. This court is adjourned," the judge said as he hit the table with the mallet one last time.

Noah looked over at Mr. Henry and said, "Thank you, Mr. Henry. I'm free to go?"

"You sure are, my friend."

"Good, because I've got things to do and I'm not going to hang around here."

Chapter 27

THE POWWOW

Noah spent most of the day riding across his ranch. He checked the herd and was concerned because it was smaller than he thought it should be. It seems they gave away more cattle to those that were hungry than the herd was giving them back in new calves.

The outside part of the house was finished but there was still a lot of work left undone on the inside. The furniture on the inside was just a make shift table and some odd chairs. He had hoped for beds and couches like what he had seen in some of the hotels in town. The front porch was still only half done.

The barn needed a little more work. The stalls had been finished but the tack room where saddles were stored wasn't complete and the corn crib was just a pile of corn stalks thrown in a corner.

Noah never got the bunkhouse started and the hands that were staying over once in a while to help slept on the floor of the front room of the house or on the ground in the barn.

He didn't know how to get all the work done. He and Clayton had used up most of their reward money and he didn't want to go back to tracking down and killing bad white people. He was tired of that way of life.

All his efforts wore him out and left him unfulfilled. He was lonely.

One gift he got from being a bounty hunter was being patient. He had so much to do but when he could remember to be patient it helped. He knew he couldn't get everything done all at once.

"Rider coming," Clayton hollered as he walked his horse across the yard in front of the barn.

Noah stepped out onto the half of the porch that was finished and sat down with his legs dangling off the end. He recognized the girl on back of this very shiny black horse with no saddle.

"Are you busy today?" she asked as she rode up in front of him and stopped her horse.

"We always have something needing to be done. Do you need our help for something, Cousin Dawn?" he asked.

"No, not help. We just need you and Clayton to come to the reservation tomorrow. It's the yearly powwow. How could you forget?"

"Where's it going to be held this year?"

"In the field next to Wounded Knee to honor our relation that died there. We're going to celebrate our people's life," Dawn said as she dismounted. "There are people coming from all over this area to join us this year. You may even find a girl to join with," Dawn giggled.

"I'm not ready to take on a wife. I don't have much to offer her."

Dawn's smile turned into a frown. "You have ten times more than anyone else I know. Killing whites has turned you into a stone. You are acting like a selfish, ungrateful boar hog."

"You're right. I just want so much all at once mostly because our people go hungry and I want to help by sharing what I have. To feel bad because I don't have enough isn't what the Great Spirit expects from me. Come on inside and eat. We have some cornbread and cooked fowl. We'll go back with you and help. It's time I bonded with my family again and start enjoying the company of our people."

Noah led the way inside where he fixed everyone a piece of the cooked fowl and handed out a piece of cornbread. He sat down and took a bite of the cooked pheasant.

Dawn said, "Now don't get mad but you want more and when is more enough? More is never enough. More is always more and enough is enough. You have become the enemy. More is the enemy. It's the evil part of being a white man not the color of his skin."

Noah said, "You're right. I needed to hear this."

"The Great Spirit has a path for each of us to follow that comes with choices to make. It is like what Chief Sitting Bull said. 'If you see a pretty rock, pick it up. When the rock gets too heavy put it back down.' All we have to do is follow the path the Great Spirit gives us to follow and we will be the person we are supposed to be," Dawn said.

"Since it's a long ride back and it would be late by the time we got there do you want to spend the night and we'll all ride over early in the morning? If you stay I could show you around the place," Noah asked.

"Okay, since I was told not to return without you, I'll stay," Dawn said.

Noah, Clayton, and Dawn rode onto the powwow grounds not long after daybreak. Noah saw there were lots of teepees in the fields next to where everyone was gathering. He saw several people he grew up with and many new faces he did not know.

"Many people came days ago. That family over there are Cheyenne and came here from the west. I've even met some Kiowa and Choctaws from the south. I heard the elders talking and they say some of these people fought at Little Big Horn and have come to give honor to the great victory they were part of," Dawn said.

"This is exciting. I want to see all my friends and family. Show me where they are camped so we can visit before the dancing begins," Noah said.

Noah spent time visiting old friends and making many new friends. That is what a powwow is all about. He saw people dressed in their tribal outfits and walking to the area where the dance was about to start. He was wearing his buckskins and moccasins and was going to dance in the men's traditional dances.

To start the celebration all the tribes went into the dance circle one at a time. A holy man named Black Bear had sage burning and as each dancer walked by he fanned the smoke over the dancer. Once all the dancers were in the circle Black Bear said a prayer.

The drums started pounding and singers bellowed loudly. The crowd quieted down and the first dancers moved into the center of the dance ring as the others stood along the edge.

The first dancers were the grass dancers. They danced and stomped down all the tall grass so the others would have a nice flat area to dance. When they finished the entire field was flat and smooth with a covering of fallen grasses that made a soft area for all to enjoy.

The call went out for the men to dance. Many of the men moved into the circle and danced in a slow step making their way around the many spears standing in the middle. These spears had special markings and different eagle feathers in a pattern or design down the shaft of the spear. They represented the different nations that were there and were placed in the middle to show respect.

Noah wanted to dance with the men but he was unsure if he should. He didn't have an outfit, only his buckskin pants he was wearing.

"Get out there and dance," Dawn said as she pushed him forward.

"I don't know. Look at what all the others are wearing. Most have full outfits. They are wearing full headdresses and have breastplates made of bone. Many have coup sticks with bear claws or antlers," he said.

Dawn looked around and found something she thought would work. She handed Noah a bright red loincloth with a string to tie it around his waist. "Now go and have fun. Enjoy life for a change."

Noah went into the dance ring and danced. He danced beside some of the greatest warriors from many different nations. He would take a step and as he did he would let the toe touch the ground then raise it and place the whole foot down and take another step. He would repeat the step with the other foot. Step, touch the toe to the ground, raise it and place the foot on the ground in front of him and do it again moving his body in a small bounce motion to the beat of the drum.

Noah saw men with their face painted with war paint. Each had his own design. Some of the men had snake skins wrapped around their arms while others wore eagle feathers on their shoulders. Many of the men had bells attached to a leather strap around their ankles to keep evil spirits away.

The drums stopped and after a short wait the drums started again with a different beat and song. Women moved into the dance circle and the men stood at the side. Noah saw Dawn dancing. She wore a light blue dress and had tiny lids from tobacco tins that were curled round and sown in rows across the dress. The tins hit together as she danced and made a jingle sound as she moved.

The women's dance was very lively. They would turn and spin making the leather fringe shake and move on the dresses as if the fringe had its own dance going on. Some of the women held eagle feathers and had shawls around their shoulders or covering their heads. Their hair was fixed with two braids, one down each side of their heads.

Noah tried to get Clayton to dance. Noah pushed him into the dance area but he pulled away. "I don't know how to do that. I'm not a dancer. Now if it was with a girl I might."

"You think you are ready to dance with a girl?" Noah asked.

A new dance was about to start. Many were standing along the side while many young men and women moved into the dance area.

"Good," Dawn said. "Let's go then."

Clayton looked surprised.

Dawn locked her arm around Clayton's arm and pulled him into the middle with Noah following. "This dance is for men and women. Just hold my hand," Dawn said.

The dancers all held hands in a giant circle consisting of boy, girl, boy, girl. The drumbeat started slowly. The dancers moved to the left by taking two steps sideways then bending their knees. They would then take a step with the left foot then the right foot and bend their knees again. The whole time everyone was holding hands. On a certain beat of the drums everyone would bend at the waist and then raise their hands over their head and gave a loud shout. Then the song would start over and each time it did the pace got a little faster.

Noah noticed Clayton was getting the hang of it when the drums started going real fast. By the time they went half way around the circle the drums were beating really fast and Noah saw that Clayton couldn't keep up and was now being pulled and jerked along completely out of step. Noah saw there were several people out of step as the drums went faster and faster.

By the end of the dance the drumbeats got so fast that everyone was almost running sideways. People where laughing as many could not keep up and had to drop out of the circle. By the end of the song only a few were still dancing and those few were breathing rather hard.

When the drums stopped everyone stopped and raised their hands high in the air and gave a loud shout. Noah started laughing. He noticed poor Clayton looked dizzy.

Dawn caught Noah alone and pulled him off to the side. "I found the right girl for you," she said.

"What?" exclaimed Noah.

"Yes, I've been talking with her ever since I saw her giving you the flutter eye."

"The flutter eye? What are you talking about?"

"You men are like hawks when it comes to hunting and bears when it comes to fighting. You see and notice everything. But when it comes to women you men are like turtles; you walk around slowly and when you see something you don't understand you hide your head in your shell."

"So now I'm a turtle?"

"Right now you would have to run to be as fast as a turtle. So, do you want to meet her or not?"

"I don't know. What nation is she with? How old is she? Have you met her family? What does she look like? Does she . . ."

"That settles it," Dawn interrupted. "Come on. You can ask her all those questions yourself. If I told you everything then you wouldn't have any reason to even meet her."

Dawn grabbed Noah by the arm and led him down the hill toward a bunch of teepees. Noah looked around to see what Clayton was doing. He saw Clayton wrestling with some other boys and it looked as if he was enjoying being with friends and children his own age.

Dawn walked over to where a mother sat on a flat stone and was mending a tear in one of the dance outfits. She was using leather lace to repair a seam that had pulled loose.

"Greetings," Dawn said.

The woman looked up and nodded her head and pointed to the teepee next to her. Noah glanced over and the teepee flap opened, a girl about the same age as him stepped out and looked over at Noah with a wide grin on her face. Dawn ran over and gave the girl a hug.

"Night Tear, this is my cousin, Noah," Dawn said. "Let's walk down to the stream and throw rocks in the water so we can talk and get to know each other."

Night Tear was a thin young woman who was taller than Noah but only by the length of an arrowhead. She had long coal black hair that hung loose and wore a braided leather headband which kept her hair from covering her face. She had a dimple on both cheeks and a petite nose. Her dark brown eyes were olive shaped and sparkled when she smiled.

She wore a light tan buckskin dress with no sleeves and it just barely covered her knees. It had a dyed yellow deerskin belt that tied in the front. Around her neck was a tiny silver chain with a small yellow transparent stone. On her feet were moccasins with the top part done in a laced patchwork pattern of yellow dyed porcupine quills.

"Your dance outfit is very attractive," Noah said as the three of them strolled down the hill toward the creek.

"Oh, this isn't my dance outfit. It's what I wear when I'm not dancing," she said with slight giggle. Night Tear walked so close to Noah that several times their shoulders would touch as they walked.

Noah said, "I can smell honeysuckle in the air."

Night Tear smiled and said, "That's my hair. I rubbed some honeysuckle over my head this morning. Do you like it?"

"Yes, I do," Noah said as he took her hand and helped her step over some rocks and down to the edge of the stream.

"I've heard so much about you, Noah Two Wolves, what is it like living with the whites?"

"I don't live with them, except for Clayton, I guess. I have a small cattle ranch just outside the reservation."

"I've heard you are a great warrior and have killed several whites not long ago. To me that's incredible."

"What about you? Is your Nation wealthy? I'm sorry, I don't mean to pry but your dress is so pretty and I guess I'm just wondering. Truth is that I don't really know what to say. I'm interested in getting to know you but I sure feel awkward," he admitted.

Night Tear took her hand and playfully pushed Noah away.

"I'm Arapaho. My people suffer the same as your people. My father is the chief and my mother makes sure I have nice things even if they have to do without sometimes. She says a princess has to look and act with a certain amount of dignity."

Dawn said, "Tonight there is going to be a full moon, the moon of the falling leaves. After dark and after the full moon rises the storyteller is going to tell one of his unusual stories and everyone is welcome to come and hear him. Noah, you can ask Night Tear to go with you and I can bring little Clayton. I bet he has never been to a story telling."

"Night Tear, would you like me to come by and take you to the story telling tonight?" he asked.

"I would love that," she answered. "Then afterwards we can stay for the other ceremony that follows."

"What ceremony is that?" Noah asked.

"The joining ceremony. We will stay and be joined together."

Noah's eyes got as big as a bullfrog's belly. "What?"

Chapter 28

THE STORYTELLER

The edge of the moon of the falling leaves could just barely be seen as it started its path across the night sky. Noah walked with Night Tear and Dawn walked with Clayton on their way over to where the storyteller would be spinning his tale.

Night Tear and Dawn broke out in laughter at the same time as if they had been giving each other signs. Dawn said, "Noah, you should have seen your face when you thought you were going to be joined tonight."

"Yes, I know. You girls got me good. The joke was on me and I don't think anyone ever pulled a prank on me the way you two did earlier," Noah said.

"What, I'm not good enough to join with you, Noah Two Wolves?" asked Night Tear.

"It's not that. We had just met moments before and that's what surprised me so much. I did believe you were serious," Noah replied.

"Maybe I was." Night Tear winked at Dawn.

Clayton pointed at Noah and said, "When you two do get hitched me and Dawn is going to get hitched with you all. We'll have a double hitch thing-a-ma-bob."

"Nice try, young-un, but that'll never happen, not next week and not next year," Dawn said as she rubbed Clayton's head to mess up his hair.

Clayton grabbed Dawn's hand to make her stop. Dawn extended the middle knuckle of her other hand and rapped the back of Clayton's hand. Clayton pulled his hand back with a grunt of pain. When he looked at his hand a knot had raised up from the minor blow he had just received.

"Okay, cut it out. We're here," Noah said.

They arrived at the top of the hill and stood at the edge of about fifty others ranging in age between very young and extremely old. It seemed everyone loved to hear the story teller. The storyteller was due to arrive as soon as the full moon could be seen in its entirety. People were talking and some were pointing at the moon.

An excited voice yelled, "There it is. The moon is all the way up!"

Noah had never been to a story telling before and was fidgety. He looked all around for whatever was going to start when he heard a horse riding fast coming toward them. The crowd got quiet and a little girl yelled, "There he is. I see him."

A black horse with a lightning bolt painted on its chest and on both sides of its rear flanks rode into the middle of the crowd. A man jumped off the horse wearing all black and he had a black cape. All anyone could see was his head, which was painted like a white skull. He gave out a blood-curling scream.

Noah jumped. The scream had scared him. Night Tear moved closer to Noah and took hold of his hand. Had she done that to comfort him or had she been startled too? It didn't matter because her being close to him and her hand in his gave his heart and body a warm feeling and he liked it.

Everyone moved close to the storyteller and sat down with him in the middle. Noah and his friends were only four or five spear lengths from the storyteller. Children cuddled up in their parent's laps afraid to move.

The white skull spoke. "Ahhheee!" he shouted and everyone jumped. One baby started crying. "Great Spirit, protect us and teach us what we need to know to be better human beings. Then give us the strength to use that teaching in our lives."

The white skull lit a bundle of sage and walked around fanning the smoke on everyone. When he finished blessing all with the sacred smoke he moved back into the middle of the crowd.

He pointed out into the crowd and said, "Someone's son will see thirty two summers but will die riding an iron horse."

Noah whispered, "I'm glad that is none of us."

"Two people here will be joined before the first snow fall this year," the skull continued.

Night Tear squeezed Noah's hand then giggled. "See? I told you."

"One of you will have a relative in the future that will become a chief." He pointed over toward the Looking Horses. "Another one here will tell stories on paper that others will keep with them. Now, if you are ready, I will tell a story.

"When I was a child, I lived far away, on the other side of the great mountains."

"Past Bear Butte?" a child asked.

"Yes, far beyond Bear Butte, across the great river."

"Across the Red River?" another child asked.

"Yes," the storyteller then chuckled. "Further than the Red River. I got into trouble because I didn't listen." He lowered his head and looked at everyone through his eyebrows. "My father left that morning to go and hunt for buffaloes. My mother told me to stay near our teepee but I didn't listen. I wanted to play by the creek so I was walking across the tall grass field heading for the little stream to play in the water.

"I heard something that sounded like thunder." BOOM sounded a drum off to the side. "And when I looked up I saw it, the giant thunderbird. It was a bird as big as two or three stagecoaches. Its head was as big as a horse. When it flapped its mighty wings they made the sound of thunder." BOOM. "It was coming straight for me. I ran but I had nowhere to hide." The storyteller flapped his black cape and spun around.

"The thunderbird swooped down and picked me up in his huge talons. It flapped its wings and I heard thunder again." BOOM. "It flew away holding me tight. Its talons clamped on to me so hard that they squeezed me and I could just barely breathe. It flew very high in the sky. The teepees below looked like dots and the buffalo were the size of ants.

"We were so high that now I held on for my life because I didn't want the thunderbird to drop me. It flew a long way high up into the mountains. On the highest mountain peak, it circled around. Below I could see a nest but instead of a nest made from sticks and leaves this nest was made from small trees and bushes.

"It drew close to the nest and opened its talons and dropped me down in the middle of this nest. The thunderbird landed on the edge and was staring at me. I wondered what it wanted with me but then I saw why it brought me here to its nest. All around me were bones; bones of many other children were at the bottom of this nest. Fear filled my heart as I realized the thunderbird was going to eat me.

"The thunderbird lowered its beak and when I saw the beak open I thought I was going to end up like the other children it had brought there to this nest. I would end up just a skeleton.

"I dove down and hide under a bush. The thunderbird's foot was scratching at the bush to find me. I climbed my way down deep into the nest. At the very bottom I found an opening and through that opening I climbed out of the nest. When the thunderbird couldn't find me it squawked and that squawk was louder than the loudest waterfall, louder than stampeding buffalo.

"I started climbing down the mountain as fast as I could climb. Once I was at the bottom I ran for home. I ran so hard my sides were hurting like they never hurt before. Sweat was pouring from my forehead. My legs felt like willow branches. I ran all day. I was breathing from my mouth. I was too scared to look back.

"I saw my teepee ahead. But just when I thought I was safe I heard thunder." BOOM. BOOM. The storyteller opened his cape. Inside the cape his body was painted like white bones and the cape was painted like giant wings. He opened the cape and flapped his wings and ran around the crowd. BOOM. BOOM.

The children were screaming and some of the women were gasping as he ran past. Even a few of the warrior men flinched and held their hands up to protect themselves as he ran by.

He stopped and folded in his cape. "The only thing that saved me was my father returning from the hunt. My father saw the thunderbird chasing me. He put an arrow into our campfire and once it was blazing he shot the arrow from his strongest bow.

"The thunderbird saw the flaming arrow coming toward him. He flapped his wings." BOOM. "The thunderbird flew high into the sky. The arrow missed but the flaming arrow scared the thunderbird and it flew away.

"I almost got eaten that day and it was entirely my own fault. If I had just listened to my mother and obeyed her then I would have been safe and the thunderbird would not have been after me."

He ran to his horse and jumped up on its back. He opened the cape again and flapped the wings as he rode away. Boom. Boom. The drums grew softer as he rode out of sight.

The following day was the day of challenges. The first challenge was the horse race. Noah brought his horse over to the starting line where seventeen other young men were lining up for the event.

He only had a bridle because in the race everyone had to ride bareback. He didn't figure that was much of a problem because he had always ridden bareback until he rode off with Dayton Colt to become a bounty hunter. His main worry was if his horse was fast enough.

At the starting line there were many big and strong horses with strong young men to ride them. He knew several of the young men but there were many horses and riders from other nations he did not know.

The race went across the rolling hills off to the south and across the river. It then turned to go over to a canyon and down a rather steep and rocky trail that went over to a long and steep hill. Once at the top it was back across the rolling hills to the finish line.

Noah looked for Dawn, Clayton and Night Tear but they had not shown up. There were many families cheering on the other riders.

Noah knew the course well and thought that would give him a big advantage in the race.

At starting time, all the riders mounted their horses and walked them to the starting line. It felt good to Noah to be riding bareback again. He could feel the horse under his legs and he liked that much better than having a saddle that prevented him from feeling the movement of the horse's muscles as he rode.

An old warrior that used a wooden carved limb to help him walk because of the gimpy leg he had sustained at the battle of Greasy Grass River years ago walked out in front of the horses with a flag. "Get ready to ride. You will start when I drop this flag and the first one back to pick it up will win," he said.

He raised the flag and the riders all leaned forward on their horse, ready. The flag dropped and the horses took off. The riders grunted to their horses and urged the horses to go as fast as they could.

Noah saw the crowd cheering but could only hear the sound of thundering hooves as galloping horses raced for the lead. They rode down the first rolling hill going toward the river. Noah was right behind the leader when the river came into view.

Ahead Noah could see a group of people off to one side watching and cheering as the horses approached the riverbank. He could hear Clayton yelling and he glanced over and saw Dawn and Night Tear waving.

The first horse jumped the bank and landed in the water. It made its way across and up the other side with no problem.

Noah's horse jumped the bank and went into the water. Noah lost his balance just for a second as his horse swam across and started up the far side. He started slipping off the back of his horse when it lunged to get its footing going up the far bank.

When the horse made it over the bank it took off to catch up with the lead horse, however, Noah was still sliding off because the horse was wet and he had to pull back on the reigns to slow the horse down. It was too late. Noah fell off the back of the horse and that scared the horse so the horse bucked and then kicked its hind legs.

Noah had landed on his feet behind the horse when the horse hooves struck Noah in the chest and sent him flying back over the bank and into the water. By the time he jumped up and ran over to get his horse he was in the last half of the pack of riders.

His face turned red with embarrassment and anger. He knew his cheering section had seen the entire mishap. He didn't allow his head to turn and see if they were watching. He swore under his breath. Because he had gotten too used to riding with a saddle made him unable to stay on his horse.

Dawn, Clayton and Night Tear greeted him at the finish line. Noah had made a good ride the rest of the race and finished third. The winner holding the flag was from Night Tear's tribe and she ran over to congratulate him making Noah a bit jealous.

The next event was the bow and arrow shoot. Everyone lined up in front of several trees each one having a small leather pouch hanging down from a tree limb. Dawn brought Noah a strong bow from her father with some of his straightest arrows.

The shooters took turns trying to hit the tiny leather pouch about thirty steps away. During the first round many had come close but no one had hit the target. There were many arrows stuck in the ground and into the trees behind the pouch. The second time Noah stood to shoot he took a deep breath and said, "Shoot to kill."

He pulled back the string and let go of the arrow and the bow made a twang sound as the arrow flew through the air and hit the leather pouch pulling it free from the tree and sticking through it. Only one other man had hit the target that round but his arrow hit in the edge of the pouch and Noah was announced as the winner since his arrow went through the center of the bag.

Noah felt he had redeemed himself. When Night Tear came over to give him a hug the anger he felt after the race left him.

There were other events but Noah had a huge bruise in the shape of a horse hoof in the middle of his chest so he sat out of the knife throwing and the wrestling. He thought it best to stop as a winner. Besides, he wanted to spend time with Night Tear and get to know her better.

After several days of dancing at the powwow Noah and Clayton rode up to the porch of the ranch house and stopped.

"Do you think you will see Night Tear again?" Clayton asked.

"I don't know. Perhaps, why?" Noah answered.

"Because I like her. She's pretty and a lot of fun to be around."

"How'd you like the powwow, Clayton?" Noah asked, changing the subject.

"It was great. I never saw so many Indians before. It made me miss my ma though. She would have loved to see that," Clayton said as he dismounted and tied his horse to the hitching rail.

"It's the same for me, my friend. Check on things here as soon as you get a chance," Noah said as he turned his horse toward the road.

"Where are you off too?" Clayton asked.

"I need a moment for myself so I'm going over to Gentle Breeze's grave. I won't be gone long."

Noah rode to the place where his mother was buried. It relaxed him and made him feel good to talk with her and let her know he was doing pretty well.

The hunting trip with the warriors to make him a man sure did that. He had no idea that day the trip would change his life so drastically.

He dismounted and tied his horse to a tree then went and knelt beside her grave. After praying he started talking to Gentle Breeze. "Mother, I have a problem. You taught me to be a warrior and I am one. You taught me how to take care of myself and I do that. I want to thank you for teaching me so much. There is one thing I do not know how to deal with, girls.

"One girl I like is so very different. I yearn to know her better and I love being around her. The other girl is different too, but in another way. She's exciting to be with. I

229

like one of these girls more than the other and I don't know what to do. How do I know which girl is the right one for me? How can I tell if either of them is interested in me or feels the same way about me?"

He jumped when he heard some horses going by. It reminded him of the first time he met Dayton Colt. He looked up half expecting to see Dayton Colt but it was someone else he saw. He saw three strangers riding by. They didn't seem interested in Noah. He noticed the horse in the middle was a white horse with small reddish brown spots down the front of its neck and on its hindquarters. After the riders passed Noah saw something that sent him into shock. On the back of the white horse's saddle hung a scalp. And the scalp had red beads tangled in the twisted hair lock.

The scalp was the same color hair his mother had and the red beads were fixed in the same pattern she always wore. Noah started shaking. He could feel emotions boiling up inside him. Soon he felt nothing but rage.

He realized that was his mother's scalp!

Chapter 29

TRACKING THE KILLERS

Noah watched as the riders went out of sight. He was too stunned to move at first. His chest swelled with air; his breathing was very hard. He made himself run to his horse. He put his foot in the stirrup and swung his body over the horse and took off in the direction the riders went just moments before. He wasn't sure what he would do when he caught up with them.

Noah rode around the cliff to find the men. He didn't see them anywhere. He was so disturbed that he forgot all logic and rode around like a mad man. He looked back in every canyon and down any trails that ran through the tree lines as he searched for the three men. He spent the rest of the morning riding back and forth trying to locate the riders with no luck.

He was beginning to think that he imagined the riders. He thought his mind must have created the riders because he was visiting his mother's grave. He turned his horse and headed back to the ranch.

Noah rode up to where a few men were still working on the front porch. "How's it going?"

"Everything is going smooth, Noah. No trouble so far today. We should have this porch done by tomorrow," one of the workers said.

Clayton came hurrying from the barn. "Heard you ride up. In the stall where someone has been sleeping I found a small ribbon and something else." He handed the ribbon to Noah.

Noah looked at the ribbon and said, "It looks like one of the ribbons that were attached to Bonnie Brai's pink dress. You said there was something else?"

"My hound dog was tied in the stall. He sure was happy to see me."

"What? That's odd. I wonder how your dog found his way here, but that isn't the first odd thing that happened to me today."

"You mean like the three riders that crossed the top of the ridge next to the herd?"

Noah straightened up. "You saw three riders?"

"Yep, they were headed toward your mother's grave and I thought you may have run into them."

"I did. Hey, this is short notice but I'm going to be gone for a while. I don't know how long I'll be away. I have some business to take care of. You take charge of the ranch while I'm gone. Can you handle that?"

"You know I will. You're going after those riders aren't you? You gonna be gone a few days or more?"

"More, I may be gone a week or two. I can't be sure right now how long this will take."

Noah went inside and made up a bedroll. He picked up his rifle and put his derringer in his boot. He took some jerky and a few biscuits from the table that was left over from the last meal. And on his way out the door he grabbed a box of bullets from a shelf near the window. He went outside and was putting his things into his saddlebags.

"If this has something to do with those riders from this morning, who are they and why are you going after them? Need me to go with you?" Clayton asked.

"No, I need you here. There's too much going on here that needs your attention. I'll tell you the rest when I get back. I'm relying on your help right now."

"Don't worry about a thing. Just stay safe," Clayton said.

Noah mounted his horse and rode back the way he'd just come from not more than an hour before. This time he would rely on his tracking skills, taught to him by the warriors of his tribe.

When he found the spot where he last saw the three riders he got off his horse. He studied the ground for hoof prints to see any special marks they made to tell them apart from other prints. He walked along leading his horse checking the ground for any and all signs.

Once Noah thought he knew the direction the riders were going he mounted up and rode on making faster time. He would stop every so often to check the tracks again so he wouldn't lose the direction the riders were heading. It looked like they were traveling to a town to the north. He would know more the further he followed them.

That night he camped. He didn't want to stop but he couldn't see well enough to find the hoof prints after dark. He also knew his horse needed a rest, food and water. He didn't build a fire. He just ate the stale hard biscuit he brought with him.

A couple of hours riding the next day brought Noah to a place around some trees where he saw smoke still rising from a camp fire that had almost burned out. He looked around the camp and saw where the weeds where bent and he could tell where the horses had been tied. On the ground close to where the horses were he saw a lone red bead. He picked it up and put it in his pocket.

Even though there were three of them he still had an advantage, the riders had no idea they were being tracked.

Noah kept looking to see if any birds flew up from the trees ahead but didn't see any. He knew then that he wasn't as close as he wished. Noah came upon a field of tall grass. A small herd of buffalo off to the side grazing looked up and watched him ride by. He could see the grass bent down from three horses that had made their way through the field. He would make good time here and gain some distance between him and the other riders.

He spurred his horse to a gallop. The trail became easier to follow now and he would get closer to the three men. He wanted to find them before they reached the town.

The setting sun found him riding on a road going north. After dark he had trouble finding the right hoof prints because there were other horse imprints and even wagon tracks along the trail leading into town. The town was only a couple hours or so ahead and he knew the riders were already there. He rode on in the dark.

When he got to town it was late and the streets were empty. He tied his horse to a post and went over and sat in a chair on the wooden path outside the saloon. He would wait there until morning.

The sun rose and with the new light came a clear and bright day. People were stirring and going into shops and opening the doors to start the day's business.

One of the white men elders walked by and sat on a bench next to Noah. He wore a flannel shirt and on his head was an old floppy straw hat that had seen better days. His cloth pants were held up with red straps that ran over his shoulders and buttoned to his pants in front and in the back where a belt usually went. He pulled out a small piece of red cedar wood and a Russell Barlow pocketknife and started cutting the wood. "Good morning," he said.

"Good morning. What're you making?" Noah asked.

"Nothing, just whittling."

"What's whittling?"

The man chuckled and looked over at Noah. "Whittling is where I shave very small slices of wood off this stick. If I can make them thin enough they curl up like this one; I don't make anything, I just find it enjoyable and relaxing. It takes a sharp knife and a certain amount of skill to get the shavings to curl up like what you see me doing."

Noah looked down and saw a small pile of tiny curled shavings below the man's seat. "Looks like you come out here and sit a spell every morning."

"I sure do. Helps me get my day started while I wait for the kitchen to bake fresh bread to eat with my ham and eggs. I can usually smell when breakfast is ready, too."

Noah looked the town over now that it was light enough to see clear down the street. There were three horses tied out front of the hotel and the middle horse was a white horse with reddish spots. He asked the man next to him, "See that white horse over by the hotel there? Don't know who owns it do ya?"

"Yep," came the reply.

He waited for the man to finish giving him an answer but then realized that was the answer so he asked, "Who?"

"You don't want to know that."

Noah frowned. He wouldn't have asked if he didn't want to know. "The horse is different and I just wondered who owned it. I would like to ask him where he bought it."

"You best leave that alone. The man that rides that horse is nothing but trouble but I'm guessing you already know that," the man said.

"What makes you say that?"

"Well, for one thing, you sat here all night waiting for the owner of that horse. This isn't my first go-a-round with young guns looking for Jeb Grains. There were many like you trying to make a name for themselves by drawing down on Jeb. They are all up at boot hill now."

"The grave yard?"

"Yep, that's where we bury all the young men that go up against Jeb. Jeb is the fastest gun in the west. Last time I heard he had thirty eight notches on the handle of his gun."

"What do you mean notches on his gun handle?"

"Each time Jeb is in a gun fight and kills the guy he cuts a notch in the handle of his gun. He does that to either keep count or else that's all the recognition he gives the gunslinger that went up against him."

"Oh, you think I'm a gunslinger."

"Either you're a gunslinger or you're a bounty hunter and you sure don't look like a bounty hunter." The elder laughed, sat forward and spit into the street. "The way I see it you can go on back home or end up at boot hill. Your choice."

Three men came out of the hotel and walked over to the three horses. One man with a dirty black cowboy hat went to the white horse and put something into the saddle bag. The men walked across the street and came toward Noah.

They were talking and walked past Noah and into the saloon. Seeing the man this close that he thought had killed his mother brought out a lot of emotions in Noah.

Tears welled up in his eyes. His mind went back to a simpler time not long ago when he was happy. His mother was very proud of him. He knew he was loved and he missed that feeling. He never even thought of a life without her. Everything was all different now.

He stood, wiped away his tears, and walked to the saloon. He stopped and put his hands on the swinging doors.

He looked back across the street to the white horse to see the scalp on the back of the saddle one last time.

The man sitting on the bench said, "Goodbye, kid."

"I'm not going anywhere."

"Yes you are, one way or the other, you're leaving. And it be my guess it's the other that bothers me. You young lads never listen."

"Mister, it's okay. It's a good day to die."

The old man frowned then nodded.

Noah looked inside the saloon, swung the doors open and yelled, "Jeb, Jeb Grains!"

Chapter 30

THE SHOWDOWN

The man in the dirty black hat stood between the other two men down at the end of the bar. At the sound of his name he didn't flinch but the other two men turned around and starred at Noah. Everyone else in the saloon got slowly up and moved over next to the far wall.

Noah said again, "Jeb, Jeb Grains."

"Who wants to know?" the man in the black hat asked without looking over.

"The son of someone you killed, that's who."

Jeb turned around, looked Noah over and said, "You must be wrong. I don't shoot old men."

"But you do kill women. That scalp tied to the back of your saddle belonged to my mother."

Noah noticed the others in the saloon were looking at Jeb to see what he was going to do. Noah saw Jeb's jaw draw tight and he looked uneasy; he looked angry.

Jeb shifted his weight and without standing straight up and still leaning on the bar he threw his shot glass high into the air. His hand went down to his revolver so fast it made a slapping sound as his hand hit the leather holster. He drew his gun and fired. The shot glass exploded in midair and pieces of glass tinkled to the ground before Noah could even move his hand off the swinging door.

"Okay, kid, I'll be out in a minute. Then I'll send you to see your mommy."

Noah was lost at what to do now. Jeb's shooting skills were impressive. He had never seen anyone that fast on the draw before. Noah didn't know how to react to being toyed with.

Jeb turned back around. "Barkeeper, another drink. I have to finish breakfast then looks like I'll have to go to work." The two men beside Jeb laughed. Jeb picked up the fresh drink as Noah slowly backed outside and turned away from the door.

"That's how Jeb does. You should have taken him right there and then, shot him the minute you saw him, right in the back. Now he has the advantage. He makes you wait, that way you'll get frustrated and very nervous until he's ready. That gives him a huge advantage, not that he needs one," the man whittling said.

"What do I do then?"

"Son, go on back home before it's too late. But I doubt you'll follow my advice. So, do you want to be put in dirt or a pine box?"

"What? Oh, if it comes to that I don't think it'll much matter."

Noah walked across the street and waited. He stood for such a long time he had to shift his weight back and forth to ease the nervousness. He walked over and sat on the edge of the wooden path next to the street. He waited some more.

His thoughts returned to why he came here. He remembered how excited he was going on the big hunt and how excited he felt about his first kill of meat for his family. He had felt sadness for the animal until one of the warriors told him how the animal had given its life from the Great Spirit to feed the Great Spirit's people. It was how the Great Spirit worked in nature.

That first hunt was full of good energies. The hunt now had a different purpose. This hunt would rid the world of evil.

He was thinking about how good his life was back then. He thought he hadn't experienced much good since then. The good energies were gone.

He took a deep breath and realized that wasn't exactly true. He had become friends with Clayton partly because he had killed Clayton's father but now they were more than friends, they were partners, family even. And then there was Bonnie Brai but she left him without even saying a good bye to return to her grandfather. He had met Night Tear but wasn't sure how he felt about her yet; he would have to get to know her better if that was possible. Last he thought about Dayton Colt and how he had trained with him to get where he was now. He sure could use Dayton Colt about now.

He almost allowed the evil energies to suck him in. There was good in this world and without Jeb Grains the world would be even better. He had an animal to take down to set things right once more. His mind remembered how much he thought his vision quest was stupid but here he was right in the middle of how true it actually became. After all he was only following the path the Great Spirit put in front of him.

Finally the swinging doors to the saloon swung open and three men walked to the middle of the street. Noah stood and stepped off the wooden path and into the street facing the three men.

"I only called you out, Jeb, not the three of you," Noah said.

"Well, if that is your mother's scalp then you already know I don't play fair. So what are you going to do about it?" Jeb had a large evil grin on his face.

Noah felt the presence of someone who had walked up and was now standing beside him. He thought it must be the old man that was whittling but what good would a man be with a small pocketknife? Noah glanced over to see Dayton Colt standing beside him with his hands just above the handle of his pistol. Noah smiled and relaxed just a little.

"You take out Jeb and I'll take the one on the left then we'll both get the one on the right," Dayton Colt said.

Noah nodded.

The street was empty. The wagons and a few buggies were held up and over to the side for the length of the road going through town. No one wanted to get in the line of fire. The whole town was waiting to see the showdown.

Someone yelled from the roof of a building behind the three gun fighters. A few gasps from some of the people on the wooden path beside the store windows could be heard all the way out where he stood. Noah glanced over and saw a man fall from the roof.

The man hit the ground still holding his rifle but he had a butcher knife sticking out of his chest. Noah saw the gunslingers peek and then look at each other nervously. All three of the men now had a scowls on their faces and placed their hands above their guns getting ready for the fight.

Noah knew for the first time that he really was a professional gunman. He wasn't nervous. This was his job and he was good at it. All his fears and feelings of revenge were over. He had a job to do and he was going to do it. He wasn't a kid any longer. He was more than even a warrior. He was a man. He felt strong and confident. He was ready.

Jeb drew first and fired followed by both men at his side. Dayton Colt had his gun out second. Noah dove for the ground as he drew. Jeb fired but missed because Noah went down and rolled over onto his side. Two more shots were heard.

The man across from Dayton Colt fell backward to the ground but so did Dayton. Noah knew it was all up to him now. Everything was happening so fast yet Noah seemed to be moving in slow motion. The only thing he could think about was, "Shoot to kill!"

Noah fired and Jeb twisted and doubled over. Blood sprayed out from his chest. He staggered a few steps then fell to the ground.

Another shot was fired. This time Noah felt pain in his arm. His gun flew away from him over to the side and out of reach. The third man was now walking up to Noah. The man fired once more and the bullet hit in the dirt in front of Noah's face.

The man stopped a few yards from him and took aim. Next the man froze and started choking; he was gasping for air. His arm dropped and he fired his gun off to the side then dropped it and raised his hands to his throat. He continued gasping for air and dropped to his knees. Noah saw the man turning a shade of blue.

Noah was flabbergasted. The man had him in his sights. Why didn't the man finish him off? Why was Noah still alive? What had happened to the man?

When the gunfighter finally fell forward he had a very small child's arrow stuck into the backside of his neck. The man kicked once then lay very still.

Noah searched for the person that could have shot that arrow but he didn't see anyone. There was too much going on. People were running away and people were running toward him. Mother's in bonnets were quickly leading children down the street away from danger. Gentlemen were running toward the street to see if anyone was still alive.

Dayton moaned and sat up. He looked toward Noah and said, "You okay?"

"I'm good. Got hit in my gun arm. You?"

"I was hit in the shoulder but I'll be okay. Did we get 'em?"

"We got our two guys but someone else got the third guy and the outlaw on the roof that was going to gun us down. I'm thinking it was the same person that saved our hide."

"Maybe we have an angel looking out for us," Dayton said.

Noah looked around hoping to see the angel. He didn't see her so he turned and yelled at the crowd, "Someone get a doctor. My friend is hurt."

A fight broke out down the street just beyond where the man with the rifle fell from the roof. Noah couldn't see what was going on but could hear the commotion. A couple people were getting louder as a struggle was taking place.

Noah took his bandana from around his neck and wrapped it around his forearm to stop the bleeding. He kept looking down toward the corner to see what was going on but there were still too many people standing around to make out what the ruckus was all about.

A short heavyset man with a bald head and a mustache came running into the street from the other direction. Noah wondered if that man had been scalped when he was younger. The man was carrying a black satchel and knelt down beside Dayton. First thing he did was pull out a bottle of whiskey, gave Dayton a drink and then took a swig himself.

Noah stood and watched as the doctor helped Dayton walk back to his office. He was going to go with them but the sheriff walked up and put his hand out to stop him.

"Can't this wait? I need to see if my friend is okay," Noah said.

"Your friend is in good hands. Doc is the best doctor in the state. I saw what happened out there in my street. Do you know what you just did?" the sheriff asked.

"Got shot?"

"You killed Jeb Grains."

"Am I being arrested?"

"No, I saw the fight and it was fair and square. You have no idea who you killed, do you?"

"No, not really. All I know is that's the man that killed my ma in cold blood."

"Jeb was the fastest gunslinger in these here parts, maybe in the entire west. He was wanted in more than seven states. Jeb had the highest reward on his head that I ever saw. You're a very rich man."

A deputy ran over to the sheriff and said, "We caught the other one and we're on the way to the jail with the shooter now."

"Okay, I'll be right there," the sheriff said.

"Hold on, Sheriff, I'm coming too. I got something to take care of first."

Noah walked over and looked down at Jeb. He took out his hunting knife and knelt down beside the dead man and cut a line from front to back on each side of the man's head then cut across the back. He made one more cut on the man's head across the front then put his knife away. He moved his hand down and took a hold of the man's scalp and jerked the top part of the man's hair clear off his head. He stood and threw the scalp down on the ground next to the man and stomped it and ground it into the dirt with the heel of his boot.

He walked over to the white horse with the reddish spots and untied the lock of hair from the back of the saddle. He stood there a moment and looked at it. He let out a long sigh and when he took a breath in it came into his lungs in three broken sniffs. He walked over to his horse and put that scalp into his saddlebag. Noah turned to go to the sheriff's office.

As Noah and the sheriff got closer to the jail the deputy yelled, "He's getting away." Noah saw the deputy run down a side street next to the sheriff's office. The deputy had to weave in and out of people to get to the street that went to the back of the stores. Noah and the sheriff quickly followed.

Noah thought he knew who the other shooter was because of the butcher knife and the small arrow but the deputy had said it was a man.

In a few minutes Noah and the sheriff caught up with the deputy back behind some stores. "Where is he? What happened?" The sheriff asked.

"The guy fell down as we were taking him in. I went to pick him up and got hit in the nose with the back of his head. Then he ran down here," the deputy said.

Looking around Noah spotted a cowboy hat, cowboy shirt, cowboy boots, and a pair of Levi pants over next to a water barrel by the corner of a building. No one else was around.

"Did you see where he went when you came around the corner?" the sheriff asked.

"No, there was only this young lady standing by the back door of this store. I told her to get inside so she would be safe."

Noah ran to the door and tried to open it with his left hand. The door was stuck. The deputy walked over and tried to help but the door was locked from the inside.

Noah ran back to the corner of the building and was met by a crowd of people coming to see what was going on. He had to maneuver his way through the crowd to get to the main street and down to the front door of the shop. He ran inside.

There were lots of ladies inside where it was safe. They were looking out the front window to see what was happening. Noah hurried through the store looking. He saw a lady in a pink dress and bonnet and he ran over to her. He touched the woman on the shoulder. When she turned around it was an older woman holding some cloth she was buying.

Noah ran back out to the sidewalk. "Did anyone see a young lady with reddish hair come out of this store?" he asked.

"I did. A very pretty young lady just left. I helped her up onto her large gray horse. She was riding side saddle," an older gentleman said.

"Which way did she go?"

"I have no idea. Once she was seated I turned back around to watch all the excitement. I didn't want to miss anything."

Noah ran to the middle of the street and looked one way and then the other way but he didn't see a lady riding sidesaddle. He didn't see any ladies except one sitting in a buggy across the street. He even thought about tracking the horse this lady was riding sidesaddle but knew there was no way to pick up the trail with so many other horses riding on the street. "Dab blame it," Noah said as he stomped his foot.

His foot hit something when he stomped and he looked down. There in the dirt was a small child's bow and a quiver of small arrows.

Dayton walked up and stood beside him. Dayton was wearing a sling for his arm and had a bandage sticking out of his shirt collar.

"Thanks for helping me out. We get to split a big reward," Noah said. "You okay?"

"I'm fine. The bullet went straight through. And you're welcome but you can have the reward. I don't need the money. I came out west to promote my handguns and you did that for me today. Once this tale hits the tabloids my guns will sell like a prairie wild fire. I may even go back east, back home, now."

"Me too, I guess. Back home to my ranch, that is."

Chapter 31

Two Wolves

Noah could see the ranch house ahead. He nudged his horse into a trot. He was looking forward to being back at home. With the reward money he could finish his house and increase the herd to the size that he and Clayton had talked about. And knowing his mother's killer was now dead gave him a sense of peace he had not experienced in a long time. He had almost everything he needed in life.

During the whole ride back home his mind was turning over the same thoughts. Why did Bonnie Brai leave? Why did she keep watch over him? Why did she help save his life and run away again? He could understand her leaving if she didn't like him. That was one thing but if she didn't like him why did she show up and get involved in the gunfight? If she did like him why did she keep running away? The only thing he knew for sure was that he couldn't figure out women.

As he got closer to the house he saw something that made him bring his horse to a halt. He looked again. Tied to the hitching post was a horse he didn't recognize at first glance. But when he looked again he saw it was a rather big gray horse and on the horse was a sidesaddle.

He kicked his horse into a gallop. He rode up to the front porch and brought his horse to a sudden stop but before he could dismount Clayton walked out the door with the widest grin Noah had ever seen on him. Noah's heart skipped a beat. He knew.

Noah swung his leg over the front of his horse's neck and jumped off. There in the doorway was a young lady with reddish hair wearing a pink dress.

Noah couldn't believe his eyes. "Bonnie, Bonnie Brai?" he said leaping up onto the porch.

"Aye, tis me," she said.

"Where in the world have you been?"

"Ye know darn well whaur Ah was."

"Welcome home," Noah said. He moved forward to give Bonnie Brai a hug but she held out her hand and kept him at a distance.

"Hold on, this be not me home."

"It could be."

"Are ye asking me to court ye or to get joined to ye?"

"Court me?" Noah didn't think that sounded quite like what he had on his mind or wanted so he added, "No, to marry me."

"Which be it?"

Noah was getting frustrated. He didn't like whatever game this was being played because he had never played this game before and didn't understand the rules. To him it wasn't a game.

"I'm asking you to marry me," he said.

"Are ye willin' to hear the answer even if it isn't the one ye want to hear?"

"Bonnie Brai, will you be my wife?"

"Maybe Ah could but thare is something in between us that is in the wye."

Noah saw Bonnie Brai looking down at the gun he wore on his side.

"My gun? But I need that to protect us," Noah said.

"Ye do, do ye? And with this 'us' which one did the protectin?"

"Why did you risk your life to help me during the gunfight? Was it because you care about me?"

"Oh, Ah care about ye but that not be the reason. Jeb was the devil that killed me parents. Now that he be dead ye don't have no use for a gun."

"But having a gun is part of who I am."

"Aye, but it be the part Ah don't like."

Clayton said, "Noah, would you rather be right or would you rather be happy?"

Noah looked into Bonnie Brai's eyes and knew the answer. He unbuckled his gun belt and without taking his eyes away from Bonnie Brai he handed the gun to Clayton. "Here, hang this inside on a peg by the front door. Now?" he asked.

"Now what?"

"Now will you marry me?"

"Aye." Bonnie Brai ran to Noah and put both her arms around his neck and kissed his face all over. Their lips met and they stood in that embrace for a long time. Clayton finally cleared his throat to remind them that he was standing there watching.

Noah said, "Bonnie Brai, I have a gift for you." He walked over to his horse and untied something from the back of his saddle. He walked back up on the porch and handed Bonnie Brai a child's bow and a quiver of small arrows.

Winter came and went. The days were getting longer and the trees were full of leaves once again. Wild flowers were in full bloom and Noah brought home some flowers every day to keep in a jar on the eating table for Bonnie Brai.

Noah and Bonnie Brai went through the joining ceremony before the first snow last year. It was held on the reservation and Clayton stood beside Noah. Dawn carried the flowers for Bonnie Brai. Chief Crazy Elk stood with

Bonnie Brai for the price of ten steers, ten blankets and a bag full of peppermint candy.

Bonnie Brai borrowed a light brown buckskin dress to wear and Noah wore a black buckskin shirt. As soon as the joining ceremony was over Bonnie Bria changed into her pink dress for the feast.

Since coming home Noah had tried to return to his original name, Two Wolves. It didn't work. It had been too long and everyone now knew him as Noah, or Noah Two Wolves, the renegade that killed bad whites even though he had retired his gun.

Noah was leading his horse across the yard when Bonnie Brai walked out onto the finished porch and sat in the chair with rounded legs and started rocking. She had one hand under her belly to help with the extra weight her belly was carrying. She would be giving birth in just another week or so.

"Whaur are ye off to this mornin?" she asked.

"I'm going to visit Gentle Breeze's grave. I need to return her scalp to her. I'll be back by this afternoon."

"Ah will be goin' with ye," Bonnie Brai said.

"No, you're in no condition to ride that far. You wait here."

"Now don't ye be tellin' me what to do. Ah thought ye would have learnt that by now. Nae man will ever own me again. That ye can be sure of."

Noah spurred his horse into a gallop and rode off alone. After only ten minutes of riding he looked back to see dust rising behind him. He stopped and waited. He knew he was being followed.

Two riders came up beside him with both parties grinning. Noah said, "Clayton, go back and get the pack mule. Bring extra food and some blankets along too. Bring anything else you can think of to make the trip as enjoyable as possible for all of us. We'll wait right here, over by that tree yonder."

"You got it," Clayton said as he turned his horse around. "Sis, I'll be back as soon as I can."

Noah took a minute to look at Bonnie Brai and thought she was very beautiful in her brown buckskin dress. He said, "My mother said she followed my father to fight Yellow Hair when she was with child. That's how come I was born so far away."

"Well, as much as ye run off Ah need to keep me eye on ye. A good woman won't let a good man get far if she can help it. That's what me mither taught me."

"Me run off? You can't chase me off with a big stick. It's you that has been known to disappear at times."

"If Ah am goin' to take in a stray animal then Ah have to watch him from afar. Ah be not one to put me hand down to his face to see if he bites."

"I'm an animal am I?"

"Ye are. Just look at me belly and tell me ye aren't an animal," Bonnie Brai said with a sparkle in her eyes.

It wasn't long before Clayton returned leading the donkey and the three of them headed for the gravesite.

As soon as they arrived Clayton set out to make up a camp of sorts. Noah helped Bonnie Brai down off her horse with the sidesaddle and walked with her over to the camp and sat with her.

"Is there anything I can do to help?" he asked.

"Nae, the ride made me start hurtin' in me belly. Ah will be okay as soon as Ah get some rest and catch me breath," Bonnie Brai said.

Noah went over and opened his saddlebag. He pulled out a twist of hair with a few red beads still tangled in the black lock of hair. He walked over to a grave and dug a hole where he had laid Gentle Breeze's head. He put the scalp in the hole and covered it back over.

"Gentle Breeze, I am no longer your little warrior. As foretold in my vision, there are good white men. And I did become the enemy to survive and I overcame all that once

I saw the enemy wasn't being like a white. The enemy was inside me.

"It is like the story you told me when I was a child. Inside each of us there are two wolves. One is mean and angry and the other is good and kind. They are in a fight to see which one will be the dominant one. I remember asking you which wolf will win. And it is very true when you said the one that'll win is the one you feed the most."

Noah wasn't the same little boy trying hard to become a warrior. He grew into one. He was comforted with the thought that he would be giving his child something he never had, a father.

A loud moan came from Bonnie Brai. "Me pain is getting' faster and harder. It's time for the baby. The beaver dam broke and the water is rushin' out."

The baby came quickly and without any trouble. It was as if he couldn't wait any longer to be with his father.

Noah and Clayton helped Bonnie Brai by holding her arms when she squatted to give birth to the newborn baby boy. Noah listened to Bonnie Brai as she told him and Clayton what needed to be done. Noah held the baby's head and pulled him free. It wasn't long before a tiny but loud cry came from the child.

Bonnie Brai told Noah how to cut the cord and tie it off. She showed Clayton how to wash the newborn and guided him with how she wanted the baby wrapped in the blanket.

Once Bonnie Brai and the baby were resting, Noah couldn't take his eyes from the baby. He asked, "What's the child's name?"

"We'll call him Lad for now 'til we find the right name."

Noah picked up Lad and walked over to Gentle Breeze's grave. "I am a warrior born of a warrior. Now, there is another warrior born from a warrior."

Noah heard a scream from Bonnie Brai. He turned quickly and saw two wolves walking through the small camp in between Bonnie Brai and himself. Bonnie Brai gasped as she pulled her feet into her side. She was looking at Noah and Lad with fear in her eyes.

The two wolves lowered their heads and tucked their tails between their legs as if they knew they were in the wrong.

Noah pulled Lad close to his chest and held him with one arm while the other hand went for his gun. "Shoot to kill," he said out loud.

But when his hand got to his side he remembered he no longer wore a gun. He had tried to draw from habit. He thought about the story of his birth and how he got his name. Calmness came over him.

"No, it's no longer shoot to kill. Now it's learn to be happy," he said.

Noah noticed how quiet and still the air was as he watched. Peace flowed into him even with the two wolves in front of him. The two wolves bumped into each other trying to figure out what to do. They started to go back the way they had come. They stopped and turned around. One of the wolves gave out a howl. The baby jumped and started crying. The wolves sniffed the air and looked at Lad then ran off into some tall grass and disappeared out of sight.

Noah raised Lad as high as he could reach and said, "Gentle Breeze, meet Two Wolves."

At that very moment a warm gentle breeze flowed through the stillness of the canyon.

Chapter 32

E P I L O G U E

Noah, Bonnie Brai, and their son, Two Wolves were allowed to live off the reservation due to a law suit brought against the United States by Chief Standing Bear of the Ponca Nation several years earlier in 1879. In the suit Chief Standing Bear was recognized as a person with certain rights under the law. Indians still weren't citizens.

The Wild Bunch's reign ended within a few years. Butch Cassidy and the Sundance Kid left the United States and moved to Argentina. The Wild Bunch was never the strong outlaw gang again after they were attacked by Chief Crazy Elk and their hideout, the Hole-in-the-Wall, Wyoming, was discovered.

Clayton remained as foreman of the ranch. The herd grew in size and helped feed many of the people in Noah's tribe and many of Chief Crazy Elk's people. Clayton married and built a house about a mile from the main ranch. They had two daughters.

The son, Two Wolves, kept his name but changed how the first name looked. He used the T but switched the w and o. He then turned the w upside down to make it look like m thus his named read Tom Wolves.

With a letter of recommendation from the Colt family Tom was educated and then trained in law enforcement. He later continued in his father's footsteps by becoming a U. S.

Marshall. He continued the family business of arresting bad white men and he also protected his tribe at the same time.

Noah and Bonnie Brai had two daughters. One daughter became a teacher and the other was an advocate for Indian rights. They both worked in a schoolhouse Noah had built on the reservation not far from where the Red Cloud family lived in Pine Ridge.

Noah and Bonnie Brai's last child was a boy. He worked for Wells Fargo as a guard and worked his way up to detective later on.

He was killed at the age of thirty-two during an iron horse (train) robbery outside Fort Wallace. He was protecting a white woman and her child. His body was brought home and buried beside Gentle Breeze.

Due to the hardships and lives of Noah and Bonnie Brai, many Indians realized they could make a difference with their lives and that their lives could have meaning once again.

About the Author

David C. Dillon attended Miami University. He has two grown daughters each having a daughter of their own. He lives in southwestern Ohio, in between Dayton and Cincinnati, in his tin can castle with his cats, Fluffy and Baby Boy. He is retired and now loves to write. His hobbies include playing poker, fishing, dancing at powwows, and traveling.

He has a great love for Native Americans and spent four summers with his family and friends who live on the Pine Ridge Reservation in South Dakota.

He has written another book called Dreamwalker: Native Guide. This book is about a war vet that has dreams that come true. The dreams turn dark and the character, Conley, goes to an Indian reservation to find his dream guide in hopes of understanding his dreams before someone ends up dead.

For more information or to contact the author visit:
www.davidcdillon.us.